*"As I said the morning we met, you Frenchmen are legends in your own minds."*

He was propped up against the edge of her mirrored vanity table, arms crossed, watching her in the low, shimmering light. "And here I was thinking I'm here to be seduced. Instead, you insult me."

She let a grin show below the mask. "I'm sorry if I imposed upon you," she said, doing her best to maintain her distance. "I have a business proposition I'd like you to consider."

"And it is?"

"I need information on who is who in New Orleans. Take Barber, for example. Although you assure me he is of no importance, what if he had been? If I'm to run a successful house, I need to know the wheat from the chaff."

"So what are you proposing?"

"That you supply me with that information, at whatever price you deem fair."

"I see." Archer studied her, then asked, "Suppose my price is that you share my bed?"

ATTENTION ORGANIZATIONS AND CORPORATIONS:
Most HarperCollins paperbacks are available at special quantity
discounts for bulk purchases for sales promotions, premiums, or
fund-raising. For information, please call or write:

Special Markets Department, HarperCollins Publishers,
10 East 53rd Street, New York, New York 10022.
Telephone: (212) 207-7528. Fax: (212) 207-7222.

Books by
**Beverly Jenkins**

*Contemporary*

DEADLY SEXY
SEXY/DANGEROUS
BLACK LACE
THE EDGE OF DAWN
THE EDGE OF MIDNIGHT

*Historical*

WILD SWEET LOVE
WINDS OF THE STORM
SOMETHING LIKE LOVE
A CHANCE AT LOVE
BEFORE THE DAWN
ALWAYS AND FOREVER
THE TAMING OF JESSI ROSE
THROUGH THE STORM

# BEVERLY JENKINS

# WINDS OF THE STORM

## AVON BOOKS
*An Imprint of HarperCollinsPublishers*

This is a work of fiction. Names, characters, places, and incidents are products of the author's imagination or are used fictitiously and are not to be construed as real. Any resemblance to actual events, locales, organizations, or persons, living or dead, is entirely coincidental.

AVON BOOKS
*An Imprint of* HarperCollins*Publishers*
195 Broadway
New York, New York 10007

Copyright © 2006 by Beverly Jenkins
ISBN-13: 978-0-06-057531-1
ISBN-10: 0-06-057531-X
**www.avonromance.com**

First Avon Books paperback printing: May 2006

Avon Trademark Reg. U.S. Pat. Off. and in Other Countries, Marca Registrada, Hecho en U.S.A.
HarperCollins® is a registered trademark of HarperCollins Publishers Inc.

Printed in the U.S.A.

10   9

To the fans of the House of Le Veq.
Enjoy.

*The true history of this war will show that...
Negroes have repeatedly threaded their way through
the lines of the rebels exposing themselves to
bullets in order to convey important information
to the loyal army of the Potomac.*

—Frederick Douglass, 1862

# **Prologue**

It was July 4, 1863, and the South was winning the war. In celebration of both grand events, the large, snow-white mansion owned by Confederate General Brandon Crete was awash with lanterns, music, and the raucous, high-pitched sounds of revelry. Most of Crete's slaves had taken to their quarters hours earlier, due to the corn liquor he'd magnanimously passed out, but inside the house, Crete and his Southern gentlemen friends on leave from the war for the holiday were being entertained by a troop of dusky-skinned ladies imported for the sole purpose of pleasure. The debauchery and drink were at their height when one of the women, Zahra Lafayette, silently slipped outside. Under cover of darkness, she moved swiftly towards her destination: one of the general's barns.

Looking around carefully for dogs, loyal slaves,

or anything else that might foil her plans, Zahra made her way through a small stand of magnolias. After a short, brisk walk, she spotted an outbuilding about forty yards away across an open field. From the description she'd been given, it was possibly the barn she was after. She held her position under the cover of the trees for a moment, ever watchful and ever wary, because necessity dictated both. Her wishing that the damned moon weren't so bright had no impact on its positioning in the night sky, so she set the useless thought aside and focused her mind on what she'd come to do.

Keeping her body bent low, she hurried across the space. When she reached the barn, she flattened herself against the side wall and waited to make sure she hadn't been seen. Fighting to keep her breathing even, she listened for footsteps or any other sounds that might herald discovery, but when she heard only the night song of the insects she began to slowly move along the wall towards the barn door. Her first step on the uneven ground turned her ankle, and she winced at the slight pain. At this moment she would have given two front teeth for some trousers and a pair of stiff brogans. Both items would have made this skulking about easier, but she'd have had difficulty posing as a pricey whore in such inelegant attire. Instead, she was dressed in a garish, low-cut, red dress and wore a pair of fashionable, high-heeled shoes that were useless in this line of work.

As she gained the corner of the barn, she peeked around to see if anyone was on the other side. Blessedly, she saw no one and thanked the ancestors for corn liquor and July 4. Hurrying now, she took one last look behind her, then hastened over to the big horizontal slat that barred the door. She lifted it with difficulty and set it back down as soundlessly as she could. She quickly surveyed the dark grounds around her to make certain her presence hadn't drawn any attention. When she was confident, she opened the barn door, slipped inside, and quietly closed it.

It was dark as pitch inside, and the first thing she smelled was urine; stark, pungent, and so strong she placed her hand over her mouth to filter her breathing. General Crete's horse barn needing mucking. She lowered her hand and called out in a hoarse whisper, "Le Veq? Are you in here?"

For a moment, there was silence, then a strained male voice responded, "Up here."

Zahra turned her head in an effort to determine his location, then began moving again. "Keep talking so I can find you. It's dark as Hades in here."

"You're a woman?" He sounded surprised.

"Sure am. Don't let your surprise keep you from talking, though."

"They sent a woman?"

She didn't like his tone. "If you prefer, I can go back and tell Miss Tubman you'd rather a man rescue you."

The curse he uttered led her deeper into the barn.

Setting her large handbag down on the straw-strewn floor, Zahra blindly reached inside for a small piece of candle and a flint. She lit the stub.

The resulting light was just large enough for her to see him. He was above her, hanging by his wrists from a beam high above her head. He had on a ragged shirt, and the muscles in his shoulders and beneath his raised arms were stretched so unnaturally, the sight made her ache inside. She set the candle on an overturned wooden bucket.

"Who are you?" he rasped again.

"The person getting you out of here, so let's cut you down, and you can thank me later."

Guided by the dim light, Zahra walked farther into the darkened barn to search for a ladder or something to stand on so she could reach him. Suddenly, the barn's front door flew open. She ducked down and very slowly slid her truncheon out of her handbag.

The visitor was her host, General Crete, and he had a lantern in his hand. Had he come to check on his suspended guest, or had he noticed her absence back at the house? He'd been particularly interested in her earlier in the evening, but she thought she'd successfully managed to fob him off on one of the other girls.

"Well, Yankee," she heard him say to Le Veq. "How's it feel knowing you're going to die in the mornin'?"

Silence.

The general chuckled coldly, "Yeah, we're going to stretch your yella neck like a Christmas goose— What the hell?"

He'd just noticed the tiny candle. Zahra could see him looking around. He swung the lantern back and forth in an attempt to find out who else might be inside. When the movement almost made him lose his balance, Zahra realized that he was very drunk. She smiled and slowly rose to show herself. "Why, General—are you looking for me?"

Although he appeared quite inebriated, there was a clarity in his blue eyes that indicated he was still sober enough to know something was amiss. Holding up the light so he could see her better, he asked suspiciously, "What're you doing in here?"

"Oh, nothing. Just looking around."

"Just looking around, huh?" His tone was skeptical.

"Sure. Why else would I be here?"

Crete swung the lantern Le Veq's way. "Him maybe?"

She sighed dramatically. "Oh, all right. I should have known better than to try and trick a smart Southern gentleman like yourself. I did come in here looking for him. In fact, his friends asked that I bring him home." She smiled even prettier then. "Be a dear and cut him down for me."

Crete shook himself as if trying to clear away the alcohol haze in order to make sense of what she'd just said. Then he puffed up. "The hell I will."

"Then how about a kiss?"

His drunken eyes widened. "A kiss?"

Still smiling, she strolled over to where he stood. Holding the truncheon, she kept her hands placed coyly behind her back. Her positioning gave him a good look at her bosom in the cheap, low-cut, red dress.

She stopped a few inches away from him, then purred seductively, "Yes, a kiss. You want one?"

He grinned and set the lantern at his feet.

"Then close your eyes—"

When he did, she placed her lips gently against his, then brought the lead club down hard on his head. He sank like a stone.

"Now," she called up to Le Veq, "where were we?"

"Who are you?" he asked again in an amazed tone.

"We can talk later." Zahra bet Le Veq was glad she was a woman now. She hastily retrieved her handbag and found a ladder. Bracing it against a vertical beam near where he hung, she climbed up, then lifted her dress and slid her pearl-handled razor out of the leather sheath hugging her thigh. She quickly sawed the blade across the thick ropes until they were cut through. He landed with a thud and a pain-filled moan.

Zahra moved to his side. She felt sorry for him, but there was no time for a long recuperation; someone from the house might be coming along at any moment in search of the missing general. Slipping the pearl-handled razor back into its sheath, she looked him in the eyes and said, "We need to leave."

According to her briefing, Le Veq had been sent to steal the plans detailing the movements of Crete's troops, but he'd obviously failed. She shook her head at the folly of sending a pampered New Orleans dandy into a lion's den like this. She helped him to his feet. "Can you walk?"

He nodded.

"Ride?"

"Yes," Le Veq replied impatiently. "Let's go."

"I was just being concerned. Forgive me," she responded tightly.

With Le Veq's heavy weight leaning against her, Zahra guided him out into the night. She was certain she'd hit Crete hard enough to keep him asleep for a while, but getting away quickly was imperative. They had to walk quite a distance, but the horses Zahra had been promised were waiting in a stand of trees. After sending up a silent thank-you to the unknown provider, she scrambled into the saddle and grabbed the reins.

He had a harder time mounting, however. The numbness in his limbs made it next to impossible for him to grasp the horn and pull his weight up. She imagined it might be days before he regained his strength, but they didn't have days.

Suddenly, barking dogs sounded off in the distance. Crete must have been found. "I hear dogs, my friend."

"Dammit, so do I. I'm trying."

He was only half aboard. Impatient, Zahra maneuvered her mount closer. Reaching out, she grabbed the waist of his filthy trousers and hauled him aboard as best she could onto the back of his horse. "Try and keep up!" she yelled. Digging in her heels, she propelled her animal forward.

Aided by the full light of the moon, they rode fast and hard across Crete's land. When they put some distance between themselves and their pursuers, she brought her horse to a halt, then dismounted quickly. "This will only take a moment."

Reaching into her handbag, she extracted a small leather pouch. "If the dogs come this far, this will make them wish they'd stayed in bed."

While he looked on, Zahra began to sprinkle the mixture of plant material from the pouch in a wide area around where the horses were standing.

"What is it?"

"Powdered red peppers."

"Where'd you learn that trick?" She could hear the admiring smile in his voice.

"My father."

"Does he know you spend your nights rescuing men from barns?"

Zahra looked up at him. Back in New Orleans Archer Le Veq probably had more money and more women than a biblical king. He was as handsome as the devil, too, and neither the dark nor the filth could mask that. She didn't answer his question. Instead, she expertly remounted her horse and said, "We need to ride."

Archer somehow managed to keep up. Through it all he was intrigued by this resourceful and apparently fearless woman. She rode beside him astride. The gaudy dress was hiked up to show legs that shone like polished ebony in the moonlight. This was no prim miss; she'd already proven that.

Once Crete and his dogs were left behind and the sounds of the darkness settled once more, she led them to a spot on the shore of a small cove.

With the smell of the water in the air and the lapping waves the only sound in the night silence, they dismounted. "A gunboat is supposed to meet us here in an hour or so," Zahra explained. How are you faring?"

"Fine," Archer lied as he sank to the rocky ground. In reality, he felt like he'd been dead for a week. The ride had sapped the last of his strength. He'd been hanging in that fetid barn for a day and a half, and he doubted he'd be able to move his arms or shoulders ever again. At this point in time he would have gladly exchanged his entire fortune for a feather bed, a hot bath, and the soft stroking of his golden-skinned mistress, Marie; he was injured, exhausted, and famished. He was thankful to be alive, though, and he owed that to his rescuer. "My thanks for getting me out of there."

Her back to him, her eyes still on the dark horizon, she responded, "You're welcome. It's good to know you have some manners after all."

Archer's eyes narrowed.

Zahra turned to face him. "You seemed pretty disappointed to be rescued by a woman, but then, I've never known a *gens de coleur* to be thankful to anyone but their own kind."

Archer heard the sneer in her voice. "What do you know about the *gens de coleur*?"

"You're slave owners."

"Not all of us."

Zahra snorted and turned her eyes back to the dark water. She hoped the gunboat hadn't been delayed. With such a bright moon, everyone involved in the rescue was at risk, but apparently her superiors thought Le Veq's liberation worth it.

Archer wanted to challenge her narrow-minded thinking, but he decided he was in no mood to fence with her right now; he was too tired. He looked at her in that flashy red dress and wondered about her true identity. She had enough paint on her face to rouge up a bordello. "Do you have any water? A blanket would be greatly appreciated as well." He was starting to shiver even though the July night was warm.

"Let me look in the packs."

Zahra walked to the animals. Her providers had had the foresight to include a couple of canteens and two dry sandwiches. The only blankets available were the ones beneath the saddles, so they would have to do. She returned to find him seated with his back propped up against a tree. She was glad to see he'd had sense enough to move out of the moon's direct light. Kneeling at his side, she placed the canteen and the linen-wrapped sandwiches on the ground. "Lean forward so I can drape this around you."

He complied, then braced himself again. He told her, "You'll have to pour the water down my throat. My arms won't lift."

Zahra looked into his assessing black eyes and saw the pain behind them. She nodded. Tilting the canteen, she slowly poured the water past his opened lips. He drank a bit, then his eyes strayed to hers. His attention made her so uncharacteristically nervous that she lost touch with what she was doing. The water splashed out and drenched his face. He ducked away from the flow, and she felt embarrassment burn her cheeks. "I'm sorry."

Without thought, she wiped away the wetness with her fingers. The beard on his cheeks was rough, yet soft. His skin warm. When she realized what she was doing, she hastily withdrew her hand. His answering smile unnerved her even more.

"Thank you," Archer said softly. He had found it interesting that such an unconventional woman could be moved by something as conventional as a touch. "You didn't answer my question back there. Does your father know what you do?"

Zahra was too flustered to reply with anything other than the truth. "He does."

"And he approves?"

"Yes."

Their eyes locked once more, but Zahra found it impossible to maintain the contact. She'd grown up around men of strength and purpose; a man like Le Veq shouldn't affect her at all, but he did. She handed him the sandwich and went back to her position on the shore.

A short while later, a light flashed out of the darkness on the water; it was the signal. "They're here," Zahra quietly called to him. "Can you stand?"

"Yes." Archer's body protested being set into motion, but he forced himself to his feet. He wobbled a bit due to the weakness in his legs.

Zahra came to his side. "Here. Lean on me. We need to hurry."

Archer knew that anyone seeing him being aided along by a woman who barely reached his collarbone would find the sight comical. He would have laughed too had he not needed her help. He forced himself to have the strength to walk down the rocks.

Two seamen in a rowboat came ashore. Zahra helped Archer get in, then stepped back. She said to the seamen, "Tell your captain thank you."

"Yes, ma'am."

Archer was surprised. "You aren't coming along?"

"No. I have another engagement."

Archer masked his disappointment. "Then this is good-bye. My thanks again."

*"Au revoir, monsieur,"* Zahra replied.

Archer smiled and politely inclined his head. As the canoe pushed off, he saw her walking back towards the horses, where she disappeared into the darkness. He asked the seamen, "Do you know the lady's name?"

"That's the Butterfly."

Archer stared back at the shore in shock. The nom de guerre Butterfly was well known in Union intelligence circles. If the rumors were true, the woman behind the name had spent the last few months posing as a house slave in the kitchens of some of the South's most important generals, feeding Federal forces valuable information on everything from troop movements to how much food the Rebs still had in their stores. The rumors also described the Butterfly as being as beautiful as a sorceress, and twice as deadly. Archer searched the horizon in hopes of a last glimpse of the

fascinating female, but saw only the dark land-
scape. Could she really have been the Butterfly?
More importantly, Archer wondered if they would
ever meet again.

# Chapter 1

October 1871
Calhoun County, South Carolina

"**B**ut I don't want the job," Zahra Lafayette
said, standing on the small front porch
of her ramshackle cabin. She let the night's silence
resettle before turning to look back over her shoulder at the person who'd made the offer. The intelligent black eyes in the gnarled dark face stared
back with a patience Zahra knew all too well. To
the world the old woman was known as Harriet
Tubman, but to Zahra and others, Harriet was
Araminta, the name bestowed upon her at birth.
"The Black Butterfly is no more," she added
plainly.

"I know, but the president wants you, or no
one."

While trying to determine how much of a verbal

14

fight Araminta would put up to convince her to agree, Zahra studied the Carolina night. The moonlit darkness was alive with its nocturnal symphony of frogs, insects and other beasties. Stars were sparkling in the clear skies above. "Under the circumstances, President Grant has quite the nerve asking me for anything."

Seated on an old cane chair, Araminta replied sympathetically, "True, and when I explained the situation to him, he promised he'd look into getting your folks back their land."

Zahra chuckled sarcastically. "He's promised to look into it. What is there to look into? My parents helped the Union fight because the Union asked them to, and now, the land that they worked from dawn to dark to pay off is snatched away like a blanket off a child."

"I know, but if you turn Grant down, they'll never see that land."

And therein lay Zahra's dilemma. She had no leverage to make the government give her parents the justice they deserved. In April 1865, her parents, like other freedmen, had been awarded land under General Sherman's Special Order 15. The order had promised each freedmen family forty acres on confiscated Reb land in an area that reached from Charleston, South Carolina, to Florida's St. John's River. The provision had also been included in the congressional act establishing the Freedman's Bureau, but the summer after Lincoln's death, President Johnson forfeited the Blacks' claims and titles.

"We Black folks are looking into the winds of a storm, Zahra," Araminta pointedy out sagely.

"That's why the president wants you to find out just how strong those winds are."

"Why choose me?"

"Because you were one of the best dispatches the Union had."

During the war, Araminta had headed up a shadowy network of Black spies the army called Black Dispatches. They'd taken on scouting assignments, helped with reconnaissance and gathered information on everything from the deployment of Confederate troops to the size and makeup of fortifications. Some dispatches had even infiltrated the household staffs of the Confederacy's generals and politicians. Zahra had been one of them.

"Why Louisiana?"

"Because the experiment Lincoln called Reconstruction almost succeeded there."

"And now?"

"Now it's like cats being thrown into a bag of dogs. Two warring Republican parties. A Republican governor passing Black Code laws like a Democrat. Bribes, scandals. You name it, it's in New Orleans."

"Along with the Union soldiers."

Araminta nodded.

Zahra thought on that for a long moment and on the heated debate being waged across the country over the soldiers' continued presence in Louisiana. "This isn't about the race's plight at all. What Grant's really after is something that will help him decide how soon he can withdraw the soldiers so that he can get Congress and the newspapers off his backside."

"Correct," Araminta replied, then added sarcastically, "but we're just poor, simple colored women. We're only supposed to see what they tell us we see."

"Like telling a blind man he's touching a rabbit when it's really a water moccasin." Zahra shook her head at Grant's lame attempt to pull the wool over her eyes.

Araminta laughed at the analogy. "True. Oh, I've missed having you in my life."

Zahra nodded. "I've thought of you often as well."

They hadn't seen each other since the end of the war. Zahra's family had been spying for the government of the United States since the 1700's, and what she hadn't learned about intelligence gathering from her parents, she had learned from Araminta. Her parents and grandparents taught her to track, to move silently, and to listen to her surroundings, but under Araminta's tutelage, she'd learned ciphers and disguises, how to blend into crowds, and to estimate the size of a Reb brigade. Most importantly though, she'd learned when hardtack, a standard Union food ration during the war, was too wormy to eat.

Araminta said wistfully as if remembering, "Even though the boys were dying all around us, we managed to do some good."

Zahra nodded in agreement, but then added knowingly, "We had some frightening times, though."

Araminta studied her. "I don't remember you being afraid of anything."

"It was '63. Near the Combahee River. We were with Col Montgomery and his Black soldiers."

"Oh, I remember that day. We had a good old time."

Zahra laughed. "I didn't. I'd never been behind enemy lines before, and I was so terrified I thought I would shake to pieces."

Araminta sounded surprised. "You didn't show it."

Zahra thought back. "You led out eight hundred captives that day."

"*We* led, but that was only because the Rebs were too busy trying to keep Montgomery's boys from burning and stealing everything in sight. Them Rebs didn't have time to fuss with us. The flames in those cotton warehouses were high as the sky."

Zahra remembered the sounds of the pitched battle, the smoke and the smells of burning cotton and wood. The memory faded, and Zahra's mind returned to the present and Grant's offer. "What worries me," she said in a serious tone, "is Grant's people using whatever I find out to pound the last few nails into Reconstruction's coffin. All the Black Codes, the White Leagues, the killings. The soldiers didn't die for this."

"I know, but the race needs to know how strong the winds are, too. So we can prepare."

"Prepare for what?"

"Folks are talking about leaving the South and heading west where the Democrats can't reach them. Everything you find out in New Orleans we'll send onto the Loyal Leagues and veteran's societies across the South. If Grant pulls those soldiers, all hell is going to break loose."

It was the first time Zahra had heard talk about leaving the South. How could she leave? She'd been born here and, before the war, had planned to be buried here. Now with all the lawlessness and violence everywhere, her future was as up in the air as the race's. "How long does he envision the job taking?"

"Depends on how much you can glean. Six months. A year maybe."

Zahra didn't doubt her abilities to handle a long-term assignment, but she would have preferred spending her time on a job that she had faith in. However, the carrot Grant was dangling before her was a powerful one. Would he really restore the title to her parents' land? She was admittedly skeptical. The president was a politician, after all, and a promise made today could be worth dirt by dawn tomorrow, yet the hope was there, and as Araminta pointed out, declining would ensure the loss of her parents land forever. "When does he want me to leave?"

"As soon as you're ready."

"Any idea how he wants me to handle my identity? I can't skulk around alleys for six months hoping to hear something."

"I've been thinking on that."

"And?"

"New Orleans is a big fancy place, but in fancy places and in little places what two things always make men witless?"

"Drink and loose women."

Araminta's face broke into a smile. "You always were smart."

Zahra grinned, "Flattery. That almost makes me afraid to ask how these loose women and drinking will come into play."

"I want you to open a house of ill repute. You'll serve liquor and have rooms for gambling."

Zahra stared and then laughed. "What?"

The old woman nodded. "Yep. Lots of sinning going on in New Orleans. Drink and loose women ought to pry open a slew of lips."

"True," Zahra replied, "but couldn't I go in as someone a bit more reputable?"

"Nope. This will work best. If we send you in as a seamstress or a cook, you won't have access to the men you need to be with. Politicians don't patronize seamstresses, their wives do, and from what I'm told the women spend most of their time shopping, so they won't be of any use."

Zahra wasn't surprised that Araminta had all avenues of escape blocked by logic; she had one of the most strategic minds Zahra had ever encountered. Zahra sighed with resignation. "Will I have to find a house on my own?"

"No. The government has that taken care of. The house you'll be using is inside the city. Originally belonged to an old Reb colonel who died in the war. Union used it as a hospital, but it's been empty since the surrender."

"Is the interior in good condition?"

"Apparently not, but the president's folks are getting it fixed up."

Zahra was taken aback by that statement. "The

work on the house has already begun? That was a bit presumptuous of them, don't you think? How do they know I'll even agree?"

"I told them you would."

Zahra went still. She stared. "But why?"

"Because of your parents, and, in spite of the Black Butterfly being dead, because you enjoy this business. Always have. Probably always will."

Zahra would be the first to admit that the drudgery of being a laundress oft times made her yearn for the life she'd led as a dispatch. Kneeling over her washboard under the hot sun and scrubbing clothes until her hands were raw helped pay the old cabin's rent and put food on her table, but did she want to do it until she was old and gray? And Araminta was right; if she could help her parents . . . Her decision made, she said, "Okay. I'll do this, but if Grant doesn't keep his promise . . ." She had no idea what she would do, but she doubted Grant wanted her masquerading as a White House servant while she came up with a plan. In that role she could wreak a lot of havoc—just ask the defeated Confederacy.

Araminta echoed Zahra's thoughts. "If he goes back on his promise, we'll handle it when the time comes. I've asked an old friend to aid you. During the war, she was known as Lilac."

"I remember people speaking very highly of her. Is she in New Orleans?"

"Yes, runs a highfalutin brothel there."

"Then why not use her and her place?"

"She and her man are active Radicals. Because of that the Redemptionists won't patronize her establishment—which means you can't declare yourself for either side. If the Democrats think you're leaning towards the Radicals they'll stop coming around and we'll get nothing out of this plan."

Zahra understood.

Araminta studied Zahra for a moment before saying, "Grant's mission aside, your most important job will be your reports to the Loyal Leagues, veteran's groups, and the township associations across the South. They are going to send trusted associates to New Orleans to help you with the Grant job but more importantly to help you spy for the race. We need to know if moving west will be necessary."

They spent a few more moments discussing the ins and outs of this secondary mission.

Araminta asked, "I'm assuming the madam of the house will not be available to the customers?"

"Correct." Zahra had no intentions of submitting herself to any of the men.

"I thought not, so be careful who you hire to do the actual deed. You probably shouldn't hire any whores from Washington. No way of knowing who else is privy to this plan of Grant's, and I don't want you taking on any Democrat spies."

Zahra agreed wholeheartedly. "But who's going to pay for all this? Surely not this laundress."

Araminta smiled, then called out, "Nelson! Bring that box."

Nelson was the young man who'd accompanied Araminta on her journey here to Charleston to see

Zahra. After dinner he'd excused himself and gone for a walk. At Araminta's call, he came out of the woods carrying a small trunk. He was a tall man, over six feet in height, but the manner in which he was bent over made Zahra assume that the trunk was heavy.

He set the box on the wooden porch, and the dull thud spoke to its weight. "I took the bedrolls out of the wagon. Where do you want them put?"

"We'll talk about it later. I'm sure Zahra will have a place for us to set up our love nest for the night."

Only Zahra's training kept the surprise from showing on her face, but she must have slipped somehow, because Araminta cackled in reaction, "You didn't know Nelson and I are married?"

Zahra shot him a quick glance before answering. "No."

"Been married since '69."

The tall and handsome Nelson Davis had to be a good two decades younger than Araminta, but then, the woman many called Moses had always been unconventional and had always lived life on her own terms. After all, her first escape from slavery had occurred when she'd only been seven years of age. Zahra could only imagine how the tongues of the old abolitionist guard must be wagging over the marriage.

Nelson told the women, "I'll be around back if you need me."

After his departure, Araminta held out her hand and said, "Here's the key. Open it up."

Zahra pushed the skinny key into the lock on

the front of the trunk. She pulled back the lid, and the moonlight fell on the stacks of money inside. She stared, stunned. "Where'd this come from?"

"President's man. It's for your expenses, bribes, whatever you need."

Zahra picked up a bundled stack. "Is it real?"

Araminta shrugged. "I suppose so. Then again, maybe it's just real enough to use."

Zahra chuckled but dearly hoped the bills weren't counterfeit. She closed the lid and redid the lock. She'd take a closer look at the cache tomorrow when the sun came up.

"That's the only key, Zahra," Araminta warned.

Zahra placed the key into the pocket of her worn skirt, then said with amused affection, "A new husband, a trunk full of money. Any more surprises?"

Araminta smiled. "None that this old mind can remember at the moment. Something may come back to me in the morning, though."

"Then I guess we should turn in," Zahra said. "How about you and Nelson sleep in my bed and I'll make do out here?"

"Are you sure?"

"Yes."

"Thank you, Zahra. Let me go fetch him." Araminta eased herself out of the cane chair and down the two steps.

As Zahra watched her disappear around the side of the cabin, her thoughts returned to the president's request. Araminta seemed convinced the race would be helped by the information Zahra would compile, but the South was so fraught with bloodshed, terror, and fear that she hoped it wouldn't come too late.

# Chapter 2

~~~⌒⌒⌒~~~

*November 1871*
*New Orleans*

**A**fter a rousing evening with his mistress,
the sated Archer Le Veq lay in bed while
she slept by his side. Her name was Lynette Dubois, and her quiet breathing barely ruffled the
silence—a marked contrast to the arias of or-
gasms that had filled the bedroom earlier. Thinking back on the erotic interlude brought a smile
to his full lips. The uninhibited Lynette was
worth every penny he paid to keep her gowned
in the latest fashions and to lease her this well-
appointed apartment. Unlike some of his past
mistresses, she never pestered him about wanting to marry but seemed content with their mu-
tually beneficial arrangement; that was worth
every penny, too.

26

Under the light of the dimmed lamp, Archer gently traced a brown finger down her golden cheek, then moved a damp strand of her auburn hair away from her face. In the days before the war, a mulattress as comely as Lynette would have been presented at one of the city's famed quadroon balls with the intent of snaring a wealthy protector. Back then, *plaçées*, as the women were known, were as common in New Orleans as bribes. Some men spent their entire lives with one *plaçée*; siring children, building her a home, and treating her as a wife in everything but name. Then there were the men who went through *plaçées* like mistresses went through hats. Archer had once counted himself amongst them. During his younger days, he'd supported three mistresses, but the expense and the physical stamina necessary to keep each of them happy had all but killed him—not to mention the ribbing he'd had to endure from his brothers each time the women bumped into each other on the street and a catfight ensued.

Now he was older and wiser. He had only one mistress; he was the owner of one of the city's finest hotels; and he had the love of his family. Were the state of Louisiana not mired in political turmoil, his life would be one of perfect contentment.

He'd just drifted off to sleep when a loud knocking on the apartment's front door roused him. The pounding awakened Lynette as well. Sleepily she made to rise, but Archer stayed her with a kiss on her forehead. "Go back to sleep. I'll see who it is."

Grabbing a robe, he padded barefoot out of the room.

It was his brother, Beau, and the worry on his face gave Archer pause. "What's happened?

"Dunn. He's taken ill. The doctors aren't giving him much time."

Archer was stunned. "We were just together the other day. He had what he thought was a cold."

"Apparently it's far worse. His wife has called in a number of physicians, and many of the Republicans are arriving. You should come."

"All right." Archer shook off the cloudiness of sleep in his mind. "I'll dress and be right there."

Beau nodded and departed.

Archer closed the door and hurried back into the bedroom.

"Are you leaving?" Lynette asked. She'd not taken his advice about going back to sleep. Her nude body shimmered in the lamp she'd lit in his absence. "Is something amiss?"

"Oscar Dunn is gravely ill."

She pulled up the sheet to ward against the night chill rising in the room. "Lieutenant Governor Dunn?"

Archer struggled into his clothes. "Yes. Beau appeared very worried."

"Has he been ill long?"

"Not that I know of."

"Then maybe he will recover quickly."

Archer quickly donned his coat. "I hope you

are right." Ready to depart now, he leaned over and placed a farewell kiss on her soft mouth. *"Au revoir,* sweet."

*"Au revoir,"* she whispered in reply.

Outside, the weather, which had been warm for the past few days, was now noticeably colder, and a frigid wind blew ominously. Chilled to the bone, Archer hurried to his carriage.

When he arrived at the Dunn home, he paid his respects to the stricken family, then went into the parlor to keep watch with the dozen other men talking quietly around the fireplace. Most were Customhouse Republicans, the Radical wing of the Republican Party controlled by Dunn, dedicated to legislative reform and championing the rights of Louisiana's Black citizens. Glancing around the room, Archer saw no one from the Conservative Republicans in attendance, and he thought that was just as well. The Conservatives were loyal to the state's carpetbagger governor, the Illinois-born Henry Clay Warmoth. As a result, Warmoth and Lieutenant Governor Dunn were locked in a bitter power struggle over which faction, radical or conservative, would control the party and ultimately the state's political machine.

But that had no bearing at the moment. Everyone was concerned about Dunn.

Over the course of the evening, crowds of concerned freedmen and other Black citizens began to gather outside the home's front gate, while inside, Archer and the others discussed Dunn's illness.

Archer and the others were still in attendance when Dr. Beach, Dunn's family physician, returned twice during the night. Upon leaving the sickroom the second time, the doctor announced gravely, "It appears his brain has been adversely affected, too." Then he slowly looked around at those assembled in the room and said simply, "Pray, gentlemen. Pray."

Archer went home at sunrise and grabbed a few hours of sleep. Then, leaving the day's operations of his hotel to his capable assistant André Renaud, he rushed back to the Dunn home.

The number of people in the house had grown. Solemn-faced relatives had arrived from the outer parishes, and there were many more Radicals in attendance as well. For the rest of the day, a cross section of New Orleans's best physicians came to call at the home offering aid, but Dunn's condition continued to deteriorate. By Tuesday morning, he had slipped into unconsciousness.

At 6:00 A.M. on November 22, 1871, forty-five-year-old Oscar James Dunn, the first Black man to be duly elected lieutenant governor of the state of Louisiana, drew his last breath.

"Such a tragedy," Juliana Le Veq Vincent declared that next evening. "He was a great man and had the potential to rise even higher."

Archer nodded soberly. He and three of his brothers—Drake, Beau, and Philippe—were gathered around the table with their mother, Juliana, as they often were for dinner. Missing was their oldest brother Raimond, who was vacationing on the island of Cuba with his wife, Sable, and their children. Also absent was Juliana's husband, Henri, who was visiting relatives on Martinique.

Drake asked Archer, "I know you've heard the rumors that Oscar was poisoned. Do you think there's any truth to them?"

The theory that Dunn may have been poisoned had surfaced as a result of the suddenness and violent nature of the illness, but in reply to Drake's question, Archer shrugged. "Many stood to profit from Oscar's death."

"Most of all Governor Warmoth," Beau pointed out.

Before his death, Dunn had challenged the governor's political power so effectively that the whispers calling for Warmoth's impeachment were now rising to shouts loud enough to be heard in Shreveport. With Dunn no longer leading the opposition, Warmoth had to be relieved.

Although Archer didn't voice his opinion aloud, he was all but convinced that Dunn had indeed been poisoned. Finding the culprit or culprits involved would be difficult, but Oscar had been Archer's political mentor and friend. As Oscar's friend, Archer felt duty bound to root out the truth, not only for his own peace of mind but also for Oscar's widow and the thousands of freedmen who'd elected Dunn with the hopes of a better future for themselves and their children.

A few days later, Archer joined Republicans of all stripes in the funeral procession that followed Oscar Dunn's casket to the cemetery. In line were five hundred metropolitan policemen and over eight hundred militiamen. The Masonic lodges in their brightly colored uniforms marched with the city's Black benevolent societies. Governor Warmoth, Mayor Benjamin Flanders and General Augustus Longstreet were also among the mourners, as were city administrators, judges, Republican ward clubs, and state legislators. It was the largest funeral gathering in the city's history.

Afterwards, a morose Archer spent the evening alone in his finely furnished apartments located on the top floor of his hotel. In his hand was a crystal snifter of his favorite cognac. The drink had dulled his sorrow somewhat, but it seemed to have enhanced the burning questions surrounding Dunn's untimely death. He raised his glass and said softly aloud, "To you, Oscar, old friend. May you find rest and peace from a tumultuous and murderous world."

He downed the rest of the expensive liquor, threw the empty snifter into the fireplace, and dragged himself to bed.

The next morning, still feeling the effects of the cognac, Archer, accompanied by Drake, rode out to the countryside to investigate yet another murder by the local supremacists. All over the South groups like the White Camelia and the supposedly outlawed Kluxers were hiding their identities beneath sheets and masks and spending the nights terrorizing freedmen to keep them from exercising their rights to vote, send their children to school, and work where they wanted. Unfortunately it was not a new phenomenon, but in Louisiana the deaths were rising. The soldiers posted in and around New Orleans were only a small deterrent, because they couldn't be everywhere.

"I think that's the place there," Archer said.

The brothers pulled their horses to a halt and slowly dismounted. The small shack in the middle of the field had burned to the ground, and the charred logs that had once been its walls were still smoldering. Archer's lips thinned angrily. He looked around but saw no one. "Here's hope that the folks who lived here fled and weren't inside."

They walked closer. Archer had seen many scenes like this over the past few years, but the fury it invoked in him never lessened. Spying something in the ruins, he used the toe of his boot to move some of the burned debris, then knelt to pick up a charred Bible. Beside it lay a child-sized metal spoon blackened and twisted by the heat. His anger increased. No one was safe from the hate of the men behind this; not children, not God. "This has to stop," Archer said tightly.

Drake nodded. "Let's see if we can find somebody who can tell us what happened here, then we'll head back."

The seething Archer mounted, and the brothers galloped off.

* * *

Because it was early morning, the narrow, dusty road was relatively free of traffic, thus allowing the tarp-covered coach to travel the last dozen miles to New Orleans at a fairly good pace. While the chatter of the women flowed around her, Zahra focused unseeingly on the miles and miles of sugarcane fields flanking the road. Every now and then she spotted small armies of Black men, women, and children tending the fields. The sight of them working the land made her think on her parents, but she set the thoughts aside. She'd dwell upon them once she and her companions were settled into their place in New Orleans.

Zahra's first and only trip to Louisiana had been in April 1861, a few weeks after the firing on Fort Sumter. She and a small band of dispatches had slipped into New Orleans to determine the strength of its militia and the extent of its defenses. A year later, the intelligence had proved useful to the Union navy, who, under the command of loyal Tennessean Admiral David Glasgow Farragut, as well as the army under General Benjamin Butler, captured New Orleans, thus bestowing upon the largest city in the South the dubious distinction of being the first Confederate city to fall back into Mr. Lincoln's hands.

Now she was returning, a decade later, but there would be no skulking this time; she would be coming in as brazen as Salome dressed in her veils. The big coach she and the women were traveling in was protected by a tarp that bore the mud and dust of the long journey across the South. Other than having to replace a wheel outside of Atlanta, the trip had been free of mechanical mishaps. Zahra was weary of riding, though. She would have preferred a saddle and horseback to the hard seat and springs they were bouncing along on, but this was the only logical way to transport herself, her five female companions, and all their trunks, portmanteaus, and hat boxes. Once they reached the city, the other reason for traveling by coach would be revealed. Araminta wanted them to attract attention, and Zahra was certain that once that was accomplished the city of New Orleans would be knocked on its rump.

Zahra had asked the driver, a man named Alfred Wilson, to halt the carriage when they reached the outskirts of the city. He did just that. When they came to a stop on the side of the deserted road, Zahra said, "All right, ladies, we have to get out and see to the coach."

The women looked perplexed. The blonde Chloe Lee, who, in her interview with Zahra, had claimed to be a second cousin of General Lee, asked in a confused drawl, "What're we going to do?"

Zahra explained. "I want us to make a grand entrance, and the coach has been outfitted to do just that, but everything is hidden beneath the tarps."

The redheaded Matilda Trent's green eyes grew large. "Sounds excitin', ma'am."

"Yes, it does," added the tall, dark-skinned Lovey France. The light-skinned, auburn-haired

Adair Rice and the voluptuous brunette, Stella Summers, nodded agreement.

Zahra replied, "Let's hope the men of New Orleans think so, too."

The tarp was secured beneath the coach's frame with ties and large buttons, which were now being undone by the coachman, Alfred. He'd been sent to Zahra by Araminta. A former dispatch, he had a mountain-sized frame with arms that looked capable of crushing anything in their grasp. He would serve as coachman, her head man, and keeper of the peace. Zahra was sure his presence in the house would quell any thoughts of troublemaking by the patrons.

Finished with the task, Alfred slid from beneath the coach and dusted himself off. "Should I change clothes now?"

Zahra nodded. He went to the seat of the coach, took down a large satchel, and headed for the cover of woods.

"All right, ladies, grab an edge and pull."

Once the tarps came free, the women stood, stunned. The apple red coach, with its gold fleurs-de-lis and elaborately decorated lacquered frame, shone like a polished jewel in the Louisiana sun.

Lovey gushed from behind her hands, "Now that is a coach for whores."

Everyone laughed. They then took a slow turn around the wondrous exterior. This was Zahra's first real look at it as well. When Alfred had driven it to the Charleston boardinghouse where Araminta had arranged for him and Zahra to initially meet, the wraps had already been secured. At the time, he'd only been able to give her a peek at the color, but now, seeing it in all its glory, she could only wonder who the craftsman might have been. Araminta claimed to have borrowed it from an acquaintance, but she'd refused to reveal a name. The still marveling Zahra decided it didn't matter. All garishness aside, the workmanship was outstanding. The red lacquer body was smooth and unblemished as glass. The gold paint bordering the doors and fleurs-de-lis looked rich enough to be real. She had no idea what it would take to keep the painted surfaces clean, but she decided she'd let Alfred worry about that.

When Alfred returned, he was dressed in the well-fitting livery of a footman. Zahra was relieved to see that he hadn't been outfitted in red to match the coach. The black uniform with its brass buttons and crisp matching hat made him look stately but no less menacing, which suited her just fine.

Once the women were done admiring the coach, Zahra sent them into the trees as well. They needed to change out of their traveling clothing and put on their gowns. When they returned she was pleased that none of them looked tawdry or cheap. The low-cut décolletage of their dresses and the paint on their faces plainly declared their profession, but the ladies had a sophisticated air about them; an air she'd been counting on when she'd hired them. Zahra's operation had to be top drawer in order for it to be successful, and she needed girls who exuded that same tone.

Alfred called out. "Horses coming."

Zahra hastened into the coach to tie on her domino. The beautiful black satin half mask with its side ribbons covered the upper portion of her face. Making free use of the money in the trunk Araminta had given her, Zahra had had masks fashioned to match each of her new gowns, and this one complemented the black satin gown and cape she was wearing. She would don the domino whenever she appeared in public so as to safeguard her true identity from anyone she'd preyed upon as the Black Butterfly.

The horses appearing over the rise were ridden by Union soldiers. Behind them were more uniformed men driving wagons flanked by walking comrades. As the column neared the red coach and the women, it slowed.

The lead soldier, an older man with a thin frame and muttonchop sideburns, studied the women from atop his saddle for a moment, then spat a wad of tobacco in their direction. "New Orleans doesn't need more strumpets!"

The feisty Lovey gave him a tight little smile, then announced for all the men to hear, "We're not going to New Orleans. We're heading to *your* house!"

He visibly stiffened, and his whiskered face turned whore red. Glaring down at the smiling Lovey, he crisply motioned his men forward and the slow march resumed. The women laughed, and Zahra saw soldiers drop their heads to hide their smiles.

Her blue eyes glittering with annoyance, Chloe Lee said, "Old hypocrite. He'll probably be our first customer."

Alfred took a low-slung basket from the space beneath his driver's seat; while they all looked on, he withdrew yet another surprise. Alfred fit the horses with new red-and-gold harnesses that were studded with rhinestones, then he placed matching red-and-gold headpieces, complete with plumes, on their heads. The women looked on with grins. The horses were as finely outfitted as ones in a traveling circus. Zahra thought they'd look smart pulling the red coach into town and hoped they would cause the stir she was after.

Once the horses were ready to go, Alfred politely assisted the silk-gowned women back into the carriage, then took the reins and headed for New Orleans.

It was afternoon when they entered the city, and the busy streets were clogged with dust, coaches, wagons, pushcarts, and people of all races. Zahra saw well-dressed citizenry and other folks wearing little more than rags. Vendors seemed stationed on each corner, hawking everything from flowers, to braised meats, to newspapers. In the air were the smells of the Mississippi, burning charcoal, and the fetid pungency of a city filled with thousands of people.

Because of the pressing traffic, the coach's

progress was slow at best, but the snail's pace worked to Zahra's advantage, for it gave the citizens an opportunity to take a good long look at the scarlet coach and its four plumed horses. From the shocked faces following in their wake Zahra was certain the city had never seen anything quite like this. Her painted girls, waving wildly from the windows and tossing sweets and candies to the young men running beside the coach, only added to the spectacle. On the walks, fashionably dressed Creole women watched, rooted to the spot, their mouths open. Men grinned broadly. People pointed excitedly, and mothers hastily covered the eyes of their children. One soldier was so entranced that he walked right into an old woman's vegetable cart, toppling her wares into the street. Other coaches maneuvered close to get a better view, and when the girls leaned out of the windows to wave, the smiling male occupants fervently responded with calls for the girls' names.

Chloe pulled herself back inside and said to Zahra excitedly, "We have a train of people following us!"

Zahra looked out of her window. Sure enough, it looked as if half the city was streaming behind the horses. She could see adolescents running happily beside the coach, and she heard Alfred barking at people to keep clear of the wheels. Zahra felt like a marshal leading a parade. The only thing missing was a band. She smiled beneath the domino, pleased with the knowledge that even in jaded and sometimes decadent New

Orleans, their entrance would keep tongues wagging for weeks to come.

By the time Alfred halted the coach in front of the fancy house the ladies were to occupy, the crowd behind them had grown larger. Men vocally competed with each other to gain the attention of the girls while stray dogs ran around barking happily at all the commotion. Peddlers were there, as were men on horseback and men driving wagons. She saw soldiers in the midst, and uniformed city policemen too, but she wasn't certain if they were there to keep the peace or if they just wanted a look like everyone else.

Men would relate later that the girls descending gracefully from the coach were as colorful as songbirds. The crowd roared appreciatively as gowns of canary and cardinal were joined by emerald, lapis, and dove gray. The women were tall, short, and in between. Five of them. All sporting earbobs, face paint, and rhinestone-accented pumps that matched their gowns. A dark one with the bearing of a queen stood next to a woman so fair her race was uncertain. There was a redhead, a blonde, and a brunette. The gowns were cut teasingly low, showing off wares that could be fully unveiled for the right price.

Zahra was pleased by all the attention. She was counting on word of mouth to start the ball rolling, and this would send it well on its way. She wanted every man of importance to patronize the soon-to-be-opened establishment, because the more the men drank, gambled, and patronized the girls, the more the men would talk. Three more girls would be arriving by train later in the week, but for now, Zahra planned to bait her hook with the five lures that she had.

"You getting out?" Matilda asked, sticking her red head into the coach through the open door.

"Yes, I am."

"Well, come on," she cried excitedly. "We want to see the inside of the house."

Zahra made sure her domino was secured, then smiled at the nineteen-year-old Matilda's youthful enthusiasm. Satisfied that her features were safe, the woman once known as the Black Butterfly stepped out of the coach.

Her appearance drew applause and whistles. She inclined her head to acknowledge the approval, and the crowd responded with more raucous hoots and hollers. A grinning Zahra turned and took her first close look at the big white house. It was a typical New Orleans design, more Spanish than French, with intricate ironwork on the front gate, the second-floor verandahs, and the two large side porches positioned on opposing ends of the place. Zahra herded her women onto the porch, which was framed by two tall white columns. Out of her handbag she took the door key that Alfred had given her, then she let them in.

The interior was done up in ivory and gold. Zahra and her companions took a studied look around, and what they saw widened their eyes. Amidst the gold and ivory upholstered chairs, settees and sofas, sculpted nudes were everywhere: atop pedestals, posing in the windows, doubling as table legs, framing mirrors over mantels. The renderings were exquisite in both form and detail. A life-sized statue stood by the winding staircase that led to the upper floors. The nude woman stood facing the parlor. An equally nude man stood flush behind her. His hand was on her breast, and her head was thrown back in the throes of passion. The piece looked so realistic that Zahra felt heat rise in her blood. Hoping to find something a bit less stimulating on which to settle her attention, she turned to view the waist-high, white-and-gold bar that dominated one corner. Behind the bar was a large, gold-framed mirror and shelves to hold the various liquors. Along the front were intricate friezes of nude men and women entwined in all manner of erotic couplings. It was a decadent, voyeuristic feast that made Zahra look away to continue her visual assessment. Above their heads hung a fancy, two-tier, cut-glass chandelier. Painted on the golden plaster around it were elaborate frescoes of nubile, nude women, their eyes sly, their smiles beckoning. Everything in the room radiated a sensuality that seemed to permeate the air. Zahra felt herself affected by the riveting décor and wondered how much time it might take before she became immune to the decidedly seductive surroundings.

Everyone's attention was then caught by a woman slowly descending the grand staircase.

She was shrouded in a brown hooded cape.

Zahra asked, "Who are you?"

The woman lowered the hood to reveal a beautiful golden face and honey gold hair. "I'm Sophie Reynolds."

Zahra walked around her companions to move closer. "May I ask what you're doing here and how you got inside?"

"I bring greetings from Minta."

*Code words.* "I hear she's doing well," Zahra replied.

"I hear she had lilacs at her wedding."

*Lilac.* "Indeed, she did."

Zahra saw the woman known as Lilac smile in response to the correctly phrased reply. Zahra also noted that the gesture seemed to bring even more light to her face, a face a bit older than Zahra had originally surmised.

The girls were eyeing the exchange curiously and looked to Zahra for explanation. "Sophie and I share a mutual friend," she said simply.

Sophie inclined her head like a queen. "Welcome to Louisiana, ladies."

The women all responded with, "Thank you."

Sophie gestured grandly at the expansive gold and white parlor they were standing in. "I took the liberty of furnishing the place. I hope it's suitable."

Stella, who was as struck by the place as the rest of her companions, whispered with awe. "Oh, yes."

"I agree," Lovey echoed.

Chloe said, "It's like being in a palace."

The smiling Sophie asked, "Would you care to see the rest of the house?"

Zahra nodded.

The tour revealed bedrooms for the girls, servants quarters and the outdoor kitchen attached to the house by a breezeway. The colonel's old study had been turned into a room for the gamblers, complete with dark wood furniture and a billiard table against one wall. One the third floor was a lovely bedroom suite that would be Zahra's, but a large room on the second floor drew the most attention.

A narrow hallway ran between the outer wall and inner wall. Although the interior was unlit they could not help noticing the glass that made up the inner room's walls. Confused as to what the room might be, Zahra turned to look at Sophie, who replied, "This is for your voyeurs. Out here will be the chairs, and in there," she explained, gesturing towards the room with its red-and-black velvet walls and matching bedding, "is where your girl and her gentleman will be."

Only Zahra's training kept her eyes from going wide as saucers.

The girls were studying the room with wise smiles and a few giggles. Sophie said with amusement, "I'm always surprised by how much men will pay just to watch."

A decidedly shocked Zahra shook herself and followed Sophie down the hall. *What have I gotten myself into?* All in all, Zahra thought the house would be perfect for what she'd come to New Orleans to do, but she was going to have to get accustomed to the place's decidedly sensual atmosphere.

"Will you be needing servants?" Sophie asked her as they made their way back down to the big white and gold parlor. The other women had peeled off to take longer looks at the rooms and the décor, leaving Zahra to talk to the mysterious Sophie Reynolds alone.

They were now outside and walking along the path that wound through the overgrown gardens in the back of the house. Zahra finally responded, "Araminta said people are being sent."

"Well, if you need more I have a few names I can pass along."

"What is your role in this?" Zahra asked.

"Just to get you settled. Answer any questions you may have. I'm really your competitor. Did Minta tell you?"

"Yes, she did. How long have you known her."

"Since right before the war. I ran a house in Maryland that was a stop on the Underground Railroad in addition to being a brothel, and I handled some of her freight."

Zahra knew that *freight* was the coded word for runaways.

Sophie stopped before a small fountain, "Do you really like the place? Minta sent me funds and said spare no expense, so I didn't. I had all of the statuary in storage. No one will know it's mine."

Zahra didn't lie. "It's a bit unnerving."

"Not what you're accustomed to, I'll bet?" she replied with a twinkle in her sherry eyes. "Don't worry. In a month's time, you won't even notice the nudes."

Zahra wasn't so sure. Even now her mind's eye refused to let go of the memory of the statue of the man and woman by the staircase.

Zahra had another question. "What needs to be done to keep the business from being pestered by the city fathers?"

"All payments and permits have been arranged. New Orleans is a very tolerant city, and as long as the right people are kept happy with the occasional *gift*, you and your establishment should be fine."

Zahra assumed she meant bribes. "I'll need to know who these gifts are to go to in the future."

"Of course. We can talk about it after you get settled. You and I will have to come up with a way to communicate, since we can't be seen as friendly by the public." Sophie added wryly, "Especially once you begin stealing my customers."

Zahra met her eyes. "Will that be a problem?"

"No. You won't be in operation long enough to put me in the poorhouse. Or at least I hope not. You have some very beautiful girls."

"Thank you."

"And hopefully your girls will be able to attract the customers who won't patronize me because of my radical politics." Sophie studied Zahra for a few moments, then asked, "Do you plan to offer yourself as bait?"

"No."

Sophie smiled softly. "I thought not, but excluding yourself from the menu will make the men even more eager for your company. They won't be able to resist the challenge you present." She then looked Zahra up and down with a critical eye. "You have a good figure. Make sure your gowns highlight that. You are a madam, and you should look like one. Now, tell me why you wear the domino."

"I was a dispatch during the war, and I don't wish to be recognized."

"I see."

They began to walk once more. Sophie asked, "Is there anything else I might help you with?"

"Instruct me on the ways of a madam. I have played bawdy women in the past, but never a madam."

"Well, first of all, you need to establish a style. There are madams who are flamboyant and loud, and others who conduct their business quietly. You have a certain grace about you that I believe you should incorporate into your Domino. Make her elegant, graceful, but most of all, intelligent enough to take on the men around her. You're not a foolish woman, and Domino shouldn't be either. Flirt, use double entendres, be playful but maintain the aloofness. You want these men following you around like lapdogs."

Zahra chuckled.

"Always protect your girls. That giant man I saw by your carriage should do nicely. Also, I'll send my doctor over so that you two can work out a schedule to have the girls checked on a regular basis. The last thing you want is disease—of any kind."

Zahra took both the safety and health advice to heart. "How will I contact you if I need to?"

"For now, send one of the servants with a note. If we need a more secure means, we can discuss it at another time. Remember you and I will be rivals. If I see you on the street or in one of the shops, I will not acknowledge you."

"I understand."

"Good luck, Madame Domino."

"Thank you."

Sophie raised the hood on her cape, and once her face was hidden, she walked away, leaving Zahra standing in the garden alone.

That evening, Zahra moved into her third-floor suite. The room was cavernous, with gleaming wood floors and a set of French doors leading outside to a verandah where she could sit and sip her morning coffee. The walls were pale gold, and accented with elaborately rendered iron sconces. The design of the sconces was repeated in the standing lamps on each side of the gleaming white, mirrored dressing table. The big wrought-iron bed dominating the room had an upholstered gold canopy and was draped with silky netting. She opened a narrow door and was surprised to see a bathing room complete with a large claw-foot tub.

Closing the door gently she looked around with a smile. The décor was far grander than anything she could ever have imagined. Her little cabin back home with its leaky roof and paneless windows

would have easily fit inside the space. To her further delight, the interior was free of the nudes
and the other sensual trappings so prominently
displayed elsewhere in the house. The beautiful
room could belong to any wealthy woman in the
country, but for the time being it belonged to her,
and Zahra was grateful to have such a haven to
retreat to.

# Chapter 3

**A**rcher spent the morning in his office at the hotel as he did every morning, going over the accounts. He studied billings from the city markets where he purchased fruits and vegetables for the restaurant; from the butchers who supplied his meats; from a plumber and his personal barber. He wrote out the bank drafts, then moved on to the second pile.

Unlike the chaotic years immediately following the surrender, Archer now had no difficulty meeting his financial obligations. Thanks to his own hard work and an infusion of funds from the inheritance the family received courtesy of his mother's Cuban uncle, the Old Pirate, the struggles he'd endured were in the past. However, other business owners in the city had not been as fortunate. After the war, real estate values had plummeted, as shipping interests had. There had been extensive damage to ships and to the port caused by the guns of the Union Navy during the May '62 battle. That and the labor problems following Emancipation had dropped the city to its knees. Recovery was slowly taking place but not in a way envisioned by the Radical Republicans. Instead of the freedmen being able to own land or contract for work under conditions that would ensure their economic independence, they were being forced into agreements with former planters and masters who paid them little more than they'd received as slaves, thus stifling any expansion of the economy. Also impacting the South's recovery were the Northern bankers who, instead of investing in and loaning money to the South, were offering financial assistance to the railroads and burgeoning manufacturing cities like Chicago and St. Louis. Because of this, the North was transforming itself into an industrial giant unlike any the world had ever seen while the South wrestled with economic and societal problems that Archer sensed would keep it mired for years.

He was signing the bill for one of Lynette's new gowns when his brother Philippe entered through the open door and gushed, "Are you going?"

Archer looked up. The excitement on Philippe's tan face was easy to see. "Where?"

"To the formal opening of Madame Domino's new house."

Archer wondered if this was how their big brother Raimond felt when set upon by his younger siblings. "Who is Madame Domino?"

"Don't tell me you haven't heard about her arrival?"

Archer studied the youngest member of the Le Veq family and sighed. "Start from the beginning."

Philippe, who'd been on his way to the docks on the afternoon in question, described to Archer the eye-popping coach.

"Apple red?" Archer echoed skeptically.

"More like ruby red. It was shining like a polished jewel. Even the horses were tarted up with plumes and red rhinestone harnesses. How could you not know? Everyone in town is talking about it."

Archer responded with his patented sarcasm. "Too busy running this hotel, I guess."

"You need to leave this office, at least occasionally, big brother. You're becoming more and more like His Majesty Raimond every day. It's rather frightening."

Not liking being compared to Raimond, Archer cut Philippe a look. "Back to this Madame Domino. Why's she called that?"

"Because she wears one. No one has ever seen her without it."

Archer opened yet another bill from Lynette's dressmaker. "Maybe she looks like a horse's ass."

"Maybe, but below the domino she has the mouth of a goddess. My friends and I are betting she's scarred or disfigured in some way."

Archer met his brother's eyes and shook his head with amused disbelief. "Surely the gamers aren't taking odds?"

"Of course they are. She's quite the mystery."

"What about the other women. Are they behind dominos, too?"

"No, but they're all beauties. The other houses are bound to lose customers once Madame Domino opens her doors."

"And when will that be?"

"Soon, according to this broadside."

Archer took the paper from his brother's hand and read the announcement. " 'The most fascinating women this side of the Mississippi. Grand Opening.' " He handed it back. "Just make sure you wear a sock."

"Lord!" Philippe cracked, "is Raimond in the room?"

Archer leveled him a look. "Out, brat. I've work to do."

They stared at each other with shocked eyes. The phrase was one of Raimond's standards when being pestered by his brothers.

Philippe drawled, "I told you, I'd see a physician about that before it spreads."

Archer pointed to the door. "Good-bye."

An amused Philippe departed.

Archer walked over to the small mirror hanging on the office wall and stuck out his tongue so he could study it in the glass. Was he really turning into Raimond? He placed his palm over his forehead to check his temperature. Suddenly, his brother Drake stood reflected in the mirror behind him. Archer turned.

Drake, whose dark skin was most like their mama's, raised an eyebrow and asked, "Problems?"

"I think I'm turning into Raimond."

Drake chuckled, "I hope not. We'll have to kill you if you do. One His Majesty is quite enough. Two is grounds for justifiable murder."

Archer grinned. "What brings you here?"

"Haven't seen you in a few days. Wanted to find out how the investigation into Oscar's death is faring."

Archer studied him for a moment. "Who says I'm investigating?"

"I know you, Archer. I also know that Oscar was a friend, so, how's it faring?"

Archer surrendered. His brother did know him too well. "I've been trying to get a look at the death certificate, but supposedly it hasn't been finalized or filed."

"Is that unusual?"

"Not really, but what bothers me are the rumors that the family turned down the offers of an autopsy."

Confusion lined Drake's face. "I'd think that if there were questions about his death, his family would move heaven and earth to get answers."

"So would I, but supposedly his family didn't want one."

"Religious reasons?"

Archer shrugged. "I've no way of knowing without speaking with someone in the household."

"Have you made any attempts?"

"One. I went to the house but was told his wife was too distraught to receive visitors."

"That's understandable. His death had to be a shock."

"To everyone."

"Maybe she'll make herself available in a few weeks' time."

"Maybe."

Drake said, "Well, I just stopped by for a second. I'm on my way to see the Ursuline sisters. There's a leak in the convent roof. They want me to see if it can be repaired." Drake's building skills were as well known as his architectural skills.

Archer nodded. "Your little brother was just here."

"He still raving about Madame Domino?"

The amused Archer replied, "Yes."

Drake shook his head. "According to all I've heard, the women made quite the grand entrance into town. Horses wearing feathers. Women wearing feathers."

"So he told me. He wanted to know if I was going to the opening night."

"And are you?"

"No. Lynette and I have plans for the opera."

"I see."

Archer heard the tone. "What?"

"Nothing. Just that the lovely Lynette has you eating out of her hand."

"Because she doesn't press me or harangue me and she's always available when I need her to be. She's the perfect mistress."

"If you like the passive type."

"Passive?"

"Yes. Do the two of you ever argue?"

"Of course not. You don't choose a mistress for her argumentative skills."

"True, but I'd rather a woman challenge me the way the lovely Sable challenges Raimond. Maybe a woman like Lynette is right for you, but I want more."

"Well, I don't. A nice, quiet woman like Lynette suits me just fine. I was the one with three mistresses, remember. I've learned my lesson." Archer then brought the conversation back to the city's newest brothel. "So, are you going to the opening?"

"I may, just to see the interior of the place. I know some of the artisans who worked on it. They say it is the most elegant whorehouse outside of Paris."

"Really?"

"That's what they said." Drake headed out of the door and tossed back with a smile, "Enjoy the opera. And please, see someone about that Raimond disease. It could prove fatal."

Archer grinned and returned to the paperwork on his desk. The next morning he and Drake rode out to investigate the results of yet another night of terror. Like last time, he and Drake found a burned-out shack, but this time they found the residents; a man and his son, hanging like strange fruit in the trees.

Over the next few days, courtesy of Araminta and her contacts, former dispatches from all over the South arrived to aid Zahra's mission. They came from Mississippi, Florida, and other places across the South to serve as house maids, kitchen maids, gardeners, and coachmen. Most were strangers. However, when Chloe escorted the newest arrival into Zahra's second-floor office, Zahra looked up from the newspaper she'd been scanning and screamed excitedly, "Wilma!"

As Chloe closed the door and quietly exited, the two women embraced with a happiness that mirrored their friendship.

"It's good to see you, lass," Wilma Gray whispered fervently. "So good."

They rocked each other for a long moment more, then broke the embrace. Zahra wiped away the mist of tears in her eyes and smiled at the rotund Irish woman. "It's been a long time."

During the war, Wilma and Zahra had spent six months living together in Alabama spying on the Confederate navy anchored in Mobile Bay. "Do you live here in New Orleans?" Zahra asked.

Wilma shook her head. "No. Boston. Got here by train last night. Spent the morning finding a decent boardinghouse, then asked around until I found someone who knew of the mysterious Madame Domino. Miss Harriet told me the plan."

"You are looking well."

"I'm old and feeling it, but you're as beautiful as ever. Have you found a man strong enough to match you?"

Zahra shook her head and smiled. "No. Doubt I will, old as I am, but it's wonderful having you here."

Wilma looked around the office. "Nice place," she said. With an amused twinkle in her blue eyes, she added, "No nudes?"

Zahra chuckled. "Not in here, thank goodness."

"The statue by the steps—the one with the man and woman, liked to stole me breath."

"I know. The atmosphere down there is very, shall we say, heady?"

"That's putting a polite name on it." Wilma ran her eyes over Zahra, then asked easily, "So tell me all you've done since we were together last."

"First, would you like some refreshment? Tea, café? We're still waiting for our cook to arrive from Atlanta, so I'm afraid I can't offer you anything of substance to eat."

"Tea will be fine."

Using the bell pull behind her desk, Zahra summoned one of the new kitchen maids, who promised to return promptly with the tea. The young woman, a dispatch from Florida named Suzette, kept her word, and when she retired, the two old friends sat, sipped, and caught up on each other's lives.

"I've been living in Boston with my son," Wilma began. "He's married to a wonderful lassie, and they have two children. Most beautiful grandchildren in the world." She met Zahra's smile with one of her own before continuing. "Have me own dress shop now, but work with the indigent, too. Many refugees are arriving north with nothing but the clothes on their backs."

"How much is your organization able to help?"

"Quite a bit, actually. Boston has a large Colored community that's been lending a helping hand for almost a hundred years, but donations have been declining, and it's making the work harder."

"The country is weary of the race's problems. They don't understand why the freedmen aren't content. After all, they are free."

"Few Northerners realize the issue is far more complex than that." Wilma sighed and shook her head. "So where are you living now?"

"Near Columbia."

"Miss Harriet said the government confiscated your parents' land?"

Zahra nodded tightly over her cup. "The president has promised to look into the matter in exchange for my help here."

"Do you believe him?"

Zahra met Wilma's blue eyes and said truthfully, "I don't know. My head says no, but my heart holds hope."

"Well, my Boston friends and I are very disappointed with Grant. All the scandals, all the graft and bribes. Not to mention him and the Republicans turning their backs on your people. It's unconscionable."

Zahra agreed.

"Have you heard from your folks?"

"No. I've no idea whether they are still on the land or not." Zahra last saw her parents right before she left South Carolina. They, like their neighbors, had armed themselves and were determined to hold on to the land by force if need be for as long as they could. She knew that if the situation became intolerable they'd return to Sanctuary, the town in the Carolina swamp where Zahra was born and raised. But the citizens of the swamps from Florida to Louisiana were also being forced out, by Rebs who didn't want Maroon communities of Blacks nearby and by speculators anxious to sell the land to anyone wealthy enough to ensure them a fat profit.

Wilma said genuinely, "Let's hope you hear from them soon."

They spent the next hour talking about the operation Zahra was putting into place. Wilma agreed with Zahra's theory that President Grant was after more than just a report on the state of the race. "The people and the big newspapers back home are calling for the removal of the troops. In their minds, once that is accomplished the war will officially be over, and life can go on."

"He can't remove the troops," Zahra said. "If he does, the Redemptionists and the Kluxers will steep the South in blood. The only thing preventing that now are the soldiers."

"I know, but the North doesn't seem to care."

Knowing that further discussion on the nation's disinterest in the fate of the newly freed slaves would only fill her with frustration, Zahra turned the conversation back to the operation. "So what role does Araminta have you playing in our little drama here?"

"I'm to be a seamstress. Araminta's contacts have found a woman who wants to sell her shop, and I've come down to be the buyer. Apparently, she caters to the elite, so maybe I can sniff out something pertinent for you."

"That would be appreciated."

"I'm also here to render whatever assistance you may need."

When they'd been together in Mobile, Wilma had assumed the persona of a mad old widow woman named Annie. Zahra had played the role of her slave companion. Every morning, wearing a tattered nightgown over a soiled and ratty day dress, the blue-eyed, wild-haired Annie would walk down the streets of Mobile arguing with herself or sometimes the occasional stray dog. Whenever residents of the city happened upon her, they either gave her a patronizing smile and left her alone, or crossed the street out of fear of being forced into a loud and embarrassing conversation on such nonsensical topics as whether inchworms could grow to be more than an inch. None had suspected that in reality, Crazy Annie, as they'd called her, had been tallying the names, classifications, and numbers of Confederacy ships in the bay, and sending the information on to Washington. A few weeks after Zahra and Wilma left the city, the intelligence they'd gathered helped the Union navy gain victory in the August '64 battle at Mobile Bay.

The two women finished their tea and stood to say their good-byes. A parting hug was shared, and Zahra said genuinely, "I'm glad you're here."

"I am, too. I should be open in a week or so, so

stop in. I can be your gown maker from here on if you'd like. I'll gown the girls, too."

"I'd like that, but the elite Creole women probably won't."

Wilma waved away the concerns. "Once they see the design and quality of my wares, I'm certain they won't care who my other customers are."

Wilma then took up the pen on Zahra's desk and wrote down the number of the house and the name of the street where she'd taken a room, then she added the address of her shop.

Zahra escorted her back downstairs to the front parlor. Wilma spent a long moment scanning the beautiful ivory-and-gold décor, then said, "All this gold and white would make you think you were in a church if it weren't for those." She pointed at one of the nude statues.

For a moment, Zahra's attention lingered on the life-sized couple embracing at the foot of the staircase. The rapture on the woman's face was riveting. Zahra could almost feel the pleasure, sense the heat of the man's cupping hand. Admittedly, her experience with men was limited to the clumsy rumblings of her youth and to the two times during the war she'd had to put herself on the lure in order to bait the fish she'd been trying to catch. However, this statue the girls had dubbed Adam and Eve touched her in ways she couldn't explain. *Could it be because you've never known such passion?* her inner voice asked. Zahra was honest enough to admit that the answer could be yes. She hastily set the thoughts aside and found Wilma watching her intently.

"Be careful, Zahra," Wilma warned gently. "A place like this can seduce even a woman of strength like yourself. Passion can dull your senses and make you vulnerable."

"I'll be fine. It's just all this"—she gestured around—"takes some getting used to."

Wilma nodded knowingly. "All right, but keep my words in mind."

"I will," Zahra promised.

They shared one last hug and Wilma was gone.

Zahra made her way back to the stairs to return to her office. As she climbed, she pointedly ignored Adam and Eve, but her mind's eye saw Eve's ecstatic face just the same.

Later that afternoon, Roland Keel, a cousin of Alfred's, arrived by train from Memphis. He'd come to oversee the gambling, bringing with him a three-person crew of barkeeps and dealers to ensure the house's games ran fairly and to keep an eye out for cardsharps.

"I wouldn't know a sharp from a Philadelphia lawyer," Zahra admitted as she sat talking with Roland and Alfred in her office.

Roland was at least a foot shorter than his giant cousin, but he had the same muscular build. "Learned all I know from my old master—one of the best gamblers on the Mississippi."

"Then you're just the man we need."

"For Ms. Tubman I'd walk through fire," he declared with conviction. "She helped my folks go north back in the fifties, and I'll always be grateful."

Zahra understood his devotion. Araminta was responsible for hundreds of people escaping captivity. "All the gambling operations will be under your control. If there are supplies you need purchased, please let me know."

"Yes, ma'am."

"You'll be reporting back to the Loyal League in Memphis?"

"Yes, and they'll be sending me any news they think you should pass on to the other Leagues."

"How are things going for the race there?"

"No better or no worse than anywhere else. The riots in '66 let us know who our friends were though, and while some progress has been made, many of us are terrified it will happen again, soon."

The Memphis riots of 1866 began harmlessly enough with the collision of two hacks on a Memphis street. One driver was Black, the other White. It evolved into a three-day orgy of hate and murder fueled by mobs, the police and the local news organs. Forty-six people were killed, forty-four of them Black. Eighty-five people were injured. $100,000 of property, goods and money, much of it owned by the Black soldiers and their families stationed at nearby Fort Pickering was either stolen or burned. When the riot ended, a local newspaper crowed, "Thank heaven the white race are once again ruler in Memphis." But the Congressional hearings convened to investigate the matter found the riot to be ". . . an organized, bloody massacre of the colored people, inspired by the press and led on by officers of the law . . ."

"Well, welcome to our odd family," Zahra said genuinely. "Alfred will show you around the place, then he can take you to some of the boardinghouses."

He nodded, and the cousins departed.

Left alone, Zahra wondered where this would all lead. Opening night was less than two weeks away, and she still hadn't filled all of her household positions. The most crucial was the cook, who'd been expected to arrive yesterday. According to the railroad agent, the train the woman was traveling on from Atlanta had experienced some mechanical difficulties and would arrive at the station today. Zahra hoped so, because they could hardly have a grand affair without food. Her staff was also on her mind. Although they all came highly recommended, common sense told her that at least one, if not two, would eventually prove untrustworthy. To believe otherwise was to be naive. Trusting Wilma seemed logical, but Zahra knew that many former friends of the race were just that—former. She also knew that if the president or Congress got wind of rumors that some leaders of the race were contemplating leading the freedmen out of the South, the ramifications would roll across the nation like a wave. Radical politicians would lose their constituencies, and planters, their cheap labor. An outraged Congress would probably hold hearings to find the conspirators responsible for "influencing" a race of people the country deemed too feebleminded to think for themselves. So, considering all that was at stake, the only counsel Zahra could wisely keep was her own.

The cook did arrive later that day, but there was a problem.

"What do you mean, she's not staying?" the confused Zahra asked Lovey, who'd come up to the office to announce the cook's decision not to take the post.

"She set one foot inside, looked around, and stomped out. You should come down and talk to her."

Zahra found the tall, chesty woman outside on the porch. Her face was sour, and her body was tense with anger. Zahra introduced herself. "I'm Domino, and you are?"

"Doesn't matter. I won't be staying."

"May I ask why?"

"This is a whorehouse!" the woman replied, as if the answer was obvious. "I'll not be working under the devil's roof."

Salome and Naomi, the mulatto twins who'd arrived three days ago from Nashville, stood in the doorway, with Zahra's other girls, looking on.

The woman eyed Zahra and declared pointedly, "I've known Harriet a long time, but that young man she's married to must have loosened her mind. She knows I'm a God-fearing woman."

"But ma'am—"

"No buts needed, miss. I'll be going back to the train station. And I'll be praying for your souls."

With that, she turned on her heel and strode off with her carpetbag in hand.

In the silence that followed, Matilda asked, "So, what do we do now?"

A grim Zahra watched the woman climb back

into the hack and be driven away. "I suppose we find another cook."

That evening, Zahra sent one of the maids around with a note to Miss Sophie explaining her dilemma and asking for the name of a quality caterer who might handle the food, since Zahra wasn't certain a replacement cook could be found in time to handle all the preparations necessary for the opening night festivities.

Sophie wrote back: *Archer Le Veq. Hotel Christophe.*

Zahra looked at the note. *Archer Le Veq?* Hadn't she rescued him from a barn back in '63? Surely this couldn't be the same one, but casting back she did recall him being from New Orleans. Zahra got up from her chair and began to pace. Would he remember her? He'd been in such bad condition when she helped him escape that he'd barely been able to sit his horse, yet his dark eyes had flustered her so much she'd accidentally poured water from the canteen all over his face; a gaffe that brought heat to her cheeks even now.

After putting him on the gunboat, she'd ridden to her next assignment certain she'd never see him again, but he'd stayed in the back of her mind for weeks after. How had he fared, she'd wondered. Had he gone back to New Orleans, or had he been patched up and sent back into the field to continue his espionage work for the Bureau of Military Information, whose purpose had been the collection of intelligence on the Confederacy. As happens with all memories her recollection of their encounter had faded over time, and she'd had no further thoughts of him until now.

Was he, like her, still gathering information for the government, or had he left that part of his life behind after Lee's surrender. Even though she'd had to rescue him from Crete's clutches, she knew better than to sell him short—Le Veq had to have been a skilled agent to be employed by BMI. If he was still an active agent, could she call on him for help in a pinch? And if he somehow uncovered her true reason for being in New Orleans, then what?

Zahra pondered Le Veq for a few moments longer then came to a decision. If Sophie recommended him there was really no reason not to hire his staff. After all, it would only be for a week or so. She'd have her own chef eventually. Le Veq's presence in the city was a wrinkle she hadn't allowed for however, especially when a part of her kept recalling the vivid power in his dark eyes.

The next morning she dressed in a fashionable indigo gown, put on a matching domino, and had Alfred drive her over to the Hotel Christophe. *Better to beard the dragon in his den.*

Archer was in the hotel kitchen trying to convince his temperamental chef, Aristide O'Neil, not to quit over the questionable quality of the vegetables delivered this morning, when André came rushing in. "You're not going to believe who's sitting in your office waiting your attendance."

"Governor Warmoth?" he asked dryly.

"No. Madame Domino."

Crystal and china hit the floor; pans were dropped, and every head in the kitchen snapped up.

"She says she has a business proposition for you."

Ignoring the eager curiosity on the faces of the kitchen staff, Archer excused himself and headed to his office.

She was standing by the window, looking down onto the busy street when he entered. The indigo silk gown, with its pleated hem and soft bustle, was highly fashionable. When she turned slowly and faced him, the dark eyes within the gilded indigo mask held his for such a long, time-suspended moment that his groin tightened in response.

"Monsieur Le Veq?"

She had a voice like black velvet.

"Yes."

"Thank you for meeting with me. I'm called Domino."

While the mask hid the upper portions of her warm brown face, he noted that the dark eyes were intelligent, the jaw nicely formed, and the mouth lush as any Archer had ever seen.

She walked to him, silk rustling sensually, and gracefully extended her hand gloved in black netting.

"Enchanté," he said, bowing gallantly over her hand and placing his lips lightly against it. He politely released her hand, then gestured to the leather chairs by his desk. "A seat?"

"Thank you."

Once again the silk whispered as she swept the gown aside so she could sit.

"May I offer you refreshment? Tea, coffee?"

"Tea would be fine."

"Then tea it shall be." He walked to the door intending to call for André, but when he opened it, the apparently eavesdropping aide all but fell inside the room.

André straightened himself hastily.

Archer raised an eyebrow, then asked, "Can you bring the lady some tea? Café for me."

"Certainly," André responded while taking peeks at the notorious visitor. "I'll return shortly."

He left, and Archer closed the door.

Domino had a small smile on her beautifully masked face. "How long has he worked for you?"

"On and off for almost a decade. When he's not eavesdropping, he's rather efficient."

Archer found no fault with André's curiosity. Were the shoe on the other foot, Archer would have been the one falling into the room. He wondered if she affected all men this way, then decided the answer was undoubtedly yes. The intrigue she exuded was hard to ignore. "André mentioned a business proposition."

"Yes. I'm in need of a caterer for the house's opening night. I'm told that your staff is one of the best in the city."

"We are indeed. Tell me what you have in mind."

While she talked, Archer listened, took notes, and discreetly studied the mesmerizing woman on the other side of the desk. She had a mouth as sensual as a French courtesan. The front of the gown buttoned high on her neck, but a diamond-shaped cut in the bodice offered the male eye a teasing view of the swells of her breasts, accented by a short ruffle of black lace. Her hair was covered by an elaborately rendered head wrap, the color of which matched her gown.

"So, do you think you can accommodate me?"

Archer looked up from his notes. The question had such a tantalizing undertone that it made him speculate on whether the double entendre had been intentional. Holding her eyes, he responded, "Accommodating a beautiful woman is one of my specialties."

The smile she gave him in response was slow and secretive.

Conscious of the lust humming in his blood, Archer heard the doorknob turn, and he watched André enter the room carrying a tray. On it sat a small teapot, cups, and a small cup of café. André set everything upon the edge of Archer's desk, nodded at Domino, and withdrew soundlessly.

"Shall I pour?" Archer asked.

"Please," she replied.

Zahra took her now filled cup, and in the moments of silence that followed admitted that although he was as handsome as she'd remembered, she'd not been truly prepared to confront him in the flesh. His skin was the color of African gold and he had entered the room with knowing eyes and kisses for the back of her hand. The touch of his lips, though fleeting, had sent warms tendrils of response up her arm, and his pointed gaze had warmed the rest of her. He exuded the aura of a man who enjoyed women and Zahra sensed that very few told him no. Over her raised cup she discreetly studied his attire. The first time they'd met his clothing had been as filthy as Crete's barn, but today Le Veq's well-formed frame was set off by a black frock coat, white shirt and red paisley vest. Like most men of the day, he wore brown trousers and buttoned his coat only at the top to better display the vest and the expensive looking gold pocket watch chained to it.

"Much is being said about your arrival in the city," he said to her after a few moments.

"Hopefully the talk is positive," she responded.

"Very much so."

"Then that pleases me."

*What else pleases you?* Archer wanted to ask, running appreciative eyes over her loveliness. "Where's home?"

"Here and there," Zahra replied with intentional vagueness. He was making no attempts to hide his interest and the secret call in his gaze was sinuously worming its way through the defenses she'd set around herself.

"A lady of mystery."

She sipped. "Not really. Most men seem more interested in my *present* than in my past."

"I'm not most men."

Her eyes raised to his. "No?"

"No. You will find that I am most distinctive."

Try though she might Zahra could not ignore his effect on her senses. He made her so warm she wanted to pick up some of the papers on his desk and fan herself. "How so?"

"In how I please a woman."

His voice sent another ripple through her, and her chin rose in response as if the gesture might somehow counteract the spell being woven around her. She tossed back amusedly, "I'd heard that you Black Frenchmen hold a high opinion of yourselves."

"Only because it is well earned."

"Or because you are legends in your own minds."

Archer smiled. "You are a very intriguing woman."

"In my profession, that is how it should be, *non?*"

"And generally, how much will such intrigue cost a man?"

Zahra paused for a moment to weigh him and her answer before looking directly into his glittering eyes to reply, "The common man need not ask because I am unavailable to him, but for a man who matches me in strength and purpose—there is no cost."

The black velvet voice coupled with her sultry eyes rendered Archer instantaneously hard. "Then I will make it my business to meet the test."

"Is that a gauntlet I hear?"

"It is."

"And your mistress?" she asked easily. "What will she say? A man as *distinctive* as you claim to be, surely has one."

Archer was struck speechless for a moment, then said with a cool voice, "I wouldn't think that a man's mistress would be a barrier for a woman like you."

Sophie's beauty and her well-run, clean house were without parallel. Until now.

Archer shrugged. "It's hard to tell with the domino she wears, but she is very intriguing."

Lynette met his eyes and studied them as i looking for something, then sighed, "All right we'll attend the opera another night, but fo the postponement you owe me one new gown Archer Le Veq."

The small pout on her face made him smile "That is a small price to pay. Thank you for un derstanding."

"Just as long as your working for her pertain: only to business." Then she added with moc| warning, "I am a descendant of Marie Laveau you know."

He did. Leveau was New Orleans's most fa mous priestess of *vodoun*. Personally he put littl stock in the cult's spells or its supposed powe over people and nature, but Lynette was a firn believer. She was convinced that her *magic wa* the reason the two of them had been togethe these past five years. "The last thing I want is on of your spells hanging over my life."

She smiled prettily and went back to her lunch

After seeing Lynette off with a passionate kiss Archer summoned André to his office to inforn him of the contract for New Year's Eve. "Madam Domino has hired us to handle the catering fo the opening of her house."

"Oh, really?" Unlike his earlier appearance a the door, André seemed to have regained hi sense of formality.

She gave him a knowing smile and said pleasantly, "For all your legendary expertise, Mr. Le Veq, you know nothing about a woman like me, so, shall we return to the business at hand?"

Archer got the distinct impression that he'd offended her. *An offended whore?*

They spent a few more minutes firming up the details of her dinner and the costs. When the negotiations were completed, he said to her, "I'll have André draw up a contract and have it ready for your review tomorrow morning if that's agreeable?"

"It is." Zahra wondered what it was about this man that made her so aware of him. Even though he was seated on the other side of the desk she could feel his heat, making it difficult for her to hold his assessing gaze for longer than a few seconds. Deciding that a retreat might be in her best interest, she gathered herself, looked away from what she swore was amusement in his eyes, and slowly stood. "I should be getting back. Thank you for the tea and for your time, Mr. Le Veq. I'm looking forward to working with you."

"I am as well." And because Archer was not ready to relinquish her just yet, asked, "May I walk you out?"

"No, that won't be necessary. I remember the way." With a brief parting smile and the rustling of silk she was gone.

Archer rose and stepped to the window of this office that looked down onto the busy street. It didn't take long for her to appear below. With appreciative eyes, he watched her walk the short distance to the ruby red carriage. It was his first look at the storied conveyance and he noted that it sparkled like a jewel in the sun, but it was the lush-mouthed Domino who filled his mind. Who was she really? He'd encountered very few women with the power to instantaneously ensnare him the way she had. Just thinking about her now tightened his groin. The coach's well-dressed driver, a man the size of Goliath, held open the door. Once she entered, the giant took his seat behind the reins and they drove away. Archer went back to his desk chair and for a moment sat there musing on the woman in the mask and his desire to see her again as soon as it could be arranged.

On the ride back to the house with Alfred, Zahra reviewed the encounter and wondered if marching into the dragon's den had been such a good idea after all. In reality she could have sent Alfred or one of the other staff members to the hotel to handle the hiring and maybe not have had to personally encounter Le Veq ever, but she'd admittedly been curious as to whether he really was the man in the barn, and that had been confirmed. On another level the visit had been necessary to prove that her reaction to him that night in Georgia had been a fluke. As if just waiting to bedevil her, the memories of the rescue's aftermath rose and she relived how Le Veq's distracting nearness had affected her hold on the canteen. Then came her fumbling attempts to rectify the mess which resulted in her being so unnerved by the warmth of his skin and his unfathomble eyes, she'd gone immediately still. In the silence that followed something passed between them that

she'd had no words for then or now; something that had stayed with her for weeks after she'd ridden away and something that had been rekindled this morning when he brushed his lips against the back of her hand.

Shaking off the echoing effects, she turned her mind back to the matter at hand. Other than verifying Le Veq's identity, this morning's visit had proven that her reaction to him back in '63 hadn't been a fluke. Then as now, she was attracted to the Black Frenchman, but even more worrisome was the knowledge that he was very attracted to Domino as well.

Later, Archer met Lynette for lunch in one of the hotel's small private dining rooms. It was a standard appointment, but today, Archer couldn't seem to concentrate on Lynette or her conversation.

"Did you hear me, Archer?"

He shook himself away from the fantasy of removing Domino's mask, then apologized. "I'm sorry, I didn't. What did you say?"

"I said, I purchased the tickets for the opera for New Year's Eve."

"I can't go."

She observed him over her small blue bowl of bouillabaisse. "And the reason?"

"Work. The staff is catering an event that evening."

"Where?"

"At the former Pierre House."

"The new brothel?"

He nodded.

"I hear the madame rivals Miss Sophie herself."

They then discussed what would be needed, the logistics around deliveries, setup, and the like. "Would you draw up a contract? I'd like to take it to her tomorrow," Archer stated.

"Of course," he replied. Then he asked, "Is there anything else?"

"Yes. Find out what you can about her. I'd like to know who I'm really dealing with. I'll do some inquiring on my own, as well."

"All right. I'll get started on the contract."

"Thank you."

# Chapter 4

That evening, Archer stopped off at his mother's. Seeing his brothers' carriages parked on the street outside the gate made him remember this morning's visitor. As he entered the parlor, he tossed his hat, cane, and coat onto an empty chair and greeted everyone, then announced, "Philippe, I'm sure you'll be happy to know that I'm catering Madame Domino's opening affair."

Every eye in the room swung to his face.

Juliana stared. "Oh, Archer, how could you? The *good* women of this city are not happy with these new doxies at all."

Archer took a seat on the edge of her chair and kissed her cheek in greeting before saying, "I'm sure they aren't, but this is business, Mama. I stand to make a tidy profit."

Juliana still looked displeased. "Couldn't you have sent her to someone else?"

He smiled. "No."

Philippe asked, "Have you met her?"

"Oh, yes." Then he added, "I believe I offended her, though."

"Mama, cover your ears," Drake instructed before asking his brother, "How do you offend a whore?"

Archer shrugged. "That's what I asked myself. Out of respect for the lovely Juliana I won't go into detail, but yes, I think I offended her." Archer was still thrown by that. He inwardly admitted having been caught off guard by her pointed question about Lynette and that he'd replied with the first words that came to mind but how was he supposed to know she had sensibilities; the woman made her living on her back for heaven's sake.

Beau asked him, "So will you be there opening night?"

"Yes, to make sure everything runs smoothly."

"What are you going to do about the opera you're supposed to be taking Lynette to that night?" Drake asked over his wineglass.

"We'll go some other time. Lynette was very understanding about the whole thing." He then drawled, "You know, brother, if you had a mistress of your own, you wouldn't have to be so concerned with mine."

"Ouch!" Beau winced aloud.

Philippe eyed the simmering Drake. "Are you going to take that sitting down?"

Juliana studied her brood. "If you two are going to fight, please do so outside. If I have to replace even one more piece of china, you'll be banned from my home permanently."

Over the years Juliana's rambunctious boys had cost her much in broken china, vases, furniture, and lamps, but because her sons knew a real threat when she uttered one, the two brothers glowered silently at each other but said no more.

"Did you see to the convent's leaky roof, Drake?" Juliana asked, hoping to defuse the grumbling by changing the topic of conversation.

"Yes, I did. The repairs shouldn't take much time."

"Good. I heard the sisters were having to put out buckets when it rains," Juliana said. "The newspapers are reporting more lynchings."

"More and more people are being terrorized by the Leaguers and Kluxers. Something has to be done."

"What are the Republicans going to do?" Beau asked.

Archer replied with disgust, "They're so busy fighting with each other, the whole population could vanish overnight and they'd not notice."

Archer was becoming more and more disillusioned with both the Republicans and politics as a whole. In Louisiana bribes and patronage ruled. Bills were passed to raise the pay of everyone from the governor down to the postmaster, but bills designed to ban the noxius Black Codes languished like a spinster at a dance. On the House floor the other day, he'd watched representatives shout themselves hoarse in attempts to get some meaningful legislation passed, but to no avail. In

the face of all the deaths caused by the supremacists, and the indifference shown by the powers
that be, many of the Black Civil War vets were of a
mind to leave the talk behind and take up a gun
to protect their families; Archer was in full agreement. He and other Republicans were patrolling
nightly in hopes their presence would deter the
actions of the night riders but they weren't being
very successful it seemed.

Zahra and the girls were enjoying the breakfast
provided by a local woman hired yesterday to be
the house's cook. While the girls chattered around
her, Zahra's mind was on Archer Le Veq. He'd
promised to bring the catering contract over this
morning and she found herself anticipating the
visit.

"Are you listening, Domino?"

Zahra swung her attention to the twin voices of
Salome and Naomi. They spoke in tandem most
of the time, a practice Zahra and the other girls
found quite amusing. "No, I wasn't. My apologies.
What did you say."

"We said, we want to work the voyeur room
opening night. That is if it's okay with you and
everybody else."

Hiding her surprise behind her raised coffee cup, Zahra looked around the table at the
smiling women dressed in their wrappers and
morning growns. "Does anyone have any objec-
tions?"

There were none.

Later that morning, Zahra was in her office

composing a letter to her parents. She missed them dearly and wanted to let them know. A knock on the door caused her to look up. "Come in," she called, and slipped the letter beneath some papers on the desktop.

It was Alfred. "Mr. Le Veq's downstairs. Shall I send him up?"

"Yes, please," she managed to say easily. "Thank you, Alfred."

He departed and Zahra used the time alone to pull on a pair of crocheted gloves to hide her still tingling hands and to compose herself. The moment Alfred announced Le Veq's arrival her heart had begun pounding, but she was determined to maintain control and not let his charm and golden good looks render her as nervous as they had yesterday. She hadn't known what to expect then, but she did now.

When he entered the office, she stood. He was again well dressed and his eyes met hers with a sparkle that seemed to look past her mask and into her true self.

"Good morning, Domino."

"Mr. Le Veq. Please, have a seat. Would you care for refreshments?"

"Café would be fine, if it's not too much trouble."

Noticing Alfred standing on the threshold for the first time, and the displeasure on his face as he studied Le Veq, Zahra said to her giant driver, "Would you have one of the maids bring us some café, please."

"Yes, ma'am."

As he turned to depart, Zahra made a mental note to speak with him later. He apparently didn't care for the Black Frenchman, and Zahra wanted to know if he had a legitimate reason, because if he did, she needed to hear it. "Thank you for coming."

"You're welcome. Your décor downstairs is quite . . . stimulating."

"It is what we are about, after all," she stated more easily than she felt. "When we're done here, I can give you a tour if you'd like."

He inclined his head. "I'd like that. Would you care to see the contract now?"

Zahra studied the clauses and terms while they awaited the coffee. The maid Suzette delivered the brew a short time later, and once she withdrew, Zahra set the contract aside and asked him, "Shall I pour?"

"Please."

Cognizant of his interest and doing her best to appear nonchalant, Zahra stood and poured the dark liquid from the pot into two cups. Cognizant also of his nearness, she congratulated herself on completing the task without incident. Handing him one of the cups her fingers brushed his and only Zahra's discipline kept her from overtly reacting to the sweet shock that erupted from the accidental touch. He was watching her too and seemed well aware of the effect he was having on her. Her sense that he was secretly amused by that knowledge made her all the more determined to maintain an outwardly show of calm even if she was becoming a wreck on the inside. Taking her seat, she picked up the contract and began reading again, hoping it would give her something to concentrate on besides him.

Archer sipped from his cup and was admittedly taken by her beauty. She was in red today and her matching domino was piped in gold. The deep cut of the gown's bodice showed off the comely swells of her breasts and he wondered if her brown skin would be as soft to the touch as it appeared. Forcing his attention back up to her face, he took in the outline of her jaw, the sensuous slope of her throat and decided that no matter how long it took, she would be his, willingly, even if only for one night. Her pull on his senses was too strong, her aura too captivating not to pursue. "Are the terms to your liking?"

"They are. It may be necessary for me to extend the contract if I can't find a suitable chef to hire soon. Would that create problems for you?"

"Not in the least. We can alter the arrangement at any time. Just let me know."

Satisfied with his answer, Zahra picked up a pen and signed her name. "While that dries would you care to see the house?"

Archer drained his cup, then stood. Bowing gallantly toward the door, he said to her, "After you, madam."

Out in the hallway, Zahra led him from her second-floor office and around the balcony that overlooked the large downstairs room. "Do you like to gamble, Mr. Le Veq?"

"Depends on what's at stake. Are you the prize?"

She looked up. "No."

"Pity."

She shook her head with amusement. "I asked that because we have a room for the gamblers and I wanted to get your opinion."

"And I asked because I'd wager my hotel to win you."

She stopped. "Really?" The skepticism in her tone matched her pose. Before he could form an answer, she asked, "What sound-minded woman would believe such poppycock?"

The golden lips twitched with amusement. "Let's just say, you'd be amazed."

Zahra enjoyed the smile gleaming in his eyes. It was apparent that he was a man who also liked to play. "How about we go and see the gambling room?"

His attraction to her growing by leaps and bounds, Archer nodded and let her lead the way.

He found the gambling room much to his liking. The dark wood tables and chairs gave the place a masculine feel. There appeared to be ample space to get up and stretch one's legs and the French doors would allow access to fresh air for those who needed it.

"So what do you think?" she asked him.

"Of the room, or present company?"

"The room, Mr. Le Veq," she replied with mock exasperation."

"I'd much rather offer my opinion of you."

His soft-toned response rippled over Zahra like a breeze in summer. "You're very persistent."

"With you, any man must be."

"Astute and handsome. That's quite the combination."

"They serve me well."

Zahra was enjoying the banter more than she cared to admit. A woman would have to be mentally adept to stay ahead of him, but she considered herself well qualified for the challenge.

Archer stared down at her masked face. He was enjoying her very much. "The gamblers will find this room most suitable."

"Good. Would you like to view more?" Upon seeing the light of mischief glittering in his dark eyes, she added quickly before he could respond provocatively, "See more of the house."

That appeared to please him, "You're learning quickly, madam."

"A necessity I'm finding."

Archer let her show him the rest of the place and he had to admit he'd never seen so such naked flesh in his life. Nudes were everywhere, but none held his interest for long. No matter how provocative the surroundings, his attention kept returning to Domino.

She then introduced him to her girls. Philippe had been correct, they were all very lovely, but in Archer's opinion none could hold a candle to the lady in the mask. She finally led him back to the office and he folded up the now-dry contract and slipped it into his coat pocket.

She said to him, "Thank you again."

"You're welcome, and thank you for the tour."

"Shall I walk you downstairs?"

"I'd enjoy that."

Zahra escorted him out of the office and then down the staircase where Adam and Eve stood posed in perpetual rapture.

He said to her, "Quite a statue."

"It is that."

She could feel him watching her, but Zahra pretended not to notice so she wouldn't have to meet his eyes, or say more.

At the door, Alfred was waiting like the doorman at a hotel and as soon as she and Le Veq approached he opened it as if signalling the Frenchman not to delay his departure. Zahra shook her head. "Alfred, will you go see if the cook needs anything before you and Suzette head off to the market."

It was a nonsensical request, and both she and Alfred knew it, but she couldn't have him glaring at the man who would be providing the food for their opening gala.

After Alfred's departure, Archer asked, "Is he just protective or in love with you?"

"The former."

"Then tell him he's doing a damn good job because he scares me to death."

She chuckled. "I will let him know."

Archer liked seeing her smile. "What excuse shall I use to call on you again tomorrow."

"I'm certain you will think of something," Zahra replied in a voice far quieter than she'd intended. She extended her hand. "Thank you again."

"My pleasure." He took her hand and raised the fingertips to his lips. The faint pressure coupled with the lure in his eyes was just enough to make her knees weaken, and when he let her go, her heart was racing.

"Until tomorrow," he promised, and then he was gone.

That evening, Chloe asked, "Do you have a program for opening night worked out, Domino?"

Zahra did not. She hid her ignorance of whorehouse etiquette by saying, "I'd hoped we could come up with a plan as a group. Any ideas? You all know your strengths better than I. What would you be comfortable doing?"

"Besides back work?" Stella Summers, the oldest of the women, asked.

They all chuckled.

Chloe said, "Well, I play the piano and have a passable voice."

Lovey spoke up next. "I do a dance an old madame of mine called the Dance of the Seven Veils."

Zahra was almost afraid to ask. "And it entails?"

"Me dancing and removing the veils one by one."

"Sounds like just what we're looking for," Zahra said, chuckling.

"Stella and I have performed on stage," Adair added. "We know quite a few ribald songs and poems."

"Well, then it's agreed. We'll put on a show opening night, highlighting our *talents*."

Her emphasis on the word evoked a few chuckles.

Matilda said, "Most places I've worked, you take the man upstairs, he pays, he leaves, and you pick out the next man. But a place like this calls for something excitin'!"

"I think so, too, Matilda. If the entertainment proves successful, I believe we shall call our establishment a gentleman's club."

Chloe said, "Sounds a lot more highfalutin than a whorehouse." Then she said in a mock haughty voice, "Madame Domino's Gentleman's Club."

Everyone laughed.

"Then let's get to work," Lovey said enthusiastically.

For the next hour Zahra and her girls put together an opening night program both scandalous and entertaining. She had no idea how the customers would view the various performances, but since they were men, she'd be willing to bet they'd be ecstatic.

The girls went off to rehearse, and Zahra headed to her office. She thought back on her meeting with the seductive and handsome Black Frenchman Archer Le Veq. For all of her training and inner strength, she'd found herself affected like a virgin with a Lothario. His voice, his eyes, the brushing of his lips across the back of her hand had been the practiced moves of a man who could tempt a woman across time. But she was here to do a job, not become Archer Le Veq's next bauble. The fact that he was *gens de coleur* was a mark against him in some ways. Granted, Le Veq and the rest of his class were known for their wealth and their ancestral ties to France and

Spain, but they'd owned slaves. They'd also considered themselves distinct enough from the rest of the Blacks in the country to have met with Lincoln during the war in an effort to have themselves declared a separate class and thus eligible for the rights inherent in such a designation, but the effort had failed. Only after the war had the Creoles of Color, as some called them, resigned themselves to the realization that their elevated status meant nothing to the country. To the nation, *gens de coleur* was just another way of saying *Blacks;* as a consequence, they'd been lumped in with the rest of the race. Zahra did applaud the Creoles for their recent efforts on the freedmen's behalf and their decision to link their fate to the race, but she wondered how strong the commitment would be had Lincoln approved their request.

The next morning, Zahra asked Alfred, "How much do you think you can find out about Le Veq with you being new to the city?"

He shrugged. "There are ways, especially if he owns a hotel here. He's undoubtedly well known. It shouldn't be too difficult."

"See what you can do." Then, changing her tone, she asked, "What are your plans for the day?"

"We're still trying to find my cousin Roland a place to let. He prefers not to live in the center of the city where most of the boardinghouses that rent to *us* are—too much crime and other dangerous carryings-on, so we keep looking."

"I hope he'll be situated soon. In the meantime, I've another task for you."

He smiled, "Does your mind ever rest?"

"Not as far as I know," she tossed back.

He shook his head with amusement. "What do you need done?"

"We need to purchase a less ostentatious coach. There may be times when I'll want to move about the city anonymously, so our candy apple coach won't do."

"I agree."

She opened one of the desk drawers and withdrew some bills, which she handed to him. "Have your cousin handle the transaction. His face isn't as known. Tell him he may use the coach as his own except for those times when I need to."

Alfred nodded. "Anything else?"

"Yes. No one is to be in this office if I'm not here. Not the girls. Not the servants. We don't want anyone nosing around our strongbox."

"Understood. Anything else?"

She ran her eyes over the large knot on the crown of his prominent nose. "How'd you break your nose?"

He smiled at her endless curiosity. "Slavery. I was a boxer. I'll tell you about it sometime."

"I'd be real interested."

"All right, I'm leaving now, Zahra. Is there anything else?"

"One more thing."

He chuckled. "And it is?"

"Must you glare at Le Veq?"

He studied her for a moment, then replied, "Yes, I must."

"And your reason."

"Don't like him. Too pretty, too Creole."

Zahra smiled. "Well, just in case we have to call upon him for something important, can you at least pretend to be nice."

He paused for a moment, then said, "I suppose."

"Thank you, Alfred."

"You're welcome."

After his departure, Zahra thought it best she find out all she could about the suave Mr. Archer Le Veq. Who knew what direction this mission might take, and if she did indeed need outside help, knowing as much about Le Veq as possible could aid her decision as to whether to reveal her plans to him or not. Having full knowledge of him might also help her deal with him on a personal level. He seemed set upon winning her and although she was flattered by his interest, she had no plans to succumb no matter how much she enjoyed his flirting. Admittedly, she'd never been pursued this way before. The eligible men back home had never kissed her hand nor showed any appreciation for her wit. Le Veq had done both and as a result she felt desirable, almost powerful in a womanly sort of fashion. She wasn't sure where those feelings would lead, but she did know that while being around Le Veq was thrilling, she hadn't come to New Orleans to be thrilled. She'd come here to do a job, and if snooping around in Le Veq's life would help her build up the defenses necessary to keep his passionate pursuit at bay, that's what she'd do.

However, the moment Lovey knocked on the door and said Le Veq was downstairs waiting, all of Zahra's resolve momentarily crumbled. She was filled with an uncharacteristic excitement that she forced herself not to acknowledge.

"Should I bring him up?" Lovey asked.

"Would you please?"

"Man like that make a woman's teeth ache just looking at him."

Zahra smiled and Lovey left.

Calmer now, Zahra walked over to the French doors to wait.

"Afternoon, Domino."

"Mr. Le Veq. Did you find the excuse you were after?"

"I did." He pulled out a sheaf of papers. "Copies of the contract for you to keep."

"Very nice," she said approvingly. She walked over to take the papers from his hand and placed them on the desk. She leaned back against the edge and asked, "Now, what excuse will you use to prolong your visit?"

He grinned. "I didn't think you required another one."

He was standing so close, Zahra could smell his spicy cologne. "I do."

"You're a hard woman, madam."

"Makes me interesting, don't you think?"

"Very much so."

Archer wanted her so badly he could taste it.

This flirtatious back and forth only enhanced matters. "Suppose I have no other excuse?"

"Then you're not as clever as I'd hoped."

His eyes held hers and Zahra's heart began beating like a drum.

"Shall I offer you a kiss in exchange for my ineptness?"

The room suddenly went warm as July or so it seeemed to Zahra. She hadn't planned on backing herself into such a volatile corner, but the determination in her nature refused to let her turn tail and run. "If that is all you have to offer, I guess it will have to suffice." Just like yesterday, her tone was not as firm as she'd intended.

He slid a slow fiery finger over the corner of her mouth, "I think it will be more than sufficient. . . ."

His touch generated tiny quakes all over her, and when he pressed his lips to hers, the power made her eyes close. Zahra had been kissed before but nothing compared to this sweet potent rendition. His mouth was warm and knowing; she was inexperienced and melting. When he eased his arm across her lower back and moved her up against the hard cradle of his chest and thighs, she lost all touch with time and space. The kiss deepened. The tip of his tongue played sensually and her defenses crumbled like sand.

"Ahem!" they both heard someone say.

The dazzled Zahra backed out of the embrace and saw a very displeased Alfred standing in the office doorway.

"Yes?" she asked coolly.

"Came to bring you your mail."

The tight set of Le Veq's jaw showed he wasn't happy with the interruption either. The two men faced each other like combatants in a coliseum.

Zahra walked over took the mail from Alfred's hand. "Thank you. Now, good-bye."

Closing the door quietly but firmly, she turned to Le Veq. "My apologies."

"None needed," he said, then drawled, "but I suppose I should go. I do have business to attend to today and it won't get done if your pet has me for lunch."

She enjoyed his wit and sense of humor. "Thank you for the contract and the kiss."

"You're welcome. Next time maybe we won't be interrupted."

"Who said there'll be a next time?" she asked softly.

"I do."

The promise in his words affected her more than she let him see.

"Good day, madame."

Before she could reply, he placed his arm across her back, eased her to him and kissed her until she was dizzy. When he released her she melted back onto the edge of the desk.

"Told you there'd be a next time," he whispered, then walked confidently to the door and departed.

The breathless Zahra knew she was in trouble.

With Christmas less than a week away, Archer decided that the time had come for a decision. His desire for Domino was all-consuming, but he had a mistress. Until meeting Domino, Lynette had been an ideal mate and the idea of casting her aside had never crossed his mind. Although she was not his wife, he nonetheless respected her enough to be faithful, and expected her to do the same even though most men would say that spending a few nights in the arms of a lady of the evening did not constitue such. To their thinking, a mistress was the meal while women like Domino were froth, and therein lay the dilemma. Domino was not froth. No man in his right mind would think that after meeting her. Granted Archer knew next to nothing about her, but what he had experienced in her company he liked. He'd seen the aloof side, the witty side, and had tasted the passion in her kiss. Lord knew he wanted to know and see more but he had a mistress. Archer was not the type of man willing to share a woman. Yes, he'd vowed to somehow make her his, yet the idea of maybe sharing Domino's charms with half the men in New Orleans did not sit well.

Looking at his choices logically, Lynette won hands down, but sometimes desire defied logic, he knew. He also knew that Domino's occupation promoted faithlessness and any man who did not take that into consideration was a fool.

With that in mind he set aside thoughts of the mysterious madam and turned his attention to the type of Christmas gift he wanted to give to Lynette. He was uncertain, but she'd hinted at a gown she'd seen at an expensive shop that had recently opened, so he decided to meet her there.

For all her loveliness, his Lynette was not shy when it came to desiring the best in everything. The more expensive the better seemed to be her motto, but he didn't mind. One mistress was infinitely cheaper to please than three. Leaving the hotel, he headed up the street. It was a cold December day, but the sun was shining, and the air was fresh off the Mississippi.

Archer loved New Orleans. He loved the crowds, the sounds, the smells. He stopped and purchased a bouquet of flowers for Lynette from a young flower girl selling blooms out of a cart, then he continued his walk. A funeral procession was moving down the street; behind them was a crowd of people known as the second wave, folks who might or might not have had a connection with the deceased but had joined the family, along with musicians playing a lively tune, to send the soul on its way. Such happenings were common in a city known for loving both music and having a good time. In the rougher parts of town music could be heard spilling from the doorways of gambling halls, brothels, and saloons from dawn to dawn. It had its own distinct sound, one heavily influenced by the varied ancestry of Africa, Haiti, Spain, and France. In New Orleans every celebration had a musical backdrop, whether the event was a birth or a death. As the funeral wound its way out of sight, Archer smiled and headed towards the dress shop where he was to meet Lynette.

She was already inside when he arrived. There were quite a few other women there as well, making the shop a bit cramped. Lynette and an older woman he assumed to be either a clerk or the owner were leafing through a book of drawings. The other customers were doing the same. Lynette raised a graceful gloved hand in greeting. He approached, handed her the bouquet, and enjoyed the smile the small token put on her lovely face. "Now, let's see this gown."

Indicating the woman at her side, Lynette said, "First I would like you to meet the owner. Her name is Mrs. Wilma Gray, and she has the most divine designs."

Archer nodded. "Mrs. Gray. I'm Archer Le Veq."

"It is a pleasure meeting you."

"Likewise."

Wilma then said, "I will leave you to look at patterns. My clerk Ann over there will assist you. I had no idea so many customers would come in at the same time."

Archer said, "All businesses should have such problems. You go ahead. We'll be fine."

Just then Zahra, followed by Alfred, swept into Wilma's dress shop. She noticed that the place suddenly went silent and that every eye was directed her way. She ignored them all, except for the pair of speculative dark eyes belonging to Archer Le Veq. She offered him a short nod, then waited for Wilma to finish helping a customer.

Lynette frowned. "Is that the new town whore?"

Archer, eyes on Domino, said, "Yes."

"She's well dressed, if nothing else."

Archer noted the green gown and the matching domino. Even with the mask on, she gave the impression of legendary beauty. He also noted that she had garnered quite a bit of attention; so much so that a few of the older women, taking umbrage at her entrance, lifted their noses and huffed out. If their attitudes bothered or affected her, she gave no indication.

Lynette groused, "You'd think Mrs. Gray would keep such base people from mingling with the cultured clientele."

Archer didn't reply. He was too busy watching Domino and the giant Alfred hovering behind her while she and the shop owner spoke. He could see Mrs. Gray smile and take a small piece of paper from Domino's gloved hand.

"What about this one?" Lynette asked Archer, pointing to an elaborate gown that was hemmed in wide pleats.

He turned his attention back to the drawing, but it was Lynette's displeased face that made him ask, "What's the matter?"

"It would help if you'd pay attention to me, Archer."

He met her green eyes. "I am paying attention to you, Lynnie."

"No, you're not. You seem more interested in the whore."

Archer swung his eyes to Domino, who was approaching him. All the desire he'd experienced before rushed over him like a flood.

Lynette whispered tightly, "You are not to

acknowledge her. I'll not be made a laughing-stock."

Zahra was indeed on her way over to speak to Le Veq. She'd seen the biddies file out in apparent protest of her being allowed to shop in the same room with their illustrious selves, but she didn't care. None of them were important in her scheme of things. On the other hand, Le Veq was important if for no other reason than their business connection, and it would be impolite for her not to offer at least a token greeting. In reality, Zahra just wanted a close-up look at the confection of a woman standing beside him. Was she a relative or his mistress?

"Good afternoon, Mr. Le Veq."

Once again he was snared by the black velvet voice. "Madame Domino."

Zahra saw fury in the face of the young woman, who seemed to be making a point of ignoring Zahra. "And who is this lovely young woman?"

Archer replied, "Lynette Dubois."

But Lynette continued to turn a deaf ear to Zahra's presence.

Zahra asked pleasantly, "Do I offend your person, Miss Dubois?"

A cold-eyed Lynette looked Zahra in the face and stated plainly, "Yes, you do."

"Why?"

"Well-bred women do not traffic with whores."

"I see," Zahra replied, looking her up and down. "Are you Mr. Le Veq's sister, cousin?"

"No."

"Then you must be his mistress."

Her chin went up.

"In that case you and I are very much alike. We both accommodate men who are not our husbands, *non?*"

Lynette went beet red, and Zahra smiled coldly. "It has been a pleasure meeting you. *Au revoir*, Mr. Le Veq. Come, Alfred."

With that, she and the giant walked away and left the shop.

The female clerk assisting Archer and his mistress was hiding a smile. It was obvious that Lynette had not intended the conversation to end with her having egg on her face, but it had. Lynette told Archer coolly, "I don't care for any of these. Let's try another shop tomorrow."

"As you wish."

Archer and the clerk shared a look, then he escorted Lynette out into the streets. He hailed a hack and put her inside. Without a word or a backwards glance, she settled into the seat and was driven away. He sighed, shook his head, and walked back to his hotel.

Once Alfred and Zahra were back in her office, she took off her gloves and asked him, "So have you learned anything useful about Le Veq?" She would be the first to admit that the encounter with Lynette Dubois had left her a bit testy. Last week the man was plying Zahra with kisses and this week he was buying gowns for his mistress. She wondered why he'd not come around to see her again, and now that the reason had been revealed she felt foolish for thinking he'd been interested in someone like Domino.

Alfred said, "Mr. Le Veq is not only prominent but his family is one of the wealthiest and most well connected in the state."

"What else?" she asked with interest.

"Mother is Juliana Le Veq Vincent. Married to her third husband. A successful broker and financier. Like many of the Creoles, she lost most of her wealth during the war but has recovered nicely. Six sons."

"So many? Where's our Le Veq in the line?"

"Born third behind eldest, Raimond, who owns a shipping company, and Gerrold, who, I'm told, died in the war."

Zahra felt sympathy.

"He's also a highly placed Radical. The family is very active politically."

"How did you get the information?"

"Went to that big city market, told a few maids there I was out of work but had heard the hotel was hiring waiters, and did any of them know Le Veq? Took me a few days, but I was finally introduced to a maid whose employer lives next door to Le Veq's mother. Very chatty woman."

Zahra smiled.

"She didn't know if the hotel was hiring, but she knew nearly everything else. If I'd asked what color drawers Le Veq wore, she would have probably given me an answer." He added, "Felt sorry for her in a way. It was real clear she didn't get to talk to folks much."

Zahra met his eyes. She was learning that this giant of a man had a heart the same size. "You've given us a start. Now, what happened with Roland?"

"Found him a place and he has the coach."

Pleased, Zahra nodded. "Good. Anything else to report?"

"Nope."

"Then I'll see you later on. Thank you, Alfred."

He nodded, closed the door, and left her in the office alone.

Christmas Eve, Archer joined his family for the celebratory midnight mass at St. Louis Cathedral, then journeyed back to Juliana's to open gifts. There would be a large meal later in the evening, but right now they were content to enjoy each other, coffee, cognac, and the small sweet treats prepared by Juliana's cook, Little Reba.

Juliana surprised her sons by gifting them all with matching black velvet vests. "I know it was a silly notion," she admitted, watching them admire the garments, "but I simply couldn't resist. I used to dress you alike when you were younger, and I suppose I never got over it."

They all smiled. The vests were finely made, and the sons were now old enough to not resent being given the same gift.

She, on the other hand, was given everything from gifts of jewelry from Archer and Drake, to an elaborate candelabra seaman Philippe had purchased on his last trip to Cuba. Beau, the artisan of the family, gave her an elaborate iron-worked trellis for her garden. As always, Juliana was moved to tears by the generosity of her boys, but she mused aloud, "I do wish Henri were here, and Raimond and Sable and my grandchildren."

"And Gerrold," Archer said somberly. Gerrold Le Veq, their second oldest brother, had given his life to the country during the war. Seven years had passed since his death, but the hole in the family's fabric was still as real today as it had been the day the tragic news had arrived.

Beau lifted his cognac. "A toast to family."

"Here, here!"

They all lifted their drinks in response, touched each other's glasses as was the tradition, then downed a swallow.

To end the quietness that always overcame them whenever Gerrold was mentioned, Beau asked his mother, "So when is His Majesty due to return?"

"Sometime after the new year."

Archer cracked, "Raimond can stay away indefinitely, but I do miss Sable, Cullen, and the girls."

Archer and the other Brats, as Raimond had christened his brothers, enjoyed the way Sable Fontaine Le Veq had upset Raimond's well-oiled life during the early months of their marriage back in '65. Raimond had tried everything to keep from loving the former slave woman, but in the end he'd been so overwhelmed by his deep feelings that he'd even agreed to adopt three children Sable had found living on the streets of New Orleans. The then twelve-year-old Cullen, his twin sister, Hazel, and the younger Blythe were as

loved by the family then as they were now. Later
that same year, Sable and Raimond added a
daughter of their own, Desiré, and she was as
feisty and as beautiful as the House of Le Veq required.

After going home to get some sleep, Archer
bathed, dressed, then set out on Christmas Day to
see Lynette. He would spend the afternoon with
her before returning to his mother's home for the
big Christmas feast.

When she answered his knock on the door,
she greeted him with uncharacteristic coolness.
He assumed she was still simmering over her
encounter with Domino. Undaunted, he kissed
her smooth cheek. "Merry Christmas, sweet-
heart."

"Merry Christmas to you as well, Archer. I have
a gift for you."

While he shed his coat and hung it on the peg
by the door, she returned with a small package
wrapped in bright blue cloth.

"Thank you." Inside he found a set of white
linen handkerchiefs. A prominent *A* had been
embroidered on the corner of each. "These are
real fine, Lynnie. Thank you."

"I hoped you'd like them. I did the needlework
myself."

"They're just what I need."

She smiled for the first time.

He eased her into his arms and gave her a soft
kiss. "What would you like to do today?"

"You pick, as long as it doesn't involve talking
to whores."

Archer ignored the dig. "How about a ride through the park?"

"No. I hear that woman has been parading around in that vulgar red coach of hers. I'd rather we didn't run into her."

"So you plan to spend the rest of your life hiding at home?"

"No, Archer, I don't. But I do wish you had listened to me and not acknowledged her."

"She's a client, Lynette. I could hardly ignore her when she walked up."

"Considering who she is, and that everyone in the shop heard the way she spoke to me, I would think you'd cut your ties to her."

Archer stepped back. "Excuse me?"

"You heard me. She's a whore, and in spite of her snippy words to me, she and I have nothing in common. Nothing!"

He studied her silently.

"And if you cared for me, you'd do as I asked."

Archer drawled, "And that would be, what?"

"Tell her you won't cater her affair. I'm sure she can find someone else."

"How about we take that drive—get some air. You're obviously distressed."

"Yes I am, and a drive is not going to cure that. She insulted me, Archer, and you just stood there."

He said tightly, "If I remember correctly, you drew first blood, Lynette. Were you expecting her to just slink away?"

"I was expecting not to have to deal with her at all," she responded just as tightly.

"Well, I won't be canceling my contract with her."

"Why on earth not?"

"Because this is business, Lynette, and you do not get to call the tune on the way I make the money that puts the jewels on your wrists or the gowns on your back." Archer was reminded of his brother calling Lynette passive. Not anymore.

"I think you should leave, Archer."

"And I agree."

He retrieved his coat, hat, and cane. "I'll call on you in a few days."

"Fine."

But as he left, they both knew this might possibly be the beginning of the end.

"What's the matter?" his mother asked, stepping out on her verandah, where he'd gone to seek a bit of solitude away from the festivities inside.

"Why does something have to be wrong?" he drawled emotionlessly.

She took a seat at the table. "Because it is cold out here, Archer, and of all of my sons, you have the warmest blood. If *you* are out here in this chill, you are distressed over something."

He smiled softly, then turned her way. She'd always been an insightful parent, and he wondered if it was the result of her having raised them alone after their father's untimely death at sea during the twelfth year of their marriage. "I think it is time to find a new mistress."

His mother's voice held surprise. "Oh, really?"

He then told her the story.

"Interesting," was all she said.

Archer turned to her. "You are dying to say something, Mama, so go ahead. I'm big enough to take whatever it is."

She gave him a small smile. "Well, to be truthful, I've never cared for her."

"Mama, you've only met her twice."

"Indeed. However, each time was in a shop, and each time she impressed me as being a tad greedy."

Archer dropped his head into his hands.

"You asked, son."

He righted himself. "I know, but why can't she understand that my relationship with Domino is strictly business."

"Is it?"

"Yes, Mama. I find the woman intriguing, but that's all."

"Well, I hope I raised you to have the sense not to become enamored of someone in her occupation."

"Don't worry." Although thoughts of her haunted him daily.

"Well, whatever you decide to do about Lynette, remember that life is too short to be unhappy. Take it from a woman who knows."

Zahra and the girls had spent Christmas Eve observing a holiday tradition unique to New Orleans. The locals called it *feux de joie*, which in English translated to "fires of joy." Bonfires were lit along the Mississippi River from New Orleans to Baton Rouge to light the way for Papa Noel. In addition to burning piles of cast-off wood, the locals built edifices like large teepees, replicas of houses, cabins, and riverboats to burn as well. Zahra had always loved spectacles. The smoky night air thick with the smell of burning wood and the various foodstuffs mixed with the beat of drums and the brassy rhythmic blares of horns made it an experience Zahra wasn't likely to forget.

On Christmas Day, Zahra, her girls, and the staff spent time together as a family. They feasted on fish, rice, and yams delivered by a local restaurant. For dessert, Roland Keel brought out a cake he'd purchased from one of the city's bakeries. They opened gifts, and Alfred played his fiddle while everyone danced. Zahra, who loved to dance, was right in the middle of the celebrating. Like everyone else, she had had a tad too much of the Christmas spirits provided by Stella and Adair, and a good time was had by all.

The next morning, they awakened with sore heads, but no one would have traded the fun they'd had for anything.

A few days later, Alfred knocked on Zahra's office door. "Someone here to see you."

"Who is it?"

"A young man. He's outside on the steps."

Curious, Zahra picked up her domino, secured it, and followed Alfred downstairs.

Zahra did not recognize the young man. "May I help you?"

"Are you the woman called Domino?"

"I am."

"Then I'm supposed to give this to you."

He held out an envelope, which a wary Zahra took from his hand. She opened it. On the small piece of vellum inside was written one word: *Sanctuary.*

Distressed, she asked him, "Who gave you this?"

"Mrs. Nelson."

Nelson was Araminta's married name. Zahra nodded. "Thank you." It didn't matter to her who the young man was or how he'd come to be at her door. For the moment, *Sanctuary* was all she could see, but even as the word echoed inside, she remembered her manners. "Can I offer you something? Food, drink?"

"No, ma'am. I have to be going."

With that, he left the porch and walked up the street.

Alfred, who had been standing silently a few feet away, asked with concern, "Are you all right?"

"No. My parents have lost their fight for their land."

"Sorry to hear that."

"No sorrier than I."

Upstairs in her office, Zahra sat silently. *Sanctuary.* The single-word message had been her parents' way of informing her of their return to the swamps that had hidden her ancestors since the nation's colonial days. She prayed they were in good health. Her first thought upon receiving the note had been to immediately set out for home to make sure. It had come to her, though, that had anything untoward happened to either of her parents, Araminta would have certainly included the news in the envelope, so she felt safe setting aside that worry. Other worries remained, however. What had her parents found upon returning to the hidden encampment of cabins and farms? Were the buildings still standing where she'd played and grown up? What about their neighbors and their families—had they returned to Sanctuary, too? There were so many unanswered questions that the urge to leave this operation behind and travel to South Carolina as fast as she could was still strong.

She couldn't abandon her post, though. Now that the house was on the verge of opening, she would have much to do. Araminta had trusted her to see this delicate, though unconventional, assignment through, and Zahra would keep her word. Her parents would demand no less.

Later that day her mood was considerably lightened by the unexpected arrival of the Hotel Christophe's chef, Aristide O'Neil. When she came down to meet him, he bowed low over her gloved hand and kissed it lightly. In French-inflected English, he gushed, "It is an honor, madame."

"I am honored as well. To what do I owe this visit, sir?"

He was a tall, reed-thin man whose straight brown hair had receded almost to his ears. His eyes were smoky gray, and his complexion was the café au lait so prominent among the Creoles. "I have come to see where I will place everything and to get a sense of the room's air."

The girls were up on the balcony looking down on him with a mixture of smiles and curiosity.

He bowed to them as well, saying, "Mademoiselles."

Their smiles turned to grins.

For the first few moments he did nothing but look around. "Very sensual place, madame."

Zahra inclined her head in silent thanks. "We like it."

"How about ice statues?"

"Ice statues?"

"Yes, a swan or two, a woman or two. Maybe something similar to the couple you have by the staircase."

He was referring, of course, to Adam and Eve. Zahra gave the couple a glance and felt the pull on her senses. "You can make them out of ice?"

"Maybe not as finely or as large, but the essence will remain."

"Where are you going to get the ice?"

"We've had an ice-making business here in New Orleans since '68. Mr. Le Veq was wise enough to be one of the initial investors, so the hotel has access to all the ice it needs."

Zahra was impressed. From the looks on the girls' faces, they were as well.

He spent the next hour looking, measuring, and making notes on a small tablet. In the middle of going over the menu, O'Neil asked, "Have you tasted Mr. Edmund McIlhenny's pepper sauce?"

"No."

"Ah, it is one of the best things to come out of

the war. I will have some for your event. It will help keep your patrons' blood hot!"

He gave her an exaggerated wink, and she couldn't suppress her grin as she asked, "And it's made from peppers?"

*"Oui,"* he responded while writing down more notes. "Peppers were the only thing left in his fields over on Avery Island after the war, so he turned them into a sauce he calls Tabasco."

"And you put it on food?"

"Yes. I promise, you have never had anything quite like it."

Zahra was skeptical, but his enthusiastic manner made her want a taste of this new sauce called Tabasco.

When he was finally done, he bowed over her hand again and said, "Madame, you are charming, beautiful, and very mysterious. You and your ladies will take New Orleans by storm."

Zahra smiled. "Why, thank you."

"I shall be visiting quite regularly as the date approaches, so expect me."

"We will."

With a wave of good-bye to the girls, Aristide O'Neil and his energy left the house, and Zahra asked, "Is it just me, or did he make you all tired, too?"

The girls laughed, then went back to their day.

As Zahra climbed the stairs to return to her office, she found herself studying Adam and Eve and trying to imagine them in ice form. Once again, she sensed the passion flowing through Eve, and immediately thought of Archer. Shaking

herself free, she redirected her thoughts to the
Hotel Christophe's chef. She was looking forward
to working with the effervescent O'Neil. She liked
him.

# Chapter 5

It was New Year's Eve—opening night—and Zahra studied her reflection in her bedroom's standing mirror. The woman staring back was hard to recognize. The daring décolletage showed off the tops of her brown breasts, and the capped sleeves left her arms bare. The white satin gown hugged her waist, then fell to the floor with yards of fabric, only to be caught up in the rear in layers of swirls and pleats over a soft bustle. The word *princess* came to mind, as did *queen*, but she wasn't pretending to be either. Her role tonight was to be the madame of a New Orleans cathouse and survive to tell about it in the morning.

She picked up the exotic domino designed for tonight's affair and tied it on with the attached white ribbons. She studied the effect. The white satin matched the gown, but the soft, jewel-toned peacock feathers outlining the eye holes and the peacock plumes adorning the mask itself would undoubtedly cause the stir she and Wilma were hoping for.

A knock at the door brought her back to the present. It was Alfred.

"You look real fine, Miss Zahra."

"Thank you. Let's hope the customers think so as well."

"Oh, I doubt you'll have any problems there."

She smiled. "How are things going downstairs?"

"That chef fella is running around like a chicken with its neck wrung, but it's all coming together. Food's here, his help is here. Roland has the gambling room ready to go, and his people are in place."

"Good." She glanced over at the wooden clock hanging on the wall. It was now eight. "We've one hour before this madness begins. Make sure you keep an eye on things once we open. Especially the girls. Any of the men cause trouble, hustle them out."

"Yes, ma'am."

"For the time being, we'll have the customers enter by the rear door. I think they'll be more comfortable with that. Many won't want to be seen entering from the street. That reticence might change once our reputation is established and we can use the front entrance."

He nodded his agreement.

"Well," she said, "I'm going to check on the girls."

"And I'll go see if that chef needs any last-minute help."

"Thanks, Alfred."

"You're welcome."

Before he could leave, Zahra called out, "Alfred?"

"Yes, ma'am?"

"You look real nice too." He was wearing a gray suit, a black paisley vest, and a string tie.

He responded by shyly dropping his eyes and smiling. "Thanks."

He exited, and Zahra went to see how the girls were coming along.

For the past week, Wilma and her hired seamstresses had been sewing gowns nonstop for Zahra and the girls—not that the girls would be wearing them long, Stella drolly pointed out. In truth, the girls were more accustomed to wearing wrappers when working, mainly for ease in removal, so in response, Wilma had fashioned some in a variety of colors and styles. All were elegant and revealing.

But now they were formally dressed. The paint had been applied to their faces, their gowns were on, and their eyes were sparkling with excitement. Perfume scented the air.

Adair was adjusting her clockworked stockings when Zahra entered. Adair stopped and said, "I've been doing this a long time, but tonight I'm as nervous as long-tailed cat in a room full of rockers."

Chloe, who was in the process of putting the final touches on her hair, added, "Domino, this is the most high-class place I've ever worked. I hope I don't embarrass you."

Zahra said, "I'm not concerned. Just be yourself."

Wearing matching gowns of rose red, the twins, Naomi and Salome, said in unison, "We can't wait to show ourselves off."

Zahra shook her head at their antics. "Well, you all look beautiful. We've less than an hour before Alfred throws open the doors, so once you're ready, stay here until he comes and gets you. We're going to make a grand entrance."

Zahra started for the door.

"Hey, Domino." It was Stella.

Zahra turned back. "Yes."

"Thanks," she said sincerely. "For the gowns, the house, everything."

Zahra nodded. "You're welcome."

Outside on the street, Archer could not believe the numbers of fancy coaches and carriages snaking their way to Domino's opening. There were as many behind him as there were in front, and at the slow rate they were all moving he thought it might be tomorrow before he reached the door. The advertised admission fee of thirty dollars had separated the wheat from the chaff, and only the elite were here. He recognized more than a few vehicles belonging to politicians, local business owners, and other prominent men in the city; he'd never imagined so many would turn out. With its being New Year's Eve, he would have thought most of the men in line would have been spending the evening with family.

Thirty minutes later, Archer finally handed the reins of his barouche over to the waiting groomsman and stepped down. He had only to follow the men ahead of him to find the entrance.

A voice behind him said, "Well, Le Veq, I'd no idea you'd be here, too."

Archer recognized the voice as belonging to Etienne Barber, a carpetbagger from Illinois and now a prominent New Orleans broker. "Good evening, Etienne. I came to see what I could see, just like everyone else."

"I hear the madame is quite beautiful."

"That is true."

"You've met her?" he asked, sounding surprised.

"Yes, the hotel is handling the catering."

"I see."

Archer had no intentions of spending the evening in the company of the oily Barber, so when they entered the crowded back parlor, he said, "Have a good evening."

"You, as well."

And Archer made his way through the crush.

The din of voices was deafening. There were so many men in the main parlor that it was almost impossible to move about easily, but not even the large crowd could hide the startling décor. Having been born and raised in New Orleans, Archer was accustomed to the decadent and sometimes seamy underside of the city, but this heady, erotic place with its elegant interior would arouse a dead man.

"Hello, brother."

He turned to see a grinning Philippe standing at his side. He had a glass of cognac in his hand. "I see you made it."

"I did," Archer shouted over the noise. "This is something."

"Yes, it is. There's almost as many people upstairs in the gaming rooms as there are down here."

"Where are the ladies?"

"They're supposed to be making their entrance any time now. Someone said there's to be entertainment first."

"What type of entertainment?"

Philippe shrugged. "No idea, but I've no plans to be chaperoned by my big brother—so I'll see you later."

Archer grinned.

Philippe made his way back through the crowd, and Archer looked over at the elegant ivory-and-gold bar, wondering how long it might take him to make his way there.

Once he had his cognac in hand, Archer sipped and observed. His waitstaff, under the supervision of Aristide O'Neil, was moving about the room with plates of hors d'oeuvres and demi glasses of spirits. The expansive buffet set up on one side of the room had everything from meat to sweets. Archer made a mental note to compliment Aristide for the sumptuous display. Off to the side, a small group of musicians added their lively melodies to the gay atmosphere.

"Gentlemen!" A voice rang out over the room. "May I present Madame Domino and her ladies!"

Everyone turned and looked up towards the balcony. On it stood five beautiful multiracial women and the stunning, white-gowned Domino, wearing an exotic feathered mask. The room erupted with cheers.

The women smiled, waved and curtsied.

Archer had eyes only for Domino. The white gown and the striking plumed mask made her even more alluring.

A voice beside Archer said, "I'm trusting you to introduce me."

Archer turned to see Etienne Barber staring up at Domino with excitement in his eyes, but Archer said with amusement, "You're on your own, Etienne."

"Why do you think she wears the mask?"

"It's the question of the day."

"Oh, here they come."

The women floated down the large staircase like royalty, smiling and nodding at the appreciative men. Domino, on the other hand, maintained her position on the balcony, a queen overseeing her domain.

The giant Alfred announced to the men, "If you will all make yourselves comfortable, the entertainment will begin."

The blonde named Chloe took a seat at the shining white piano. She began with a rendition of the bawdy song "Buffalo Girls" but changed the name to "Louisiana Girls." By the time she got to the chorus, men were singing along boisterously, *"Louisiana Girls won't you come out tonight—come out tonight!"* She then sang "Jimmy

Crack Corn," "Pop Goes the Weasel," and "Jennie with the Light Brown Hair." When she segued into "The Bonnie Blue Flag," one of the most popular songs among the Confederate soldiers, and followed that with "Johnny Comes Marching Home," the Union army standard, it was obvious to all in attendance that Domino was not playing political favorites. Archer thought that a brilliant move on her part.

Chloe stood and received the adulation of the crowd. Blowing kisses, she sat again and was soon joined by two women who'd been introduced as Stella and Adair. They sang some hilariously off-color songs, then playfully recited some of the most ribald and suggestive poetry many of the male ears, including Archer, had ever had the delight of hearing. One in particular titled "The Budding Rose" had a stanza that went:

> See his amorous lips and hands,
> Fondle all her naked part;
> And his upright vigor stands,
> In her open ravished heart.
> Shift and shirt are off together,
> Naked is the sweet embrace,
> Not one part concealed by either
> All's as naked as your face.

While Stella and Adair took their bows, Archer shook his head with amusement. The men roared and raised their glasses yet again.

Next up was a tall, dark-skinned woman named Lovey. Unlike the other women dressed in elegant gowns, Lovey had entered the parlor wearing nothing but scarflike red veils, much to the appreciation of the boisterous multitudes. As the musicians began a slow, sensual tune, Lovey danced while slowly and erotically removing the veils one by one, until she was as naked as the statues in the room. Every eye stared transfixed at her enticing performance. Archer stretched his tie a bit, swearing the temperature in the already warm room had risen even higher.

He heard Etienne whisper, "Amazing . . ."

By the time Lovey grabbed her discarded veils and left the room, the whistling and applauding men knew that this was not the ordinary, everyday brothel many had frequented in the past. Domino's place was novel, and Archer was certain that once word got out, customers would be lined up from New Orleans to Baton Rouge trying to get in.

Zahra didn't know about anyone else, but the heady atmosphere was affecting her in ways she found impossible to ignore. She attributed it to this being the first night and to her not being accustomed to so much sensuality. She told herself she'd be calmer in a few days once the novelty wore off, but in reality she wasn't sure. She surveyed the crowd from her position above the floor. The sheer number of customers pleased her, as did their reaction to the entertainment; if she could survive the next few hours, she might be okay. As a dispatch she'd played at many things, but nothing as challenging as this.

Surveying the room, her eyes locked with the

wry, dark eyes of Archer Le Veq, and she mentally jumped. Of course, she'd expected his attendance, but not the knowing look on his entirely too handsome face as he stood below her. He flashed her a smile, then lifted his glass in silent tribute. Dressed in a formal coat, his presence seemed to dominate the room. In spite of the crush around him, he was all she could see, and he was viewing her as if he had the answers to all of her secrets. Knowing she couldn't afford to be distracted tonight or show favoritism to any one man so soon, she gave him a short nod in response, took in a deep breath, then turned her attention to the men in line to greet her.

Zahra smiled at the next one. He was tall, light-skinned, and had pock scars on his face. He bowed low over her hand. "Etienne Barber, at your service, madame."

"It's a pleasure meeting you, Mr. Barber."

"You have quite a place here."

"Thank you."

"I'm a broker—here's my card."

Zahra took it, scanned the writing on it for a moment, then handed it to Alfred, who pocketed it inside his coat.

Barber appeared to want to protest, but he seemed to catch himself before saying, "I transact real estate, loans, investments. If you are ever in financial straits, I am at your service."

"I'll remember that. Thank you. It's been a pleasure meeting you."

He met her eyes and said with quiet assurance, "I could make it much more pleasurable. What must a man do to get a date with the madame?"

"The madame doesn't date," she said, smiling falsely beneath her mask.

"Oh, really," he replied skeptically, his eyes on her bosom. "A pity."

"One must sometimes choose business over pleasure, Mr. Barber."

"I see." He ran his eyes over her again. "Now where did you say you were from?"

"I didn't. Thank you, Mr. Barber. Take a stroll around and see the other delights we have here."

It was obvious he wasn't pleased to be given such short shrift. "Until we meet again, madame." A bow later, he was walking towards the gambling rooms.

Standing by the bar, Archer sipped cognac and watched the men lined up to pay their respects. There had to be fifty at least. All were given smiles by the beautiful Domino. Some were even gifted with her soft laughter, but he noticed that none were allowed to remain at her side. Each was given no more than a few minutes of her time before the giant in the gray suit politely moved them on and beckoned the next man in line. Archer wondered if she would send him packing if he joined the lemmings, but he didn't bother. The men of the House of Le Veq lined up for no one, not even a woman as beautiful and as challenging as she was.

He saw the tight-jawed disappointment on Barber's face when Domino sent him packing, and for Archer that was well worth the exorbitant price of admission. Barber was a carpetbagger, and now that the Democrats were *redeeming* the South by reinstituting segregation and other antebellum atrocities, men like him, no matter how successful, were treated with a scorn the Rebs usually reserved for the freedmen. In truth Blacks had no use for his kind, either. Carpetbaggers had looted monies for schools, land, and other federally funded programs designed to aid the freedmen. That the abrasive and condescending Barber was a *Black* carpetbagger ranked him somewhere below Mississippi sludge.

While Domino continued to receive tributes from her minions, Archer climbed the stairs. He saw her eyes slide to his, but he simply nodded and headed to the gambling rooms.

Zahra chastised herself for being disappointed that Archer had not joined the line, but she told herself that the farther she stayed away from him, the better. As the next man stepped up and whispered suggestively and crudely in her ear, she pasted on a smile and wondered why Araminta couldn't have sent her on a more cut-and-dry mission like breaking into someone's home and stealing a military code. In comparison to this madhouse of sex, arousal, and twins performing for all to see, the former was far easier.

The air in the gambling rooms was thick with cigar smoke and the smells of stale cologne mixed with liquor. Archer, seated at one of the tables, had been playing poker for just under an hour. As the man across from him, a Republican from out of town, dealt the next hand, the man asked, "Did you see the show?"

"I did."

"Phenomenal. Don't you think?" asked the third man at the table.

"I was impressed." Archer looked at his cards.

Their fourth, a politician who said he'd come all the way from Shreveport, asked Archer, "Have you been down the hall yet?"

"What's down the hall?"

"The Voyeur Room."

Archer stared.

"Ten dollars gets you a seat. The women are *twins!*" he exclaimed.

Archer chuckled. "Every man's fantasy."

"Oh, most definitely."

They all laughed and began to play.

After another few hands, Archer pocketed his winnings, gave his seat to a man waiting to play, and made his way through the crowd to the Voyeur Room. He'd seen rooms like it before in France, Cuba, and Haiti, but like most men, he was still curious, so he paid the ten-dollar price to the man taking the money at the door, took a seat, and watched the erotic play of the man and the two beautiful, uninhibited twins on display. The man, his back to the watchers, had wisely donned a domino in order to mask his identity, another common practice. However, mask or no, Archer knew his baby brother with or without his clothes, and the realization that the man on the bed was Philippe made Archer choke on his cognac. Were Raimond in Archer's position, Philippe would be snatched up, thrown his clothes, and escorted out, but Archer was not Raimond. Archer also had no desire to watch his baby brother's technique, so he excused himself. Seeing Domino standing behind the crowd he made his way over to her.

Zahra had wandered in to get her first look at the twins in action, and the sight of the two young women making love to the well-endowed man—and, shockingly, to each other—had her riveted. She watched lips and hands caress and fondle; saw heads thrown back in a passion reminiscent of the Eve statue, and when the various positions seamlessly melted into a heated eroticism, she found it hard to breathe.

"Are you enjoying yourself, Domino?" came a husky, familiar voice.

She didn't need to turn to see who the caressing voice belonged to. "Are you, Mr. Le Veq?"

"I am." Aroused by her nearness and by all he'd seen this evening, Archer wondered just how long it might be before he could pleasure Zahra the way Philippe was lustfully pleasuring the twins.

Zahra had seen Le Veq enter the room only moments before. The man on the other side of the glass was now slowly stroking the straddling Salome while the passion-eyed Naomi twined around them both like sensual smoke. Forcing her voice to as normal a tone as she could manage, Zahra said to Archer, "You didn't spend much time in your seat."

Feeling the warmth of her white-gowned body teasing him, Archer asked quietly, "Are you keeping time on all of your guests, or just me?"

"Just you." Only then did she turn and meet his eyes.

"I'm flattered."

"You should be. I'm keeping time on you with the hope that I'd have the opportunity to say thank you for your help. Your chef and his staff have performed admirably." She had no intention of referencing their prior encounters.

"You're welcome."

Suddenly, Etienne Barber was at her side. "Ah, Madame Domino, just the lady I was in search of."

"Hello, Mr. Barber."

"May I have the honor of a dance? The band has promised to play a waltz."

Zahra had no intentions of letting Barber monopolize her time. "No, I'm sorry. I was just talking to Mr. Le Veq about a slight misunderstanding we seem to have in the contract drawn up for tonight. We were on our way to discuss the matter." Then she added, "Once again, Mr. Barber, business before pleasure."

Archer fielded Barber's angry eyes with an amused smile. He then asked Domino, "If you're ready, madame?"

"I am."

Zahra placed her hand gently on Archer's extended arm and let him escort her away. When they were out of earshot, she asked, "Is he powerful enough to give me problems?"

"Only if you owe him money."

"I don't."

"Then you should be fine."

Zahra could see the looks of surprise and, in some cases, outrage on the men's faces as she walked with Le Veq. "You're the envy of everyone here, Mr. Le Veq."

"Let's just hope you won't have to pull any knives out of my back."

"No violence of any kind is allowed on the premises. In fact, Alfred is outside explaining just that to a customer who pulled a razor after losing quite a bit at the poker table."

On the main floor, the girls were holding a lottery. The winners would get to bring in the New Year with one of the girls, and any interest in Domino and Archer was immediately lost.

"Where are we going?" Archer asked.

"To my bedroom."

Shocked, Archer stared down.

She smiled up. "Isn't that where you've been wanting to take me since the first time we met?"

He looked down into the feather-trimmed eyes and shook his head and smiled upon seeing the mischief sparkling there.

Zahra had come to a decision. Gathering the information the president needed was going to be too difficult if she had to spend the next six months trying to figure out the players. Potential pests like Etienne Barber and the other crude men she'd met tonight made that clear. She needed to know the difference between those she could shove off the pier and those she had to smile at and tolerate as soon as possible. Not knowing her parents' fate made it imperative that she get this job done quickly and efficiently.

Because the door that led to her room was on the far side of the house, few if any of the revelers saw it open, and she and Archer disappear inside.

The sconces on the wall of the narrow staircase softly lit the way. Zahra was very conscious of him climbing the staircase behind her. The vivid performances of Naomi and Salome continued to haunt her.

Zahra ushered him into her bedroom and lit a lamp. She saw him looking around and wondered what he'd think if he saw her real bedroom back home.

"Beautiful room," he said to her approvingly.

"Thank you."

She saw him eyeing her bed, but she looked away and walked over to the French doors instead. Opening them let in the cold December night, but after the heat of the twins' performance and humidity everywhere else in the house she relished the chill of the fresh air.

"Feels good," Archer said, eyeing her lovely presence.

"It does, doesn't it? Besides getting away from Barber, this is the real reason I wanted to come up here."

"I'm disappointed."

She met his eyes and smiled even as she felt them stroking her like a hand. "As I said the morning we met, you Frenchmen are legends in your own minds."

He was propped up against the edge of her mirrored vanity table, arms crossed, watching her in the low, shimmering light. "And here I was thinking I was invited here to be seduced. Instead, you insult me."

"Thank you for going along with the ruse."

"You're welcome."

Silence settled between them, and with it came memories.

Doing her best to maintain her distance, she said to him, "I have a business proposition I'd like you to consider."

"And it is?"

"I need information on who is who in New Orleans. Take Barber, for example. Although you assured me he is of no importance, what if he had been? If I'm to run a successful house, I need to know the wheat from the chaff."

"So what are you proposing?"

"That you supply me with that information, at whatever price you deem fair."

"I see." Archer studied her, then asked, "Suppose my price is that you share my bed?"

"Then I will find someone else."

In the undulating light, she looked confident, fearless, and so temptingly beautiful that he found himself wanting her more with each tick of the clock that was the only sound in the otherwise silent room. "Suppose I amend that and just ask for the pleasure of your company?"

The eyes in the bird mask studied him. "I'd prefer a monetary agreement, Mr. Le Veq."

"And I prefer your company. You're very mysterious, Domino, and I'd like to know you better."

"To what end?"

"Seduction, of course."

Her nipples tightened of their own accord. "You're very bold, sir."

"If you wanted meek, you would be waltzing with Étienne Barber."

He was formidable, but she'd already known

that. "Have you ever had a woman not succumb?"

"Not that I can remember."

"I am tempted to agree just to show you that
such women do exist."

"Is that a gauntlet I hear?"

The words mirrored the conversation they'd
had in his office. "I believe it is."

"Then may I suggest we go riding? Maybe a
morning later in the week? I can tell you about the
city and answer any other questions you may
have. We'll let the seduction play out on its own."

"I don't plan to be seduced, Mr. Le Veq, but
people will think I'm your paramour. Are you
prepared for that?"

"For that and more." Again Archer fantasized
about removing her mask while kissing her succulent mouth.

"What of your mistress, the lovely Lynette?"

"Lynette is not at issue here." And in truth she
wasn't. He'd broken it off with her.

"I see. Then I will agree to your terms."

"I'll send my card around to inform you of the
date."

"That is acceptable."

"Excellent."

Zahra had no idea what she'd really agreed to,
but nevertheless, she was determined not to succumb to his charm or his kisses, no matter how
tempted she might be. "We should probably return to the party. Alfred will be looking for me."

"How long have you known him?"

"Not long," she said vaguely as she led him to
the door.

In the silent hallway that led back to the noise and people, he said, "I'll be taking my leave now."

"So soon?"

"Yes. You have business to oversee, and I'm not one for being one amongst many." He bowed. "Until our ride, madame."

In his eyes she saw a directness that touched her core. "I'm looking forward to it."

"No more than I."

# Chapter 6

"We did well," Zahra declared as she and Alfred went over the previous evening's receipts. She and the rest of the household had only gone to bed when the last of the drunken guests had staggered out around four that morning. They'd slept the day away. "The gaming tables and the bar made up for the girls being allowed to keep most of their takes."

Alfred was pleased. "Good."

"The twins brought in a small fortune."

Alfred dropped his head and shook it dramatically.

"What's the matter?"

"I've just never been around women like them before."

"They are something, aren't they?"

"That and more."

Zahra's mind's eye could still see the twins

entwined in the erotic tableau. Any uninitiated persons viewing their performance had received quite an education. Personally, Zahra's limited experience in the bedroom had been greatly expanded as well.

"So where'd you disappear to last night?" Alfred asked. "I couldn't find you after I tossed out the fool with the razor."

"I was with Le Veq."

Alfred eyed her skeptically.

"Don't look at me that way. It's part and parcel of having to amend this plan of ours."

"Why?"

"Because I need to get the information for President Grant as soon as possible so that I can return home and determine what is happening with my parents."

"I understand that. So?"

"So, the fastest way for me to learn the rules of the game and its players is to use someone who is already at the table. Otherwise we may still be here next year this time."

"But why him?"

"Why not?" she asked with a shrug. "He's a Republican, his family is prominent, and he's handsome. No one would expect me to be seen with Etienne Barber, for instance."

"True, but Le Veq worries me."

"He worries me as well, which is another reason why I'm enlisting his aid."

"To keep an eye on him."

"Correct. In fact, he and I will be going riding in a few days."

"Are you sure he won't find out why we're really here?"

"No, but it's all I have for the moment, so we'll cross our fingers and see what tune comes out of the horn."

"All right, but watch your step."

"Advice I have already given myself."

And she had, reminding herself as she sat in a rocker on the verandah outside of her bedroom later that evening. Bundled up against the cold, she mused on the past few days. Only now would she admit that she'd been dreaming about him; hot, erotic couplings that left her damp and restless when she awakened. Last night, he'd come to her as the statue Adam and she'd been Eve. Even now, Zahra could feel the warm weight of his hand cupping her breast; as if to offer proof, her nipple hardened shamelessly. She also willingly admitted that were she not engaged in this charade for Araminta and the president, a liaison with Le Veq might prove intriguing. He was as tempting as any other man she'd ever met—the kind that could make a woman lose her religion—but Zahra could not let herself be so dazzled by him as to lose sight of her true mission. She'd always prided herself on being strong-minded, and in the days and weeks to come she sensed she was going to need every ounce of it.

Unlike Zahra, Archer's thoughts weren't on the present but on an event of the past; Oscar Dunn's official death certificate had finally been published in the local newspapers. According to the document, Louisiana's first Black lieutenant governor had died of congestion of the brain. That evening, Archer discussed the findings with his brothers as they ate dinner with Juliana.

"I talked with Coroner Creagh over at his office this afternoon, and, according to him, the poisoning rumors were so rife he went to the Dunn house the day of the death and told the family that because of all the rumors, the law demanded an inquest and autopsy.

"But what I didn't know was that Doctor Avilla, the chief police physician, wasn't allowed to see the body either."

"The police were kept away too?" Drake asked.

"Yes."

Beau remarked, "This is beginning to smell, Archer."

"I agree."

The conversation turned as Juliana announced she'd gotten word from Raimond. He, Sable, and the children would be returning later in the week, but the silent Archer continued to muse on the mysterious circumstances surrounding the death of Oscar Dunn.

Drake said, "Mother, I—"

But his words were drowned out by a cacophony of noise flooding in from the streets. Curious and confused, they all left the table and headed to the door, where they were alarmed by the sight of a large crowd of men marching by. Archer estimated there were at least two hundred in the noisy throng. In their hands were banners, lit torches, and signs proclaiming supremacy held aloft on pieces of wood. They were also carrying clubs, guns, and lengths of pipe; On their faces were masks and bandanas to hide their identities. The power of their voices and marching feet shook the ground as they chanted in unison, "Redemption! Redemption!"

The brothers shared an angry glance. Their neighbors came out to investigate.

One of the marchers looked towards the Le Veqs and yelled, "You Sambo Republicans better leave town or you'll wish you had!"

His comrades roared agreement. A shot rang out, then another, shattering the window behind Juliana and making the Le Veqs scramble to shield their mother. Archer drew a pistol, and Juliana screamed, "No! They're trying to provoke a riot! Don't shoot back!"

She was right, of course; provoking a fight and then murdering the victims had become one of the supremacists' most hated tactics, but Archer was so furious that he felt capable of killing them all with his bare hands.

The marchers laughed, then journeyed on, shouting their hated chant.

As the men faded into the distance, the brothers drew in angry breaths and saw that all of them had drawn their pistols. Philippe helped Juliana to her feet.

They all crowded around to make certain she hadn't been hit by the lead.

Archer asked, "Are you hurt?"

Her eyes blazed. "Just my pride. Having no recourse but to watch those mongrels go by is the most humiliating, I believe." Then she added a declaration. "Gentlemen, if the government doesn't put a stop to this madness, I will leave this god-forsaken country and live out the rest of my days in Haiti."

That said, she went inside.

The still seething brothers cast malevolent eyes at the shattered window behind them. Archer said, "She could have been killed."

The enormity of that was not lost on any of them.

Archer eyed his brothers. "Some veterans are proposing arming themselves and fighting fire with fire. I believe they just got four new recruits."

"Five," Philippe contradicted. "When Raimond comes home and finds out those sheet-wearing cowards shot at his Lovely Juliana, all hell is going to break loose."

The next afternoon, Archer was eating his lunch at his desk and reading the local newspapers when a report on a fire at the home of one of the city's most vitriolic Democratic officials caught his attention. It seemed a band of mounted hood-wearing men swarmed over the estate in the middle of the night tossing torches into the house and into the estate's cane fields. The terrified family swore the bandits were men of color. The mansion was totally destroyed.

The morning of Zahra's scheduled ride with Archer finally arrived. The part of herself that had been a successful dispatch was confident and assured, but the female self that was admittedly attracted to him was somewhat nervous, mainly because there was no guarantee that he'd be as malleable as she needed him to be. As a dispatch she'd never been attracted to a player in the ruse before, but she hoped admitting that fact would make her proceed with caution.

She adjusted the green domino that matched her bustled green gown, then viewed herself in the mirror. Satisfied with her reflection, she picked up her cape and handbag, and left her bedroom.

Downstairs, the girls were sitting around in their morning clothes, enjoying coffee and beignets.

As Zahra descended the staircase, Adair asked, "Where are you off to so early?"

"Riding with Archer Le Veq," she responded, pulling on her signature net gloves.

"Oh, my," an impressed-sounding Matilda said with a smile.

"May we go along?" the twins asked, grinning.

"No," Zahra said with mock ferocity. "He's mine, at least for the morning."

They sighed, "We'd love to get him in the room."

"He's here, Domino," Lovey called out from her position at the window, then added appreciatively, "Lord, that man is easy on the eyes."

The women laughed.

The twins ran playfully to the big front door, pushing each other out of the way in an attempt to reach it first. Once again, Zahra shook her head at their antics. In the end, they opened the door together, and as he entered, they bowed dramatically. Zahra noted that his answering grin seemed to light up the room.

*"Bonjour,* ladies," he said in greeting to them all.

When his eyes met Zahra's, his intense gaze warmed her blood, as if they were the only people in the room. *"Bonjour,* Domino."

"Good morning, Mr. Le Veq."

"How are you?"

"Well," she responded, wondering why the room seemed to be so warm all of a sudden. "And you?"

"I'm well." For a second or two, silence reigned, then he asked in that same dulcet tone, "Are you ready?"

"Yes." Finally breaking free from his spell, she turned to the girls and said, "Be good while I'm gone."

"You, too," Stella tossed back knowingly.

Heat seared Zahra's cheeks. Ignoring the female giggles behind her, she took hold of Le Veq's properly extended arm and let him escort her outside.

As they moved down the walk to his waiting black-and-brown barouche, there stood Alfred. With a scowl on his face, he opened the carriage's passenger side door. Zahra gracefully lifted her skirts and stepped in. Once she was seated beneath the half moon roof and Archer had taken his spot behind the reins, Alfred warned, "Treat her nice, or you'll have to answer to me, Le Veq."

A displeased Zahra turned to speak, only to have Archer say first, "I plan to."

Making a mental note to remind Alfred that although she appreciated his concern, she already had a father, Zahra and Le Veq drove away from the brooding giant, who was left standing at the curb.

The January day was bright but cold. Zahra was glad she'd worn her heavy cape and even more grateful for the heated bricks he'd provided for her feet, in addition to a thick blanket that warmed her from waist to toes.

"Warm enough?" he asked, looking her way.

"Yes."

"Good. I wouldn't want you to catch a chill."

"Neither would I."

It was small talk, a natural occurrence on first dates, because neither was sure how or where to begin again.

Archer didn't have to wonder why she attracted him the way she did. The mystery surrounding her identity was only enhanced by the beauty he sensed lurking beneath the green satin rhinestone mask. He found her so fascinating that he was willing to put up with the whirlwind sure to begin once he was seen with her this morning. Never a slave to public opinion, he planned to enjoy her company for as long as she extended him the privilege. More than a few male noses were going to be put out of joint by her largesse, but that didn't bother him either. "Shall I show you the city?" he asked.

"I'd like that."

"This is the famous *Place de Negroe*," he said to her as they stopped near a large open field near Ramparts Saint. "When the French and Spanish ruled New Orleans, free Blacks and slaves were allowed to come here on Sundays to market their wares, meet their neighbors and families, and generally have a good time. There was music, drums, and dancing. In the old days, this was a gathering place for the native tribes. Over the years though, the name changed to Congo Plain but is now called Congo Square. We celebrated the Emancipation Proclamation here, and gathered here to mourn when Lincoln died. Crowds still gather on Sundays for the festivities. People come from all over the world to see the dancers and hear the singers. I'll have to bring you here one Sunday afternoon so you can see it for yourself."

"Sounds like fun."

He nodded, then signaled the two horses so they could move on. He showed her the Ursuline convent, the beautiful opera houses, and the building housing Straight University.

"It was charted for the race's higher education by the state legislature in '69," Archer explained.

"So it's new?"

"Very."

Looking at the impressive structure filled Zahra with pride as she thought about the bright young minds gathered inside honing their intellectual gifts.

"The school's named for a man named Seymour Straight," Archer said, admiring her even more than the celebrated university. "He donated the land, and the Freedman's Bureau donated twenty thousand dollars."

Zahra was even more impressed.

Leaving the school, he drove them to a less prosperous section of the city—the Mississippi shoreline, where squatters had set up tents and wooden lean-tos, and where the smells from cooking fires floated on the air. Most of the residents were destitute, homeless freedmen. Zahra saw no beauty or brightness there, only mothers and children wrapped in newspapers, sleeping on the ground; men with vacant eyes who'd spent the night sleeping beneath wagons. In spite of the gains made by the race in the years immediately following the war, the big cities of the South were awash with shantytowns just like this, filled with residents with no hope in sight. "So, where does the race stand here?" she asked as they headed back to the main area of the city.

"On a very slippery slope. Just like in Memphis, the rioting here in '66 is not far from our minds."

The New Orleans riot of July 30, 1866 began when thugs, many of them Confederate veterans, descended on the city's Mechanics Institute to oppose a convention of Blacks and Whites called to amend the state's harsh Black Codes. Aided by firemen and police, the Rebs shot at delegates marching to the meeting then broke into the building to attack the attendees already inside. Thirty-seven of the delegates were killed, three of them White. During a hearing on the event, the 39th Congress determined that in addition to the deaths, hundreds more had been injured.

Archer continued, "The fact that the city's police force is more than one-quarter Colored shows there has been positive change, and many of the sheriffs in the parishes are also men of color, but Governor Warmoth is trying to reinstitute segregation on all levels—transportation, the schools, lodging. He probably would be impeached by now but for the death of our Lieutenant Governor Dunn back in November."

"How did Dunn die?" Zahra had read bits and pieces in the city's newspapers, but she wanted to hear his view.

"That's the question of the day." He then explained to her as much of the mystery as he knew personally.

"So do you believe he was poisoned?" she asked.

He nodded. "The evidence so far points to arsenic, but whether it really was or not, only an autopsy would tell."

Zahra found the story of Dunn's death very interesting. "But you said Dunn was originally a supporter of Governor Warmoth."

"Yes, he was, much to the chagrin of many of the Radicals, but Dunn refused to support the man my circle supported."

"Who was?"

"Francis E. Dumas."

"Why wouldn't Dunn support him?"

"Dumas was one of the state's largest slaveholders before the war."

"Ah. Was he a man of color?"

"Yes. Officially, an octoroon, but he supposedly treated his slaves well."

"Not well enough to give them a wage or set them free?"

Archer could tell by her tone that he was tipping in quicksand, so he didn't address that; instead, he asked, "where were you born?"

Zahra met his eyes. "Baltimore," she lied.

"Fred Douglass is from Maryland."

"So I hear."

He smiled, and Zahra found herself charmed. "What's the smile for?"

"You. So mysterious."

"You may not be interested if I reveal everything."

Their gazes met long enough for them both to be touched, then he drove her back to the house.

As they sat out front, Zahra said, "Thank you for the drive. I know much more about the city than before."

"Make sure you take that giant with you when you're out and about. Supremacist thugs are becoming bolder and bolder. They're not above targeting a woman."

"Thank you for the warning." Zahra was indeed glad for the advice, but she rarely left the house without her pistol or the razor strapped against her thigh, and she was well trained in the use of both.

"Will you have dinner with me this evening?"

The request caught her off guard. "Where?"

"My hotel."

Zahra studied him for a long moment. In spite of her previous vows, she wanted to spend more time with him. The morning ride had been quite enjoyable. "What time should I be ready?"

He gave her that easy smile. "Seven?"

"Seven, it is."

He came around to help her out, and as her hand met his, the warmth slid up her arm and spread. "I had a wonderful time, Mr. Le Veq."

"Name's Archer."

"Archer," she replied, softly smiling. "I'll see you this evening."

"I'm looking forward to it. Is there something you wish for Aristide to prepare for this special occasion?"

"Surprise me."

"Oh, I plan to."

With that, Zahra left him and moved gracefully to the door. Even though she was tempted to look back at him, she didn't.

That afternoon, Alfred came up to the office. "How did it go?" he asked.

"Fine. No problems. Did you know that Lieutenant Governor Dunn may have been poisoned?"

"I read the rumors in the newspapers, but I assumed they were just that—rumors."

Zahra then told him what Le Veq had told her.

Alfred said, "Very interesting."

"I thought so as well. And I think we should send a note to all the Loyal Leagues letting them know. This is the kind of information I'm sure Araminta would want us to share."

"I agree."

"Now as to Le Veq and myself. I appreciate your concern, Alfred, but I will be fine. I need you to stop growling at him whenever he comes around."

"Man like him is accustomed to women eating out of his hand."

"I'm aware of that, but I can take care of myself."

He didn't look convinced.

She decided to change the subject. "Tell me about you. You were a boxer during slavery?"

"Yes, I fought other slaves, and I was owned by the family that once owned Tom Molineaux back in the 1780's."

"And he was?"

"Probably the most famous slave to be a boxer."

"I'm afraid I've never heard of him."

"He earned his freedom boxing."

"So were you freed, too?"

"Nope. Ran soon as the troops came through. Since I'd traveled all over Alabama boxing and knew the area, the army made me a scout."

"Are you married?"

"Not anymore. Had a wife during slavery, but when I went back for her after the war, found out she'd taken off with a man headed to Ohio."

"I'm sorry."

"Me, too. She was a fine cook."

Zahra smiled. She now knew a bit more about her giant right-hand man. "Well, no boxing Le Veq, you hear?"

"Yes, ma'am, but if you need me, I can make his nose look just like mine."

Zahra chuckled, "Let's hope that won't be necessary."

"I'll go over to Wilma's and have her send the messages on to the Leagues and to Mrs. Tubman."

"Thank you, Alfred."

Zahra watched him go, glad he was on her side. She definitely wouldn't want him rearranging her nose.

When Alfred returned, he brought Zahra a message sent to Wilma by Araminta. Zahra read the short note, then asked, "Who is Henry Adams?"

"No idea."

"She wants me to meet him tomorrow evening." Zahra handed him the note. "Do you know where that address is?"

"No, but it shouldn't be too difficult to find."

"Tell your cousin I'll be needing the coach tomorrow then."

"I will."

"I'm having dinner with Le Veq tonight at his hotel. If there's anything to report, I'll let you know when I return."

He didn't look happy but he nodded, then departed.

Zahra spent a few more moments wondering about the man named Henry Adams. How was he connected to Araminta, and what role might he play in what she and Alfred had been sent here to do? In the end she decided to let the matter rest. She'd know more when they met tomorrow. In the meantime she decided to go downstairs and join the girls for their afternoon game of dominos. The time had come to enlist their aid in her search for information.

While watching Naomi and Salome, who always played as a team, go up against Lovey, Zahra said casually, "Ladies, I need a favor."

"What is it?" Stella asked while looking over Lovey's shoulder.

"I need to know who is who in this town, and I want you all to help. If you can, find out what our customers do for a living and what their politics are. With the election coming up, I don't want us to be caught in a cross fire."

"That doesn't sound too hard," Chloe responded.

"But be sly about it," Zahra warned. "We don't want them to know we're nosing around."

"Of course," said Adair. "As much as men like to brag in bed, it should be easy."

"Good, because I need you to tell me everything. Even if it doesn't sound important, tell me anyway."

"Will do," Matilda replied.

Pleased that enlisting their assistance hadn't been difficult, Zahra spent a while more watching the game, then told them, "Le Veq and I are having dinner tonight."

"You could do worse," Stella said with a knowing grin.

"Yes, like that Etienne Barber," Lovey declared. "He wanted me to do the Dance of the Seven Veils last night before I took him to bed. I made him pay me an extra twenty greenbacks."

"Good for you," Zahra replied.

"Afterwards, he tried to ask me a lot of questions about you. I told him he wasn't paying me to be your biographer, too."

Zahra smiled. "Thank you."

"Man's a pest," Lovey pointed out, "but a wealthy one, it seems. Maybe I'll send him to the twins next time."

"Please do," they offered while studying their bones. "Once we're done with him he won't have the energy to ask anyone anything."

"Amen to that," Matilda testified, and everyone laughed.

"Do you plan to make New Orleans your home?" Archer asked.

Zahra looked up from the bowl of flavorful crab bisque she'd been enjoying and met his eyes through the wavering flames of the candles centering the beautifully set table. "I haven't lived here long enough to decide either way. My original plan was a two-year stay."

"Why only two years?"

"My feet begin to itch if I stay in one place too long."

He showed the soft, engaging smile that undoubtedly had been snaring females since his nursery days. "Personally, I can't imagine residing anywhere but New Orleans."

"Really?"

"I was born here and hopefully will be put to rest here."

Zahra was reminded of thinking the same thing about the Carolinas. "It is a very vibrant city. One of the most lively I've ever visited. I've never heard so much interesting music, either."

"We are most proud of that."

Zahra was wearing a low-cut gown of black satin and her matching rhinestone mask. She had hoped he would be too busy staring at the tops of her bosom to notice that she wasn't offering much information about herself but was having trouble concentrating; not that he'd said or done anything overtly forward, but she kept remembering his kisses. "Do you have family here?" she asked. Although she already knew the answer, she wanted to keep him talking about himself.

He told her about his brothers, mother, nieces, and nephew, Cullen. He then asked, "And you? Any siblings?"

"No," she replied truthfully. "I am my parents' only child."

"Where do they live?"

"I'm not sure. We've been out of touch for some time."

"I see." By nature Archer was a curious man, but he decided not to dwell any further on her parents. Having no idea what had caused a family schism, the last thing he wanted was to offend her again or make her angry.

While they savored their bisque, Zahra discreetly watched him from behind her mask. As Lovey had waxed so eloquently this morning, *Lord, the man was easy on the eyes*. From the well-cut lines of his black coat to the shine on his expensive boots, Archer Le Veq was the epitome of the *gens de coleur;* wealth, breeding, privilege. Zahra knew that were it not for her fancy clothes and mysterious persona, a man of his class wouldn't spend two minutes with a woman of her class, let alone invite her to his private suite for an intimate candlelit dinner. Having posed as a house slave in Southern mansions on numerous occasions during the war, she knew all about fine furnishings, crystal, and the like, but she'd never imagined she'd see such equally fine things in the house of a man of color. There were Brussels carpets on the floors, elegant lamps, and beautiful brocaded upholstery. Framed artwork decorated the walls.

An upright piano stood across the room, and the table they were eating on was topped with marble. She tried not to gawk but felt like the proverbial rube at the fair. "How long have you owned the hotel?"

"Almost eight years."

"Do you enjoy it?"

"I do. I get to meet a variety of people from a variety of places, and I like that."

Mindful of her mission, she smoothly led him in another direction by saying casually, "Some think the elections this year will be as violent as '68. What do you think?"

"I hope not. Many freedmen were killed in the days leading up to the one in '68."

"And many more were so terrorized they didn't vote at all," she added.

"Every city in the South is experiencing it, but how about we discuss something lighter."

"Such as?"

"Who you really are. Why you wear the mask and when you'll let me make love to you."

That last part jolted her. "You are direct if nothing else, Archer." Steepling her fingers, she assessed him through the flickering flames of the candles on the table. "You want to make love to me."

"Very much so."

"Of course I'm flattered. But if I say yes, all of the mystery you find so intriguing will vanish and in the end you will return to your young mistress and I will be forced to take my morning drives with Etienne Barber."

Archer laughed. "Your wit is equal to your beauty."

"Thank you."

The banter pleased Archer because she seemed to be softening a bit. When Arisitide O'Neil entered the room pushing a wheeled cart topped with silver-covered dishes, Archer was not pleased with the interruption.

"Did you enjoy the bisque, madame?" Aristide asked Zahra.

"I did indeed."

"Good. The rest of the feast is just as wonderful. And why are you scowling?" he asked his employer while removing the soup bowls from the table and replacing them with the dishes for the main course. "Your face reminds me of your brother, Raimond, when I created the lovely Sable's dessert."

"Thank you, Aristide," Archer said coolly.

"You're welcome," he replied, his tone equally cool. He then bowed towards Zahra. "If you wish anything else, madame, let me know."

"I will. Thank you."

Upon shooting Archer a superior look, he left them alone.

"How long has he worked for you?"

"Too long." Archer knew that what he was feeling was jealousy. He'd never been prone to it in his life, yet for some reason Aristide's entrance and conversation with Domino had rubbed him wrong. *What in the world am I doing feeling possessive over a known whore?* She was beautiful and intriguing, but she was a soiled dove. No man in his right mind would attempt to capture the heart of such a woman. But watching her fill her plate with Aristide's delights, Archer did want to make love to her, if only to melt the barrier she seemed to visibly wear between herself and mere male mortals like himself.

Zahra could feel his intent, could see it in his eyes. He wanted her and was not ashamed. She wondered how many women succumbed after the first charming volley of shots and guessed most did. Zahra was not most women, however.

Archer had come to that same conclusion. He was not accustomed to a woman who did not jump into his arms when invited. His name, good looks, and wealth had always been more than enough, but not with Domino. In a way, the challenge she presented was exhilarating. He'd been with Lynette for so long he'd all but forgotten the thrill of the chase. "Do you think men are easily led?"

She looked up from her plate. "Under what circumstances?"

"The circumstances of a beautiful woman."

Zahra met his eyes and searched them for his intent. "I don't believe she has to be beautiful, but she does have to be interesting. If she is, she can lead a man wherever she wishes him to go. Was your Lynette interesting?"

"Only if new gowns or hats or jewelry are involved."

Her smile formed beneath her mask. "Why did you ask the question?"

"Just curious about how you would respond."

"And how do you respond?"

"That men are easily led. Take me, for instance. No offense intended, but a man like me shouldn't be interested in a woman like you."

"Most men like you are always interested in women like myself, but what they fail to see is this is my *job*, it isn't necessarily who I am. People tend to meld the two and fail to realize that distinction."

Archer was fascinated.

Zahra continued, "Just because women whore doesn't mean they don't have hopes or dreams or desires of their own. There is little glamour in taking strange men into your bed. Most women in this life barely make enough to live on."

"And that's why I wish to know who you are. I've already made that distinction. Who is the real Domino? What are her dreams, her personal desires?"

"The answers to those questions will be for the man who earns the right to hear them. Until then . . ."

Archer observed her over his stemmed crystal and raised it to her in admiration.

Zahra met the silent tribute with an almost imperceptible inclination of her head, after which they returned to their meals.

But Zahra found herself watching him; his hands, his mouth, the sure way his fingers curled around the stem of his wine goblet. How many women had those hands caressed? He was as golden as an idol, and over his lifetime had probably had more worshippers than Baal. She had no intentions of becoming a devotee, but she could not deny his overwhelming male aura. It began with the way he looked at you; so sensual, so male, and ended . . . Unbidden, the statue of Adam and Eve suddenly filled her mind; that's how it would end, she reminded herself, then steered her thoughts to safer waters.

Archer asked her, "What pleases you in a man?"

She didn't hesitate. "Intelligence, honesty."

"Not fortune? Not looks?"

"Intelligence and honesty." She turned the tables then by asking him, "What pleases you in a woman?"

"Challenge."

His tone and powerful gaze through the flames opened her in a way she'd never experienced before donning the role of Domino. In the lengthening silence, a pulse beat at her throat and her breathing seemed to be both fast and slow.

"I want to make love to you in a hundred ways, fill you, kiss you . . ."

Her breath stopped and her nipples hardened.

"Ride you and let you ride me," he whispered boldly. "One night, Domino. This night."

Eyes closed, Zahra fought to bring her shaken body under control, but he was slowly rising to his feet, and her heart began to pound.

Standing by her chair, he extended a hand, and there in the shadows, she looked up and saw unbridled desire in his eyes. Entranced, she took the hand and slowly stood to meet him.

For a long moment, they stood a breath apart and Zahra could feel the air thickening and crackling like the prelude to a lightning storm. Then, ever so slowly, his fingers moved to her lips, mapping the outline, lingering over the shape, the curves, the way they felt as they parted with passion. Her eyes slid closed and the touch wandered lower, over her jaw, then down her trembling throat. He lightly grazed the tip of his finger horizontally across the base of her collarbone, then leaned in and gently placed his first kiss there.

Zahra's knees dissolved, and she sucked in a shaky breath. He pressed another kiss there, teasing the nock with just the tip of his tongue before moving his kisses up to her ear. "Now is the time to say no if you don't wish for me to continue . . . I've never forced a woman . . ."

But all the while his hands were roaming over her soft curves, and it took all Zahra had to remain standing and not melt into a puddle on his beautiful blue rug. Her nipples hardened under his masterful teasing, and all she could do was implore herself to breathe.

She knew she shouldn't want this; it was not what she'd come here to do. But his hands were so sure, his fleeting kisses on her neck and the edge of his jaw were so filled with fire that she, who had never been pierced by passion before, gave in and let herself feel.

When she trailed her fingers down the solid set of his jaw, and then sensually explored the shape of his mouth, Archer sensed her acquiescence, and his manhood flared. He took one of her fingers into his mouth and boldly sucked the tapered tip. Her eyes closed, and he placed his finger in her mouth, and she sucked him in heated response. His blood fired. Withdrawing his finger, he circled the dampness down her throat, over the silken flesh above her low-cut gown, then plied her berried breasts with touches that made her croon softly.

He continued his fondling. He watched her masked face in the flickering candlelight fall back, and he enjoyed knowing that he was the man bringing her pleasure. The front of her dress was tied closed with a ribbon that opened easily. The halves melted away and the black French corset beneath filled his eyes. She was cinched so tightly the tops of her lush breasts were presented with a lusciousness he could not resist. Trailing kisses across the enticing mounds, he worked one breast free and sucked until she gasped and moaned. Wanting more, he worked his tongue around the straining bud, while his hand slid up her thighs, squeezing and savoring her tempting behind. The rustle of silk and their breathing were the only sounds in the low-lit room. Still pleasuring her breasts, he slid her gown this way and that over her limbs, her hips and then in between her thighs with a brazenness that made her part her legs so she could feel more.

By now, Zahra was on fire everywhere, and he fed that heat with his mouth and his knowing hands. When he raised her gown, she didn't protest but stood there in her black clockwork stockings and garters and let him tease her through the opening in her white silk drawers.

The moment he touched her damp, swollen flesh, she climaxed with a raw scream. Twisting, she rode out *la petite mort* while he whispered in French the many ways he planned to pleasure her next.

Without a word, he untied her drawers, eased them from her shaking legs, then picked her up. Crossing the room with long, sure strides, he carried her out of the dining room and down the hall to his bedroom.

# Chapter 7

Archer gently placed her on the bed, then freed the buttons on his shirt. The moonlight streaming through the windows illuminated her so seductively that he was forced to close his eyes and take in a deep breath to forestall coming right there and then. Her dark-nippled breasts, bared by the disheveled gown and corset, coupled with his thoughts of the damp gate waiting beneath all that silk aroused him to such a fevered pitch that he wanted to fall on her like an untried youth, but he held. His skills in pleasuring a woman were legendary, and he planned to treat her to that expertise until neither of them could draw breath. She'd undoubtedly been with innumerable men innumerable times. The only way for Archer to be remembered above all others was to give her as much pleasure as one night could hold. With that in mind, he tossed his shirt aside.

Wearing only his trousers, he joined her on his big four-poster bed.

As the mattress gave beneath his weight, she welcomed him by cupping his cheek. Kneeling next to her, he turned her hand to his lips, placed a soft kiss in the center, then guided her hand to the root of his pleasure. He felt her hesitate for a moment, as if she'd never offered such a caress before, and it increased his fervor. He loved playing games in bed, and if she wanted to act the role of a woman with little experience, the pleasure would be all his. "Grasp me, *chérie*," he instructed in a passion-gruff voice. "Feel what touching you has done. . . ."

Rather than let him know she'd never done this before, Zahra took hold of a man for the first time in her life and felt the hard promise burn her palm through the soft wool. She almost pulled away, but she held as he whispered, "You play the innocent well, Domino. Shall I teach you love?"

She realized he thought her reticence an act. Her inexperience would not be questioned, which gave her a modicum of relief, so embracing her role, she responded with a truthful, "Yes, *monsieur*. Teach me all. . . ."

In response to the black velvet voice, Archer's manhood increased, and he placed his hand gently atop hers. "Like this . . ." he husked out and slowly began to guide her in the way he wished.

Blood pounding, he threw back his head to savor the way her hand was now moving with passionate confidence. Every cell in his body wanted to climax, but he forced himself away. "You learn quickly, *ma chérie*," he told her, his eyes glittering in the moonlight. Needing to touch her again, he made her nipples rise to his fingers' sweet command, then dropped his head to taste them.

Still wearing her mask, Zahra braced herself with her arms and leaned back. She didn't know where to settle her mind. Should it be on the hot mouth making her nipples plead, or the hand moving sensually up and down her leg beneath her gown? Each was filled with its own vivid sensations and she was in no frame of mind to choose, so she gave up and just soared.

Then his big hands were sliding the gown up her legs, exposing them to his hot eyes, the silence, and the moonlight. He teased a finger over the small red rose centering the garter holding up her stockings, then over the trembling bare skin above. Worshipping caresses moved over her limbs, then up the insides of her thighs; mapping, exploring, tempting. When his fingers found her this time, she groaned, and her legs parted shamelessly.

For Archer there was something wickedly decadent about pleasuring a woman in a gown. The feel and the sight of her nakedness against the yards of rucked-up silk made him even harder. Bending, he placed a kiss against the warm brown flesh of her inner thigh, and when she jumped as if surprised, he smiled. With a finger he slowly teased the passion-wet core, then asked her softly, "Have you never had a man pay you tribute, *ma chérie?*"

His hands were moving so marvelously and erotically over her that Zahra, who had no idea what he was asking her, found it hard to respond, but finally she whispered, "No."

"Good . . ." he said, making her hips respond to the soft circles he was drawing.

When his tongue tasted her, she threw her head back, having never received this before, and it was glorious to behold. As he boldly parted her, then teased and lingered, her core pulsed hotly. His kisses were so scandalous, his fingers so carnal, that it didn't take long for her body to break under the passionate conquering, and her shuddering cries of *la petite mort* pierced the silence.

Only then did Archer remove the rest of his clothing. Watching her and touching her as she lay there savoring the fading throes of her orgasm aroused him so much that he knew if he didn't have her now, he'd spill his seed like an adolescent. Tracing her parted mouth, he bent to reacquaint himself with her kiss-dampened nipples, then pulled her atop him.

Zahra gasped as he slowly filled her. He was big. His earlier preparations had let her accept him without pain, but it was the heat he set off inside that made her groan with pleasure. He reached up to the ties of her mask, and she quickly stayed his hands with hers. "No," she whispered.

For a long moment they stared at each other in the moonlight, then he said finally, softly, "Okay, my mysterious *chérie*. I will let you keep your secrets . . . for now."

Running a palm over her bared breasts, he eased her forward so he could make sure her nipples were as hard as he, then he lowered his hands to her hips. He began to tease her with a soft, enticing rhythm that tempted her body to join in. No, Zahra had never made love this way, but an age-old awareness of how to respond awakened within, claiming her, fueling her. She rose and fell to the impaling bliss and let him guide her as he would. Soon, they were in the winds of the storm, his rhythm hard, faster. Then they were straining for all they were worth and Zahra answered with a hard and fast rhythm all her own. Her scream of completion filled the moonlit room and was followed by his own shouts of glory. Needing to brand the moment in his mind and hers too, he guided her hips in a frenetic pace and thrusted until she screamed again.

In the silent aftermath, the still impaled Zahra lay bonelessly on his chest with his arms wrapped around her. She could hear his heart pounding beneath her ear and feel his manhood throbbing dully inside her. Instinctively, her inner muscles answered with a series of soft contractions that made him place his hands low on her bare hips so he could give her a few more growling thrusts, then he went still. Never wanting to move ever again, Zahra lay there, sated, tired, and amazed by the wildness of her pleasure. Raising her head, she looked down into his face and saw that he was smiling. She asked, "Am I to assume you are pleased?"

"Oh, yes," he responded, slowly tracing her mouth, "but the more important question is, are you?"

"Yes."

"Good, because you are made for pleasure."

Somewhere in the dark interior of his house, a clock chimed the time. "I must go," she said. The sadness she felt surprised her, but then again, maybe it didn't. This night would undoubtedly haunt her for the rest of her days, and truthfully, she didn't want it to end. But being with him left her vulnerable. Under the mesmerizing spell of his lovemaking, she could easily imagine herself allowing him to remove her mask. She couldn't chance it or the ramifications it might bring.

"The night is still young," he said to her. The large, warm hand circling her hips was a tempting one.

"Stay . . ." he invited with an ardent whisper. "We both want more."

And in reality, Zahra did.

He was beginning again; feasting on her nipples, squeezing her behind, touching her heat where their bodies were joined while his manhood slowly awakened and filled her yet again. As it rose, she savored the solidness of his strength. All thoughts of leaving were set aside so that she could rise and fall to his enchanting strokes.

Her education was thorough, seductive, and so filled with pleasure that Zahra lost all sense of time and place. When he whispered for her to open her legs, she did. When he invited her to turn around and then filled her from behind, she came again with his hands clutching her breasts. Zahra never knew a woman could be given so much pleasure and live. Each time he touched her she caught fire, and when they had finally had enough, Zahra let him drive her home.

As she entered the quiet house and climbed the

stairs, she passed Adam and Eve. The bliss on Eve's face was no longer a mystery. Zahra *knew*. And because she did, she could never let Archer Le Veq make love to her again.

The next morning, as Archer drove across town to visit with Speaker of the House George Carter, his thoughts were on Domino. To say that she'd been made for love was an understatement. Just thinking about the torrid night tightened his groin. Her playacting at innocent had lit a fire within him that still burned. Initially he'd thought one night would satisfy his desire for her, but he'd been wrong. The only thing making love to her had accomplished was to heighten his need for more. The need to discover her true identity had also become acute. None of the inquiries he'd sent out to friends and former war associates had come back with any information. As far as he could tell, the woman who called herself Domino had no past, but he hoped her future would be gracing his bed.

When he arrived at Speaker Carter's home, his knock was answered by Carter himself. Archer had never visited him at home before, but he saw that the place was well furnished, and the horsehair sofa Carter directed Archer to was comfortable.

Once they were settled and had shared the latest political gossip, Archer said, "Tell me about your illness."

"The day Oscar died, I was frightfully ill, too. Prolonged stomach cramps, nausea. I feared I'd been dosed."

"What did you do?"

"I was at the *National Republican* newspaper office when the sickness came over me, so I decided to lie down on a sofa hoping it would pass."

The *National Republican* newspaper had been founded by Dunn and others allied with the Customhouse wing.

"Did it?"

"No. It worsened. I made my way home and went to bed. I was soon wracked by fever, vomiting, and then delirium."

Archer's shock filled his face.

"I was for the most part unconscious when Dr. Austen came to see me. I was so ill, everyone here was certain I was about to join Oscar, but Austen filled me with hot drinks, put steaming poultices on my belly, and mercifully, I began to recover."

"What was Austen's determination?"

"That I was simply ill. He even published a signed statement saying that although I'd been a very sick man, he didn't believe I'd been poisoned."

"And you? What do you believe?"

"I was poisoned, Archer, and I'll swear by that until the day I do die."

At dinner that evening, Archer told his brothers and mother the rest of Carter's story. "It seems others suffered from similar symptoms around that same time."

"Like whom?" Juliana asked.

"Supposedly Warmoth, but he visited Oscar three times the night before Oscar died, and he appeared fine then."

Drake added, "Warmoth was also a pallbearer at the funeral, so I think that rumor about him being poisoned too can be laid to rest."

Philippe asked, "If all of these men were actually poisoned, any idea who might be behind it?"

"Besides Democrats, Knights of the White Camelia, and the White Leaguers, you can take your pick."

The Knights of the White Camelia had been terrorizing Louisiana's Black citizens since 1868, and although Congress recently passed the Ku Klux Law forbidding the wearing of disguise with the intent of depriving persons of their rights, new groups like the White League continued to spread across the South, targeting Black office holders, prominent Black farmers, businessmen, and average citizens. Archer knew the only thing keeping supremacist violence from tearing Louisiana apart was the solid presence of the Union soldiers.

Juliana said wistfully, "The times held such promise after the war. Who would have thought we'd have five men of color in Congress today, and yet . . ." Her voice trailed off, and she shook her head sadly. "Kluxers are breaking into our homes, burning down our schools, killing our teachers. I wonder what kind of country my grandchildren will grow up to see?"

For a long moment silence reigned, then Drake said, "Speaking of grandchildren—have Raimond and Sable returned?"

Juliana's beautiful face brightened. "Yes. Earlier this evening. They'll join us for dinner tomorrow."

Even though the brothers made it their business to aggravate Raimond, they'd missed their overbearing eldest sibling—but they couldn't wait to tell him they'd missed his wife and children more.

Zahra was wearing a drab gown and an equally drab cloak with the hood pulled up to mask her hair and face. Under the light of a sputtering streetlamp, she paid the cabbie his fare, then arranged for him to return in an hour. He drove off into the night, and Zahra crossed the road to the small house whose address matched the one in the note she'd received from Araminta.

Alfred had wanted to accompany her on this rendezvous, but Zahra had nixed the idea. Because of his size and the notoriety of his employer, Alfred's face had become quite well known in some quarters of the city. Zahra was not wearing her mask tonight, and she didn't want his presence drawing attention to her.

Her knock on the door was answered by a short, older woman wearing a flowered head wrap. "Yes?"

"I'm here to speak with Mr. Adams."

"And you are?"

"A friend."

The woman stepped back. "Please, come in."

The house's interior was small and the furnishings worn and few. Zahra followed the woman through the house, then back outside into the night. Surprised but not alarmed yet, Zahra saw a small shack about a hundred meters to the left and deduced by the path the woman was taking that it would be their destination.

"Go on in. He's inside."

"Thank you."

The tiny place was lit by a stub of a candle that cast a wavering glow over a man seated on a stump. The candle was on a large rock near his feet. When she entered, he rose, and she saw that he was of medium height with a small build. "I'm Henry Adams."

"Pleased to meet you."

"Shall I call you Domino?"

"That's acceptable."

"Araminta has cast you as the spider in the web, I hear."

Zahra nodded. She liked his description. "And what role do you play?"

"I bring food to the spider to pass along the web."

"I see. And what do you bring today?"

"News from across the South and from Kansas."

For the next half hour, Zahra listened as Adams related troubling news. The hopes of Reconstruction were all but dead. From Mississippi to South Carolina to Texas and Tennessee, the race was under siege. To Zahra's surprise, he talked of a group of veterans who, over the past year, had gone to every Southern state in the Union to assess the conditions the freedmen were facing.

"How many of you are there?"

"We started out with five hundred, but only one hundred and fifty do the actual traveling."

"And your people are all common folk?"

He smiled. "Yes. No *politicianers* of any color. We figured if we told the Black Republicans, it wouldn't be long before one of them told a White Republican and soon the White Leagues would be after us."

Zahra agreed with his assessment. An undertaking of such magnitude was not something to be bandied about over cognac and squab. The killing of Black leaders had come to be called *bulldozing*; had the identities of Adams's men gotten out, they might very well have been the next victims in a long and bloody line. "What have you found?"

"That the freedmen are being cheated out of their wages and crops, made to work sometimes for no wages at all, and that more and more of our people are being terrorized by day and by night. Tens of thousands have been killed, and the county courthouses are filled with Black widows coming to report the murders of their men. We've also uncovered something even more unsettling. Death Books."

Zahra had never heard the term before. "What are they?"

"Books holding the names of the men the Kluxers and the Leagues plan to bulldoze."

The hairs stood up on the back of Zahra's neck. "How widespread is this?"

"As widespread as the lynchings. I need you to get word to Araminta and her friends to be on their guard. My volunteers pose as drifters, laborers, small farmers, and we've never made ourselves known to anyone outside of our circle. We don't plan to change, so we need a spider."

Zahra understood. That as many as five hundred Black men were acting as shadowy investigators right under the noses of both the government and the supremacist groups earned her admiration. The Death Books were troubling, however. Were there Death Books in New Orleans, and if so, whose names were listed? She'd start sending coded messages out to Araminta and the others as soon as she returned to the house. "Is there anything else you wish me to relay?"

"Only that we have members in Kansas assessing conditions there. They are touring town sites, weighing housing possibilities, and discreetly buying land. The race may need to flee the South, and we must have a place to go."

"So you are considering Kansas."

"And Nebraska and Colorado. Even as far west as California. We must and will survive."

As she promised Henry Adams, Zahra sent coded messages by way of Wilma to all of the contacts on Araminta's list. Zahra also sent some of her house's staff back to their homes across the South to relay information to their local leaders firsthand about the dreaded Death Books. She and Alfred planned to find out if any existed in New Orleans or the surrounding parishes. Were she able to present one of the books to the president, it might go a long way in convincing him of the race's plight and of the necessity of keeping the troops in Louisiana.

The crowds visiting Madame Domino's Gentleman's Club had started to fall off a bit, but

Zahra didn't mind. The core of fifty men she considered regulars were wealthy enough to pay the thirty-dollar entrance fee night after night and still have ample funds left to gamble, pay for the girls, and buy drinks. One was a man named Mitchell Isenbaum. He was a Democrat, and Matilda was his girl of choice. According to her, Isenbaum boasted of ties to the White League. Zahra encouraged Matilda to learn as much as she could about him, discreetly of course, and to report back.

Zahra didn't see Isenbaum in the club that evening, but she did see Etienne Barber. According to Archer the man was a carpet bagger, and Zahra had no use for anyone who preyed on the race. However, she was the hostess here and Barber was a paying customer so seeing him approaching her now, she pasted on an encouraging smile and waited for him to reach her side.

He bowed. "Good evening, Domino."

"Good evening, Mr. Barber."

"Etienne, please."

She inclined her sapphire blue mask. "Are you enjoying yourself?"

"As always, but I'd enjoy it more if you would waltz with me."

She could hear the strains of a waltz rise over the sound of glasses, voices and laughter. "I'd love to," she lied and wondered if he'd paid the musicians to play the selection.

He was an adequate dancer but his breath smelled of cigars and drink. His hand on her waist was tighter than she cared for and every-time he turned her he pressed his body against hers suggestively. "Would you like to spend the weekend at my cabin on Lake Ponchatrain."

She smiled up at his gaunt pocked face. "Haven't we discussed this before, Etienne?"

He smiled, showing off a set of brown mishapen teeth, "But I'd hoped you'd changed your mind."

"I haven't, sorry."

As they continued to dance their eyes held and she saw his jaw tense. His hold on her waist tightened painfully and he pulled her flush against him. "I'd think a wealthy man like myself would be just what you're after," he countered coldy.

She tried to back away but he was stronger. "I may not be Creole but I'm good enough for the likes of you."

"Good evening, Domino. Etienne."

The brittle voice belonged to Archer.

Barber released her immediately.

Zahra stared up at him angrily. "Get out or I'll have Alfred throw you out."

He was glaring down. She didn't care. The men nearby were watching curiously. She didn't care about them either.

Barber's chin rose as he met Archer's wintry eyes.

Archer said to Zahra, "The giant sent me to fetch you. He has something he wants you to see. Excuse us, Etienne."

Archer escorted her towards the staircase and once they were out of earshot of the still ogling customers, he said, "I will kill him for you, if you'd like."

She started to smile but his face was set so seriously she stopped and searched his face. He remained silent. For the first time Zahra sensed the dangerous man beneath the charm. Archer Le Veq was far more faceted than she'd believed. "The next time it happens we'll flip a coin."

He smiled.

When they entered her office she could see Alfred was upset. "What's happened?"

He held up a small dirty drawstring bag.

Zahra looked on curiously.

"It's filled with bones. Old bones. Mr. Le Veq thinks it's juju."

Zahra turned to Archer. "As in voodoo?"

He nodded.

Alfred said, "Found another just like it yesterday."

Zahra was puzzled. Of course this was New Orleans and some of its citizens set much faith in the mysterious practices but she had no idea who might have left the bag. "Do you think it was left for me or for the house?"

Archer shrugged. "You've apparently made an enemy."

"So what do I do?" She'd never had to deal with something like this before.

Alfred said, "I'm going to keep a close eye on the place for the next few days. Maybe we can catch whoever's responsible."

"Good idea."

Archer turned to Alfred and said, "I'd suggest you also keep an eye on Etienne Barber. He was being very aggressive with Domino when I walked up."

Alfred looked to her. "Did he harm you?"

"No, but we may have to bar him if he does it again."

"I'll go speak with him and make certain he understands."

"Thank you."

"What do you wish done with the bones?"

"Burn them." Archer answered first.

Zahra was surprised by that.

Alfred nodded. Taking the bag, he said, "Will do. Then I'll find Barber."

He left and closed the office door behind him.

"Thank you for intervening with Barber," she said to Archer sincerely.

"My pleasure."

"Do you think he may be the one responsible for the bones?"

"There's no way of knowing at this point."

He was right, of course.

Archer told her, "I have to go up to Baton Rouge for a couple of days. Republican Party business."

"That's not too long."

"Long enough when you'd rather be with a beautiful lady."

The sensual memories of all they'd shared rolled over Zahra like an ocean wave. "Will you think of me while you're away?"

"Probably day and night."

She smiled. "When are you leaving?"

"I should be already gone but I wanted to stop by and let you know. I'm glad I did."

She closed the distance between them. "So am I."

A beat later they were sharing a passionate

kiss and Zahra wondered if there would ever be another man in her life whose embrace felt so right.

When the kiss ended, he placed a parting kiss on her brow. "Take care of yourself while I'm away."

"Yes, sir."

He grinned, gave her one more simmering kiss then departed.

Before Archer left town he stopped by Lynette's apartment. He knew it was late but he needed to speak with her. They hadn't spoken since the severing of their relationship.

His firm knocks on her door were answered by her a few moments later. She looked sleepy and when she saw him on the threshold her face became sullen. "What do you want at this hour? You're no longer sharing my bed, remember?"

Archer ignored that. "Someone is leaving ju ju bags at Domino's. Do you know anything about them."

"Of course not." She slammed the door shut again.

Tight-lipped, Archer walked back to his barouche.

Etienne Barber must have taken Alfred's talk with him to heart because he sent Zahra flowers every morning for the next two days. This morning, the third day since since the incident, another spray arrived. The arrangements were very beautiful, but she didn't want flowers or anything else from him. Even though he was spending a small fortune on flowers Zahra was not impressed. At least he'd gotten the message that he couldn't deliver them to her personally as he attempted to do the first day. Zahra was grateful for her giant Alfred and his grim manner because had he not been around to stop Barber at the door, the man might have pushed his way into the house and Zahra would have been forced to shoot the carpetbagger.

Taking the flowers into the kitchen, she added them to the other bloom-filled vases obscuring the dining table.

When Barber arrived at the house that night, the place was fairly crowded. Zahra managed to avoid him for a time, but he finally cornered her in her office. Not pleased that he'd entered her sanctuary uninvited and unannounced, she said pleasantly through her displeasure, "Guests aren't allowed in here, Mr. Barber."

He closed the door behind him. "Did you receive the morning's flowers?"

Even more displeased that he'd had the audacity to close the door, she replied, "Yes, I did, and as always, they were beautiful." With the lower half of her body hidden behind the desk, it was easy for her to reach into the hidden pocket of her indigo gown and slide her pistol out unseen. Although she wondered about Alfred's whereabouts, she knew she could handle Barber on her own should it become necessary to do so. "I have some work needing attention. I will see you later, Mr. Barber."

"No, you will see me now." He reached back and threw the lock. "You're a whore, nothing more, and if I have to have you by force, I will."

She shook her head at his male stupidity. "Now that you've locked the door, Mr. Barber, there is no way for you to escape."

"Escape what?"

She raised the gun. "This."

He froze.

"Now, are you going to leave as I asked?"

"You won't shoot me."

The ball that exploded from the gun hit him in the shoulder and spun him to the carpet. He screamed in pain. Lips pursed angrily, Zahra stood and came around the desk just as the door splintered and Alfred burst in.

"Find out if there's a doctor here tonight," Zahra spat out. "Then escort this *waa'ment* out." She was so angry that she had unconsciously slipped into Gullah, her father's tongue.

As if he understood the intent of the foreign-sounding word, Alfred replied, "My pleasure."

He yanked Barber up, which caused the wounded man to cry out again. "You bitch," he spat at Zahra.

She responded easily, "But I'm an armed bitch. Remember that for the future."

Alfred threw him roughly towards the splintered door. "Let's go."

On the heels of their exit, an angry Zahra sat back down and placed the pistol on the desk. She looked up to see Matilda and Stella shooing away the curious crowd that had gathered outside the door. The only man who remained was Archer Le Veq.

He stuck his handsome head in through the hole in the door and said, "Good evening, Domino."

Her adrenaline finally slowing, she said, "Hello. How are you?"

"Not sure. You shooting everyone tonight, or just Etienne?"

She couldn't stop her smile from showing. "So far, just him."

"Good to know." He entered the office fully, saying, "Are you all right?"

"I am." Just thinking about Barber and his devil-may-care boast of rape started her simmering yet again.

"I think you need a bracing bowl of Aristide's crab bisque. My carriage is nearby. Care to join me?"

Zahra found him as tempting as gold must have been to King Midas, and her nipples tightened as if they eagerly agreed. "No, I think not."

He dropped his head. "I'm disappointed."

She grinned. "I'm certain it won't be for long. Go see the twins."

"I'm not interested in seeing the twins. Only you."

"We had our one night, Archer. Remember."

"I do, but do you?"

The intensity in his eyes touched her like a hand, and the memories of being in his moonlit bed rose unbidden.

"If I can't convince you with the bisque, how about we walk outside for a breath of air? I'm sure you could use some after all the excitement."

Zahra thought that a grand idea. Never mind that she'd vowed to keep her physical attraction to him under wraps; it wasn't working. Resisting him seemed to be futile. "A walk sounds fine, but

I must wait until Alfred returns so he can secure the door."

As if cued, Alfred and Caleb, who was one of the gardeners, returned with wood and tools. She saw Alfred and Le Veq eye each other for a long moment before Alfred turned from him to say to her, "One of the doctors in the gambling room is patching Barber up. I'll put him out when the doc's done."

"Good. Mr. Le Veq is going to escort me outside for some air. I'll return shortly."

Alfred nodded, but she saw his grim visage trained on Le Veq as they left the room.

Outside, they headed for the quiet of the gardens. They could hear the revelry going on inside the house, but as they walked further, the noise faded to silence.

Archer said, "He doesn't care for me much, does he?"

"Who?"

"Your man, Alfred."

She smiled. "Alfred doesn't care for any man I walk with under the moonlight. He's very protective."

"I'd hate to get on his wrong side. He looks strong enough to break a man in half."

"He was a pugilist during slavery."

"And won many a bout, I'm sure."

They were now out of sight of the house. When she spotted the stone bench set near the trellises in the winter-bare rose garden, she took a seat. She was glad she'd grabbed a shawl before venturing out. It was chilly. "When will the weather warm?"

"Soon. Mid-February usually brings the spring temperatures."

"Good."

"So, you were raised in the South."

"I never said that."

"You didn't have to. If you were born up North, this weather wouldn't bother you."

"Your first clue," she said.

"No, second."

"What's the first?"

"That you are a very passionate woman."

He was seated beside her on the bench close enough for her to smell the faint notes of his spicy cologne. Doing her best to ignore the effects of his nearness on her senses, she said, "I mustn't forget how quick you are, Archer."

"Not if you plan to keep your secrets."

Hoping to turn the conversation to something more mundane, she asked, "And how is Aristide?"

Instead of answering, his finger began to lightly trace the rich curves of her mouth with a slow, lingering possessiveness that caused her to shimmer in answer to his silent call. "As much as I want to kiss this mouth, I won't until you remove your mask. . . ."

Leaning in, he licked the tip of his tongue against the corner of her mouth. The sizzling sensation made her want to remove her mask there and then. He leaned in again to set the other corner afire, then traced her parted lips with a magical finger. "But I will kiss other parts of you, Domino. . . ."

Putting action to words, his lips found her jaw and the sensitive lobe of her ear. Brushing his mouth over the soft skin beneath, he stirred her passion to life.

He kissed his way down her throat. Her gold shawl slipped down her shoulder, and he moved his tribute over the bared skin just long enough to fill his senses with the smell of her perfume, then across the yielding flesh above the low-cut indigo gown. "You enchant me, *chérie*. . . ."

The warmth of his hands moving over her breasts made up for the loss of her shawl. She didn't feel the chill in the night air—only him and her body's burgeoning reaction.

When he freed her breasts from her gown and began to feast, her earlier pledge to never let him make love to her again became nothing more than hollow words. Because of her inexperience, she had no way of controlling the heat spreading through her like warmed molasses, nor could she keep her croons of desire from rising to become one with the night air. When he lifted his head to place his lips against the nook of her trembling throat, she could feel the chill on her damp nipples from his heated play.

The kisses against her throat burned her so badly that her head fell back and his hand slipped down her body to her thighs. He palmed her boldly through the layers of indigo silk, searing her there and coaxing her to open. She surrendered willingly, felt her skirt rising and then his hand on her stocking-encased leg, moving, squeezing, caressing as it sought her ultimate warmth. When he found her through the slit in her silk drawers, she crooned gratefully, then gasped as he slid his long finger inside.

In an inviting voice as thick as the night, he said to her, "Look at me."

All the while he was seducing, teasing, making it hard for her to even open her eyes, let alone speak. He withdrew, and she moaned with soft complaint.

He smiled, "You must look at me, my greedy *chérie*, so that I can watch you take your pleasure . . ."

He impaled her again, and she writhed scandalously. She forced her eyes to his, and the heat in them made her passion roar higher.

"Wider, *bébé*."

She complied without complaint because the pleasure was so glorious. He slid the dress up on her waist and then pushed in another finger with such masterful skill that she shuddered and came, screaming hoarsely.

"Shhh, *ma chérie*. They will hear you in Paris."

*"Ah go dahhh!"* Zahra cried out in Gullah as the orgasm tossed her about.

Setting aside for now this second instance of her speaking in a foreign tongue, Archer watched her through the desire gleaming in his eyes. He could have her this way twenty-four hours a day for years and it would not be enough. Gently bringing her back to herself with soft touches and kisses on her jaw, he politely set her dress to rights and said, "Now. Ready to go back?"

Hardly able to move, let alone walk, she smacked him in the arm. "You are an awful man, do you know that, Archer Le Veq?"

He pretended to flick a piece of lint from his shoulder. "Who, me?"

"Yes, you."

"You didn't seem to think I was so awful when you were shouting at the stars."

Embarrassed to her toes, she looked away.

Archer studied her with surprise. "You're embarrassed." It was a statement.

Zahra grabbed hold of herself. "No, I'm not."

He turned her face to his and looked down into her eyes. Even though she met his gaze without flinching, Archer's sense of something being out of kilter was strong enough to touch. "Why would a woman who claims to be a madame be such an innocent sometimes?"

"You said you liked it when I pretended."

"Are you that good an actress?"

"Yes, I am. Fooled you, didn't I?"

Archer wasn't convinced. He wished he could see her face better. It was night, true, but the damn mask hid her eyes just enough to keep him from being able to see their true nature.

"I should get back before Alfred comes looking."

"Who are you really?" he asked quietly.

"Domino."

"I'm going to find out eventually."

"There isn't anything to find out." Kissing him on his cheek, she whispered, "Thank you for the pleasure, Archer."

Picking up the hems of her gown, she hastened back the way they'd come.

Archer watched her go, but instead of following, he sat there alone in the dark for a very long time.

# Chapter 8

Zahra lay in bed, but she wasn't asleep. Every time she closed her eyes, the face of Archer Le Veq appeared, and her body would echo with heated remembrance. Having a man haunt her thoughts no matter where they turned was new for her; new and, in its own way, uniquely disturbing. How was she to conduct business when all she could think about was him raising her gown and filling her with his lush magic? The interlude in the garden had left her weak-legged and damp for the rest of the night. Even now, just thinking back tightened her nipples and inflamed her core. She tried not to dwell on the memories, but her mind couldn't help reliving the sensual moments. What was she to do with the wanton ache that seemed to come over her whenever she thought of him? Believing she could surrender to him without entangling parts of herself had been

191

fueled by her own naive arrogance. Henry Adams had dubbed her the spider. Well, the spider was caught in Archer Le Veq's web of sensuality, and she had no idea how to break free.

Since sleep seemed to be fleeting, she got up and walked to the French doors, opening them to the chilly night. After wrapping herself in a quilt, she took a seat on one of the verandah's wrought-iron chairs and looked up at the stars. Another problem haunting her was the fate of her parents. She'd written to them a few days ago via Wilma, who would forward it to Araminta. From there the letter would wind its way to Sanctuary in a journey that could take weeks or even months, depending on the circumstances. She prayed they were doing well and that she'd be able to see them soon. She wondered what they would think of Le Veq if they met him. Her father, James, would be wary at first—after all, Le Veq was *gens de coleur*—but she sensed that once he and Archer began discussing politics, the wariness would fade. Her father had been a staunch Republican after the war. He'd voted in the bloody national elections of 1886 and had encouraged others to do the same in spite of the death threats he'd received. As the head man of their small community, he'd helped organize the school and the communal association the local farmers had formed to jointly sell their crops. He'd also instituted Republican meetings, which had been held every Saturday. The meetings had always been well attended by people of all ages, who had gathered to discuss politics and to hear Republican and Black newspapers read aloud. James, like the other men in his line, was a descendant of the original James, a slave owned by William Armistead of New Kent County, Virginia. The Armisteads' James was also the family's first spy. In 1778, with Armistead's permission, James did reconnaissance work for the young Marquis de Lafayette, who'd come to America to help in the fight against British troops under the command of infamous traitor Benedict Arnold. During the time they worked together, James and Lafayette found much to admire in each other—so much so that after James was freed by the Virginia Assembly in 1786 in reward for his meritous service, he took the surname Lafayette. Zahra's family had been Lafayette and spies for the United States government ever since.

Now here she sat in the chilly night air of New Orleans, continuing the family legacy in an operation that she was certain would make no difference to the country one way or another. The minds of President Grant and the members of Congress were probably already made up on how to proceed, and no one would be offering to ease the freedmen's plight. Her talk with Henry Adams had been valuable, however, in the sense that at least someone was trying to fight back. He and his volunteers were doing the work the government should have been doing in surveying conditions and offering solutions, but the country was ready to move on and apparently didn't care about those being left behind.

Zahra got up and went back inside. Discarding the quilt, she poked at the fire roaring in her grate, then crawled back into bed. When sleep finally descended, her last thoughts were not of her parents or the president but of Archer Le Veq.

There was something about Domino, Archer mused as he lay in his bed, that wasn't right. He could feel it in his gut. Her reticence and underlying innocence in bed seemed too real to be an act. So what was at foot here? Was she really a madame? Had she inherited the string of girls somehow? Was there a pimp, and if so, had he put her on display just for window dressing? Archer quickly ruled out that theory. After seeing what she'd done to Etienne this evening, he didn't think she could be manipulated or forced into anything against her will. And why the mask? Was it simply for show, or was she wearing it for a specific reason? He was reminded of the ongoing speculation that she could be scarred, but what if she weren't? During Carnival season masked balls were all the rage and most people donned the disguise simply for fun, but others hid their faces for the express purpose of anonymity. Which category did she fall under? The realization that he was no closer to finding out her true identity than he'd been on the first day he'd met her in his office was frustrating, but Archer loved mysteries almost as much as he did beautiful women. *I'll figure it out sooner or later,* was his last thought as he drifted off to sleep.

Have you ever heard the word *waa'ment* before?" Archer asked his brother Raimond the next morning. They were in Archer's office, and the dark-skinned Raimond had his large frame comfortably settled in one of the upholstered office chairs.

Raimond echoed the word *waa'ment*. He mused on it for a moment, then asked, "Are you sure that's what she said?"

Archer nodded. "Fairly certain. I was standing just outside the door, and I heard her clearly."

"And she said it after she shot Barber?"

"Yes."

"I'll bet Etienne wasn't happy."

"Not at all. Called her a bitch."

Raimond raised an eyebrow.

Archer added, "I got the impression that the word wasn't a compliment, either. She was rather angry at the time."

Archer watched Raimond muse on the conundrum for a few silent moments more, then softly repeat the word over and over as if weighing the syllables on his tongue and in his mind.

Raimond said, "Okay, let's leave that one for a moment. Tell me about the other phrase."

"She said, as close as I can remember, *'Ah go da,'* or something similar, and the *da* sound was elongated."

"Like *daaaa?*"

"Yes."

"What was she doing?"

"None of your business."

Raimond cocked his head. "What do you mean, none of my business?"

"You heard me."

Raimond sat up, "How the hell am I supposed to help if—"

"We were making love."

Raimond's eyebrows rose. "I see." He studied Archer's tight face, and then he began to laugh.

"What's so funny?"

"You. You're becoming obsessed with this woman, aren't you?"

"No, I'm not."

"I leave here for a month and Don Juan here falls for a whore."

"Stow it, Rai. I don't think she is a whore."

Raimond looked incredulous. "What do you mean, you don't think so? The sign outside says Madame Domino's Gentleman's Club. The girls inside aren't the sisters at the Ursuline convent."

Archer sat back against his chair and folded his arms. His voice was cool as he stated, "You thought your wife Sable was a Reb traitor when you first married her."

"But that was different."

"How?"

Raimond opened his mouth but closed it again, unable to think of a way to back up his claim.

Archer said, "I'm of the belief that Domino is not who she's claming to be."

"Based upon what?"

"Let's just say a man can tell a lot about a woman in bed."

Rai dropped his head into his hands and said, *"Sacre bleu."* Then he said, "The lovely Juliana is going to have my hide for helping you with this. She's not happy with the rumors flying about you and your Domino, but as you noted, I thought Sable was someone she wasn't, so . . ." And he shrugged, as if no further explanation was necessary.

"So are the phrases familiar to you at all?"

"Yes," Raimond admitted. "Sounds like Gullah."

"Gullah? The language spoken in the Sea Islands?"

"And in other coastal parts of the country."

Archer knew that after the war Raimond and André Renaud had spent time with Harriet Tubman and the freedmen in the Sea Islands. "So if it's Gullah, what do the words mean?"

"*Waa'ment* is a Creole corruption of the word 'varmint.'"

"And the other phrase."

"Well, brat, whatever you were doing to her at the time must have been good, because loosely translated, *ah go da* means 'I'm going to die.'"

That said, he began to laugh again, and a pleased Archer simply smiled.

Later, after leaving his office at the end of the day, Archer stopped off at Lynette's before venturing across town to Juliana's for dinner. Lynette had sent a message around earlier in the day saying she had something of importance to speak with him about, so he'd come to hear what she had to say.

She met him at the door wearing a white dressing gown so transparent that her light brown nipples and the shadow of hair at her thighs were unabashedly displayed. "Thank you for coming."

Archer stepped inside and followed her to the parlor. He had to admit that the sight of her hips swaying seductively beneath the gown caught his eye.

"Do you like it?" she tossed back over her shoulder.

He smiled. "What man wouldn't?"

With a saucy smile, she poured him tea from the pot on the table and offered him a cup. Once she had a cup of her own, she took a delicate sip, then set the cup down on the white china saucer. "I've decided to give you one last chance."

Archer placed his cup down. "One last chance— to do what?"

"Come to your senses. I talked to my aunt about the problems we're having."

Archer had never cared for familial interference in his affairs, but Lynette felt differently. "And she said?"

"That I should let you sow your wild oats and not worry. She assured me that once you get over the novelty of that masked whore, you'll come back to me."

"I see."

Lynette was smiling, as if she'd just solved the world's most pressing problems. "So, I am content to wait. It won't be that long."

"Why not?"

"Because you'll eventually come to your senses and realize that she's as used as an old handker-chief. Really, Archer, how can you go where so many other men have been before?"

Archer didn't respond.

"Since I refuse to be the laughingstock of the city, I'm going to go visit my granduncle in Haiti for a few months. By the time I return, you will have gotten over your obsession and we can pick up where we were before the whore came to town."

"Is your uncle paying your passage?"

"No, silly. You are. It's the least you can do, considering the circumstances, don't you think?"

"No."

Surprise etched her doll-like face. "What do you mean, no?"

"No, Lynette. I am not paying your passage to Haiti, or anywhere else."

She stared. "What has gotten into you?"

"I'll pay the rent here for the next three months. That should give you ample time to find another protector and a new place to live."

"Archer?"

"It's over, Lynette, and I'll admit to it being my fault."

She laughed. "You can't leave me. The root I put on you won't allow for it."

"What root?"

"The strongest root there is. My woman's blood."

Bile rose in his throat. "You put blood in my food!"

"How do you think I've kept you with me all these years? Woman's blood. Each month I put a few drops of the flow in your food. The magic binds you to me. You can't leave me."

Nauseous, Archer stood.

"I will kill her if you leave me. I swear I will."

Archer walked out of the room.

She scrambled off her seat. "Come back here!"

At the door, he stopped and turned to say, "I've

changed my mind. You have two weeks to pack up and vacate, or stay and be evicted."

He walked through the door, his stomach roiling queasily in response to her admission. Outside, he almost made it to his carriage before having to stop and vomit. When he drove away, she was standing in the doorway, smiling.

The next morning, while the girls were at Wilma's being fitted for new gowns, Zahra called her staff together. Some of the eight faces had changed since she'd arrived in New Orleans, but they were all dispatches, and she finally had something worthy for them to undertake.

"We're looking for Death Books," she told everyone. When she explained what the books were, there were more than a few startled gasps.

"I need your ears and your eyes open when you're in the markets, on the streets, at parties, or simply talking to other servants. If you hear anything of import, let me or Alfred know. One of Matilda's customers, a man named Isenbaum, claims to be a high muckety muck in one of the White Leagues, so we're going to put him under surveillance. Ideally we'd like to get someone inside his estate to pose as a servant, but right now, we need to find out as much about him as we can."

She looked around until she spotted the two faces she'd been looking for. "Jesse and Caleb, you two take the surveillance of his home." Jesse was from Biloxi and Caleb from Atlanta. Presently they were posing as members of Zahra's gardening staff. "Choose whatever disguises you deem suitable." Then she added, "As we all know, cowards like Isenbaum and his friends rarely conduct their dirty business during the day, so we're more concerned with where he goes and who he visits, or who comes to visit him, after dark."

She assigned two house maids, Suzette, from St. Augustine, Florida, and Clare, from Boston, to handle Isenbaum's servants. "Find out which market they patronize and who their delivery people are—maybe that knowledge can get us a quick way in. We need to know about the house's interior. Specifically the location of his study and bedroom. If he has a Death Book in his possession, it's likely to be in one of those two places. Everyone else here without a specific task will be asked to comb the streets for whatever clues may be out there."

She scanned the men and women and noted the serious set of their faces. Once again she wondered if any of them would be Judas. "Does anyone have questions?"

Silence.

"Okay. You have your assignments. Please keep Alfred or myself aware of your comings and goings. If you get into trouble, we want to be able to send help as quickly as possible."

The meeting adjourned, and Alfred and Zahra were left alone in the parlor. She looked to him and said, "You know, Carnival season begins soon. Most of our targets will be attending balls in the evenings, and their homes will be empty. Be a perfect time for the two of us to do a little nosing around, don't you think?"

He smiled. "I think, yes."

Zahra felt as if the meeting had gone well.

Archer, Raimond, and Raimond's beautiful wife, Sable, were having lunch in the restaurant inside Archer's hotel. Waiting for their food to come, they passed the time in pleasant conversation. Sable was well known around the city for her work with orphans and was about to tell them about a fund-raiser she had planned when a hush fell over the crowded room. A confused Archer looked around to find the cause, and there stood Domino, talking with the nearly swooning André Renaud. Archer froze.

"Is that her?" Sable whispered.

Archer nodded while wondering how a woman whose face he'd never seen could be more beautiful with each passing day.

"She looks very mysterious," Sable said to Archer. "I love the emerald gown. Who's her dressmaker?"

Raimond looked at her as if she'd lost her mind.

Archer, his eyes still locked on Domino, replied, "Wilma Gray. New shop."

Sable smiled. "Archer, I've never known you to look so struck, and I must know why. Invite the lady over to join us. I wish to meet her."

Raimond raised his coffee cup and said, "*Ma reine*, the woman's a whore."

"And so was my best friend, Brigitte, for a portion of her life, and as I recall, you've never complained about the things I learned from her."

Raimond spit his coffee onto his plate. Sable ignored him.

Archer was ignoring them both; André was escorting Domino towards the table, and she was all he could see. The confident way she held her head, coupled with her beauty and enigmatic manner, had every man in the room mesmerized.

Archer was already standing when Domino and André reached the table. Sable planted a subtle elbow in her husband's ribs, and a stormy-faced Raimond rose to his feet as well.

Archer spoke first. "Good afternoon, Domino."

"Archer."

"Would you care to join us?"

"I wouldn't think of imposing. I simply wish to speak to Aristide about a birthday cake for the twins. Mr. Renaud seemed to think I should interrupt you, though, and say hello."

Archer said, "This is my brother, Raimond. His wife, Sable."

She nodded a masked greeting, then said, "Please pardon my interruption. It was a pleasure meeting you."

"No," Sable insisted. "Please, join us. Have you eaten?"

Attempting to gauge the woman's intent, Zahra studied her for a moment. Seeing nothing but friendliness in the green eyes, she replied with as much respect as she could muster, "Mrs. Le Veq, the gossips will tear you apart should I accept your invitation."

"Madame Domino, I am an escaped slave who married into the storied House of Le Veq. There is nothing they can say that hasn't already been said." Sable gestured her to a vacant seat.

A smile touched Domino's lips. "Okay. If you

put it that way." Offering a nod of thanks, Domino joined them.

"So," Sable said, once they were all settled in, "welcome to New Orleans. Are you enjoying the city?"

"I am. It's very vibrant here." That Sable had once been enslaved made Zahra alter her preconceptions about the *gens de coleur* Le Veq family. She looked over to find Archer watching her, and her core tightened of its own accord. She looked away only to behold the still grim face of his eldest brother, Raimond. Unlike his wife, the dark-skinned Le Veq didn't appear to be happy with the charitable invitation.

Zahra told him, "Mr. Le Veq. My apologies for embarrassing you. I know you are a member of high standing in this city, and my dining with you has to be awkward."

"It is," he said, meeting her eyes, "and I appreciate that you at least realize it, even if no one else here does." He glowered at Sable and Archer.

Her mind made up, Zahra gracefully pushed back from the table, then stood. "Thank you for your kindness, Mrs. Le Veq, but I must go."

"But I thought you were going to join us."

"I did too, but I can't. You shouldn't be sullying yourselves with the likes of me." Zahra turned to Archer. "Which way is the kitchen?"

He stood, saying, "This way. Come, I'll show you."

"Thank you." Domino then said to Raimond and Sable, "It was nice meeting you both."

They inclined their heads, and Zahra let Archer escort her away.

Once Domino and Archer disappeared through the kitchen door, Raimond said to his wife, "Oddly enough, I like her."

"I do, as well, and I don't believe she's a real whore either. Let's hope Archer can get it all sorted out. She'd make a nice sister-in-law, I'm thinking."

Raimond stared. Sable smiled serenely, then turned her attention to the waiter arriving with their food.

In the kitchen, Archer stood back and watched Domino make the usual ill-tempered Aristide melt like pralines in her hand. That Aristide seemed as awed by her as every other male in the city was always surprising, because as far as Archer knew, Aristide was awed only by Aristide, yet he fawned over Domino like royalty come to visit. She then thanked him with a kiss on the cheek that made the fair-skinned chef turn apple red.

She was still smiling when she met Archer's eyes, and he thought his heart would swell out of his chest. Her smiles were as rare as diamonds on the streets of the city and twice as priceless to a man who had no business wanting her.

Archer offered to drive her home. "Unless the giant is outside waiting."

She shook her head, and her eyes sparkled from within the emerald mask. "No, he isn't, I took a cab. So a ride back would be appreciated." Zahra wondered if he or his brother knew anything about the Death Books. Because of their government connections and their prominence in the city it was highly possible that they might, but until she could devise a way to ask without giving everything away, she chose to rely on the plans she'd already set into motion.

Outside, the day was bright and sunny, and the temperature higher than it had been in weeks. By no means was it close to being summertime, but at least the cold winds seemed to have disappeared. Riding with him through the crowded streets, she basked in the warmth of the sunshine. "It's a beautiful day."

"It is indeed." For Archer everything seemed even brighter with her at his side. "Have dinner with me tonight."

The uncontrollable warmth his presence always seemed to ignite rose in immediate response. "Your place or mine?"

"Mine."

"Then your place it is."

Their smiles met, and he turned his attention back to his driving.

When they reached the house, there seemed to be some kind of commotion on the steps. The girls were yelling and arguing with, of all people, Lynette Dubois and an older woman dressed in a black mantilla and a black gown, whom Zahra did not recognize. "Looks like we have guests," she drawled. Alfred and the men were out in the streets of the city searching for clues to the Death Books, but the girls appeared to be holding their own in the argument.

As soon as he pulled the brake, Zahra threw the door open and stepped out. "What's going on here?" she demanded as she walked up.

Matilda said, "We found these two sneaking around outside the house."

"They were trying to hide this in the rose garden," Chloe said, showing Zahra a small urn. Zahra lifted the top and saw what appeared to be ashes.

"Then there's this," Stella added, handing Zahra a brown porcelain jug. Zahra removed the top and saw something wedged inside. She fished it out and held up a small, crude doll wearing an even cruder domino where the eyes should be.

"You're much prettier," Adair tossed out, sipping coffee from the cup in her hand. She then made a face. "Fooling with them has made my coffee go cold."

Zahra assessed Lynette's angry face, then turned and showed the items to Archer, silently asking for an explanation.

He walked up. Giving Lynette a withering look, he said, "It's called Doll in a Jug. The jug with the doll is supposed to be taken to a cemetery and buried in the breast of a grave. What's in the urn?"

"Ashes."

He turned cold eyes on Lynette. She curled her lip but looked away. "The ashes are supposed to be buried in the backyard of the victim to hasten the spell."

"What's it supposed to do?"

"Kill you."

The old woman, her face lined by time, asked the simmering Lynette, "Is this the whore?"

Lynette met Zahra's eyes. "Yes, *Tante*."

The old woman began murmuring a singsong incantation accompanied by movements of her hands. Before her performance could gain any momentum, Zahra reached for the coffee mug Adair was holding and calmly tossed the lukewarm contents in the crone's face.

The woman howled with outrage, and the wide-eyed, angry Lynette looked about to pounce until Zahra pressed a gleaming, pearl-handled, straight-edge razor against Lynette's trembling, pale neck.

"Now," Zahra said to her softly, "if you come around here again with this silliness, this root in my hand will come to your house in the middle of the night and slit your childish throat. Do you understand me?"

Lynette nodded elaborately.

"Good. Now take this old woman home before she comes to harm."

The two left hurriedly. Both were furious, but Zahra was putting the now-folded razor back in the sheath she wore below her garter and didn't care.

Straightening, she noticed that the girls were all staring in wonder and awe. "What?" she asked.

Adair said, "Domino, if I ever questioned whether you were a real madame or not, I do beg your pardon."

Everyone laughed.

Zahra met Archer's eyes and saw that he was watching her, too, but what he might be thinking was impossible to tell.

The girls flowed back into the house, happily rehashing the incident, leaving Zahra and Archer alone.

He said, "A pistol, and now a razor. Are you always so well armed?"

"Most times."

"You're a formidable woman."

"These are formidable times."

"Do you still wish to have dinner?"

"Yes, but it will have to be after we close."

"You can't slip away."

"The last time I slipped away with you, I wound up trysting in the rose garden."

"Is that such a bad memory?"

Desire licked at her like a flame. "Not in the least, but slipping away with you always involves something else."

He gave her that grin. "I told you before, you were made for pleasure."

Her senses bloomed under his intense dark eyes. "Are all of your brothers as audacious as you?"

"Yes, madame. It's in our blood."

Zahra had to admit she'd never met a man quite like him. She gave him a soft kiss on his cheek. "Thanks for driving me home. I'll see you this evening."

Once she was in her room, Zahra stripped off her gloves and tossed them onto the vanity table. Her anger over her confrontation with Lynette still simmered. Being from the swamps, Zahra had plenty of respect for the old ways and those who lived their lives according to the tenets, but Lynette and her bumbling attempt to manipulate the forces of life and death drew nothing but Zahra's contempt. She hoped she'd scared the young woman into thinking twice before trying to hex someone else, because if it happened again, Zahra was not going to be nice.

That evening the house opened for business and the customers began arriving with grins and handshakes for their male acquaintances, and smiles and kisses on the cheeks for the scantily glad girls. Zahra standing on the balcony noted the entrance of Mitchell Isenbaum. As usual, he was alone. According to Matilda, he was twenty-five years old and unmarried. He'd grown up the wealthy scion of one of the state's largest sugar-cane plantations and boasted of having owned three hundred slaves before the war.

Zahra watched him approach Matilda, who greeted him with her patented sultry smile. Isenbaum, with his dark eyes and curling hair, was quite handsome, Zahra had to admit, but only on the outside. His ties to the White League made him ancillary to the deaths of hundreds of Blacks in the state, and the numbers were rising daily. The New Orleans newspapers were filled with reports of the killings and atrocities committed in the name of supremacy, yet Isenbaum appeared as cool and detached as a prince of the realm.

He whispered something in Matilda's ear that made them both smile, then she took his hand and led him away. Now that Zahra and her people were shadowing his moves, it wouldn't be necessary for Matilda to continue her discreet search for information. Zahra would tell her that in the morning, but in the meantime, Zahra planned to keep an eye on him.

Since leaving Domino's after the ill-fated Lynette incident, Archer was filled with the nagging sense that he was supposed to remember something, but he had no idea what that something might be. Dressing now to go and get her for their late dinner, the feeling gnawed at him like a bad tooth. Tying his tie in the mirror, he cast his mind back to the commotion on the steps. In his memory he relived their arrival, then the confrontation with the coffee cup, and then he saw Domino slide the razor back into the sheath around her thigh. Suddenly the hair stood up on the back of his neck. *It was the razor!* Where had he seen it before? His mind raced; seeking, sifting, frantically searching for the answer, and then he remembered a fetid Georgia barn and a remarkable woman. The enormity of the theory stopped him cold. Could it be? But how many women carried pearl-handled razors in thigh sheaths? His broad smile reflected in the mirror. What in the world was the famed Butterfly doing in New Orleans posing as a madame? He couldn't believe he'd actually stumbled onto Domino's true identity, but he knew as sure as his name was Archer Antonio Le Veq that Domino and the Butterfly were one and the same.

She'd saved his life that night in the barn. There was no doubt in his mind that had she not been sent to fetch him, his mother would be mourning not only their brother Gerrold's death but Archer's as well. He couldn't wait to thank her in person.

"Oh my sweet *papillon*," he said softly, translating the word "butterfly" into his native French. "What a night we're going to have."

Grinning like a kid at Christmas, Archer finished his preparations, then, whistling like the pleased male that he was, left his suite to collect his carriage.

# Chapter 9

$\mathbf{A}$fter having taken a quick bath to rid her skin of the smells of men, liquor, and cigar smoke, Zahra stepped into the gold gown she'd picked out to wear for her meal with Archer. As always, Wilma had designed the neckline to be low and teasing. The edges were scalloped and the gown itself sumptuous enough for royalty.

Knowing he would undoubtedly entice her into engaging in that "something else" they'd made reference to out on the steps this afternoon, she'd boldly left off her corset in favor of a gossamer, waist-length shift instead. Society would call her shameless for forgoing the traditional undergarment, but that was how Archer made her feel; shameless, reckless. In truth, she never wore a corset in her role as laundress, but being Domino meant forcing herself into the cinching garment day after day, having the whalebone cut into her flesh and the binding hinder her breathing. To-night she'd be able to breathe in as deeply as she wanted, and knowing Archer, Zahra was certain she'd be needing each and every one.

Giving herself a final approving look in the mirror, she picked up her handbag, gloves, and shawl, then went to wait downstairs.

As she descended the staircase, she saw that he'd already arrived and that he was formally dressed. He was talking to the twins. Now that they were done performing for the night, they were wearing long flannel nightgowns. The two looked prim enough to be the daughters of a pastor, but Zahra and half the men of New Orleans knew better.

When he glanced away from the conversation for a moment and saw Zahra, he stood, and his smile of greeting warmed her insides. "Good evening, Archer," she said, crossing the room to where he and the twins were, "or should I say good morning?"

It was, after all, 2 a.m. She asked him about his attire. "Did you just come from a ball or the opera?"

He looked down at himself. "No. It's what I felt like wearing."

"I'm flattered."

He took her golden-gloved hand and kissed the back. "And there's much more to follow."

Pierced by the desire blazing in his eyes, a pulse began beating in her throat. Noticing the twins gazing at them like two engrossed adolescents, Zahra said to them, "Go to bed. I'll see you two later."

They stood, gave her a knowing look, then said in unison, "Don't stay out too late. Unless you have to."

Giggling, they ran off and raced each other up the staircase.

Zahra shook her head. What a pair. She would dearly miss them when this assignment ended.

"Ready?" he asked.

Zahra saw Alfred standing on the balcony. "Mr. Le Veq will bring me back later."

The big man nodded, and Zahra and Archer departed.

As they drove through the nearly deserted streets, he asked, "How did the evening go?"

"It went well. The twins were in rare form. The customers were happy. A madam couldn't ask for more. How was your evening?" she asked.

"Uneventful until I began dressing to come and meet you."

"More flattery?"

"No," he replied casually, "just the truth."

A contented Zahra sat back against the seat to enjoy the rest of the ride.

They entered his suites through his private entrance, which was accessed by an iron stairway on the back side of the hotel. In the front parlor the flames in the big fireplace danced in the darkness. The hush in the room reminded her of her last visit.

Archer said, "Let me light a lamp."

Soon the parlor's interior was softly illuminated, but the hush in the room remained.

"How about you take a seat and I'll add some wood to the fires. There's a chill in here."

While he went about the task, Zahra looked around. The furnishings were as impressive as the last time she'd visited. A framed portrait on the wall drew her attention. She didn't remember seeing it last time. "Who's this beautiful lady?"

"My mother, Juliana. The artist delivered it a few days ago."

The regal beauty, with her dark skin and salt-and-pepper hair, was posed at an angle so that one could see the strength in her jawline and the warmth in her eyes. The face showed wisdom and the hint of a smile. Zahra thought it too bad that she and Juliana would never meet. Mrs. Le Veq would undoubtedly be an interesting woman to know. "I've heard she's a broker?"

He came to stand by Zahra's side. "Yes, she is. Beneath all that loveliness lies the heart of a shark. She buys properties and bonds like most women buy hats. My brothers and I would walk through Hades for her, though."

Zahra continued to study Juliana's strong face. "I'll bet you were a trial for her growing up."

"No denying that. Having to raise a brood of boys alone couldn't have been easy. Our father died at sea."

"I'm sorry to hear that."

"She made the best of it, however. We never wanted for anything, and no matter how many deals she had brewing, she always had time to spend with us."

"She sounds like a great mother."

"She is. She'll like you, I think."

Zahra responded with a shake of her head and

a smile. "Archer, I'm never going to meet your mother. I'd never do that to her."

"*Never* is a strong word, Domino. Life often has a way of negating *nevers*."

"Well, still, don't bet your hotel."

He grinned and escorted her into the dining room.

Once again, there were candles on the table, along with elegant china, gleaming silver, and crystal flutes.

"I didn't think you wanted a heavy meal this time of morning, so Aristide prepared a simple bisque and baguettes."

"Sounds wonderful."

He helped her with her chair. "You look lovely, as always."

"Thank you."

As he took his seat across from her, he raised his flute of wine and said, "To a memorable morning."

Touched by his tone and the desire in his eyes, she raised hers in response.

It didn't take them long to consume the light meal, and when they were done, Archer cleared the table.

"How about we move to the fire."

They sat side by side on the sofa. He draped his arm across the back, and she laid her head on his shoulder. Enjoying the companionable silence and closeness of each other, they were content to watch the flames.

Finally, Archer said, "You've led me a merry chase these past few weeks."

"Humility is good for the soul."

He smiled and placed a soft kiss on her forehead. "So I'm learning."

"Women have obviously come to you too easily."

"That's not been the case with you."

"I'll take that as a compliment."

His fingers were idly stroking the edge of her jaw and the side of her neck. Each languid pass stoked the embers of her desire.

Then he asked, "Where will you go when you leave New Orleans?"

She shrugged. "I don't know. West maybe."

Archer didn't like the idea of her leaving, but because he knew her true identity, he also knew her leaving would be a foregone conclusion. "What would make you stay?"

Zahra looked into his eyes. The seriousness she saw there gave her pause. She knew the answer he sought, but she had to tell him the truth, for once. "I can't stay, no matter what is offered or promised."

"I admire your honesty."

He reached out and slowly traced her mouth. The sweet sensation closed Zahra's eyes. "Do you know what the word *papillon* means in English, *chérie* . . ."

Before she could respond, he leaned in and placed a humid kiss against one parted corner of her lips, then offered the same kiss to the other side of her mouth. His fingers slid down her throat and then across her collarbone.

"Do you?" he whispered, lifting her chin so he

could see what he could of her eyes in the golden mask.

"No," she finally responded. Sensations were spreading though her like warm sunlight.

He placed his lips against her ear and husked out, "It means . . . 'butterfly.'"

Zahra stiffened. For a moment, she wasn't sure what this meant, but when he winked at her boldly, she leaped off the sofa. "Damn you, Archer Le Veq."

But his smile remained. "What's wrong?"

"Who told?"

"No one."

"Then how'd you find out?"

"From you."

Archer could see the confusion on her face. "It was your razor. The one you scared Lynette with is the same one you used to cut me down in that barn."

Zahra threw up her hands. Trust him to have such an acute memory. It had never crossed her mind that something as mundane as a razor would be her undoing. "Dammit!" she swore.

He chuckled.

"This isn't funny, Le Veq."

"Maybe not to you, but I knew you were a fraud from the moment I placed your hand on me. You'd never held a man like that before, had you?"

She didn't lie. "No."

The heat in his eyes made her desire return.

He walked over to where she stood and fit himself against her rigidly set back, then wrapped his arms gently around her. He kissed her cheek. "Why're you so upset?"

She turned to face him. "Because I've never had my disguise breached before. Never."

"Your secret is safe with me."

"That's not the point." Once again she whispered, "Dammit!"

Smiling, he studied her masked face. He reached up to the ribbon ties, and his eyes silently asked for permission.

"You may as well."

The ties loosened easily, and a moment later her face was revealed. Archer would be the first to admit that he had no clear memory of her features, only that she'd been a beauty. Now, five years later, he realized he'd been correct. The brown face was regal, the features almost feline. The skin, so soft, drew his fingers down her cheeks. "Thank you for saving my life . . ." he husked out.

In that moment, Zahra's emotions changed; gone was the frustration, in its place a familiar tightening of her core. "You're welcome."

The kiss that followed had been simmering since the day they'd met. The heat of their lips meeting overwhelmed them with its sweetness, its fire. He pulled her closer for a better fit, and she wrapped her arms around him in return. They nibbled, licked and placed kisses against passion-parted corners in urgent response to their need. Hands roamed; mapping, enticing, fueling a desire that made the kisses deepen and the sounds of their breathing rise in the otherwise silent room. He blazed a trail with his lips down the column of her throat while his hands teased her breasts.

Archer thrilled to the feel of her softness inside the gown. "Where's your corset?" he asked, boldly easing down the neckline of her gown, then commanding the exposed nipple with his magic hands.

"In the wardrobe drawer. Ohh . . ." she cried out sensually as he took the prepared bud into his warm mouth. He loved her with a series of sucks and licks that had her twisting and groaning, arching and flowing.

"And you want to leave, this," he accused heatedly.

He exposed her other breast and treated it to the same fiery loving. No, she didn't want to leave *this*, but she couldn't stay with him, no matter how thrilling the kisses stealing her breath or the fingers playing lustfully with her tight, damp nipples. Her allegiance was to her parents, not to this virtuoso playing her body like a rare and costly violin.

Archer wanted to make love to her until the end of time. Her perfumed skin, the way her breast filled his hand, the soft sounds she made when he circled his tongue around her nipple all set him ablaze. Even if he did have an eternity, he knew it would not be enough to bind her to him, or make her stay, so he planned to brand her with his loving; that way she'd never forget the feel of his hands, the taste of his kisses, or the passion fueling them both.

He undressed her then; slowly, lustily, and completely, until she was left standing with her back to the fire, wearing only her garters, stockings, and low-heeled mules. He began again; kissing, teasing, fondling. Working his way down her body like an acolyte making love to his priestess, his touches between her thighs caused her to widen her stance in wanton welcome. When the first long-boned finger went in, she sucked in a shuddering breath, and her head fell back bonelessly. He worked her marvelously, erotically, making her hips circle with a rhythm as ancient as Adam and Eve. While she preened, he added another finger to the impaling, and her answering gasp was loud, strangled. He plied her with lusty, languid thrusts that made her raise herself to him shamelessly. Lowering himself to his knees, his fingers still moving, he spread the fingers wide, and, groaning, she spread her legs in response. Only then did he bend and taste and give her his tongue. His expertise was so staggering that Zahra screamed a joyful completion only moments later. Shattering, the orgasm rolling through her, his fingers still pleasuring, she came again, to his great delight, and he picked her up and carried her to his room.

Snatching off his clothes, Archer feasted his eyes on the voluptuous picture she made lying on his bed, still in the throes of her fading pleasure. Nude now and unable to resist, he kissed her soft mouth and eased his rampant manhood into the tight, warm channel that was love's delight. Feeling her close around him so completely, his groan broke the silence. Grabbing one of the bed pillows, he placed it strategically beneath her hips, then began his strokes.

Because of the pillow, Zahra could feel him so much better than last time, something she hadn't dreamed possible. She never knew a man could worship her this way, nor that passion could be so wild. She ceased to be Zahra, or Butterfly or Domino, and became Archer Le Veq's lover, and for the moment that's the only woman she wanted to be, because he was kissing her mouth, using love-gentled teeth on her nipples, the edge of her throat and the lobe of her ear. The strokes intensified in pace and in power, so she was again in the winds of the storm, matching him measure for measure. He filled his hands with her hips, and the glory of his increasing thrusts made her arch her waist and let him love her with as much fervor and force as he craved.

Soon, she was screaming and he was roaring, and *la petite mort* was consuming them like kindling before wildfire. Then they collapsed; breathing, throbbing, content.

In the quiet aftermath, Zahra lay against him while he held her close. Her disguise had been breached, collapsing Madame Domino's house of cards, but at the moment she didn't care. Only her sated body and the feel of his heated skin against her own mattered.

He kissed the top of her hair, then softly asked, "Shall we talk now?"

She knew he was referring to the reason she'd come to New Orleans, and there was no way she could deny him, not now, not after what they'd shared. She also trusted him to keep his word. He'd been involved in reconnaissance and knew the dangers involved. More importantly, he'd deciphered the riddle of Domino and had earned the right to the truth. So she turned over on her stomach to better see his face in the dark and told him the story.

Archer found the tale fascinating, almost as fascinating as its narrator. He yearned to make love to her again, but they both needed to regain their strength, so he listened instead. It didn't surprise him that Harriet Tubman was involved. He knew how passionate she was about the race's survival and that her flair for planning secret missions during slavery and the war was legendary. "Do your girls know your secrets?"

"No. Only Alfred and the servants."

Unable to keep from touching her, Archer trailed a finger over her silky cheek. "Would you have ever told me the truth?"

"No."

Archer smiled, admiring her strength. "Then it's good I figured it out."

Zahra still didn't know if it was good or not, but it was done and she was never one to cry over spilled milk. "Have you ever met her?"

"Mrs. Tubman? No. My brother Rai worked with her during abolition and in the Sea Islands. He has a lot of respect for her." He traced a worshipping finger over a nipple. "Speaking of the islands, where'd you learn Gullah?"

Once again he made her freeze.

He smiled softly. "You've spoken it twice since we've met."

"When?"

When he told her, she hung her head, then

shook it with a sigh. "Dammit!" she whispered fiercely again.

He grinned. "We really need to expand your cursing vocabulary."

"No we don't. It's extensive enough. I'm attempting to be nice."

Studying him then, she said, "I suppose I should be grateful you were the one to figure me out and not someone like Barber or Mitchell Isenbaum."

"Isenbaum the Leaguer? What do you know about him?"

She then told him about the Death Books.

"My Lord," he whispered. "Are there any in New Orleans?"

Without revealing Henry Adams as her source of information, Zahra told Archer all she knew. "So I have a few of my men shadowing Isenbaum. If I could place a book in the president's hand, it might make a difference."

Deep in thought, he replied, "You're right." Then, thinking back on something else, he said, "I wish I'd known about these books earlier."

"Why?"

"We would have searched those houses before torching them."

She studied him for a long moment. "You're responsible for all the fires in the newspapers?"

"Not all of them, but friends and I have done our share."

Zahra knew she couldn't judge him. Times being what they were, someone had to take up the sword and fight back to counter the supremacists bent on annihilation, because that truly was their goal, and they were proclaiming it proudly, and without shame, to anyone who'd listen.

"I want to talk to my friends about these Death Books. Is that all right with you?"

"Yes, if they are trustworthy."

"Good, then that's what I shall do." He pulled her back against him and said, "With men of color in the Congress and numerous others serving in state Houses, it's imperative that we get a look at those lists and see who the supremacists have in their sights."

Zahra agreed. Was Fred Douglass on the list? What about the Mississippian Hiram Revels, the first Black man to serve as a United States senator? Had he been targeted? All over the South, Black men were in state legislatures, were elected sheriffs, and acted as spokesmen for communities large and small. The race couldn't afford to lose even one of them, because they represented the hopes and dreams of their people. She said, "How about we meet at the house this evening, bring whoever you think might aid us, and we'll talk about it. With the house being closed tonight as it is on Monday and Tuesday. We shouldn't be disturbed."

"That's a good idea. I'm sure my brothers would want to attend."

"Good. Shall we say around eight?"

He nodded, then said to her, "Now that we have discussed business, will you answer one more question for me?"

"I'll try."

His hands were moving over her with a slow

intent that let her know what would be coming next. "What's your true given name?"

"Can't tell you."

He rolled over and lowered his mouth to her nipple. "Why not?"

She whispered in the midst of rising desire, "It's a secret."

He slipped a hand between her thighs and began to play. "Why?"

"Because when we part we shouldn't see each other again."

Archer raised up and looked down into her eyes. His voice concerned, he asked, "Suppose I wish to?"

She shook her head. "That's your lust talking. We're from two different worlds, Archer. You're wealthy, well bred. I'm not. I'm also not cut from mistress cloth. If you were the man of my heart, I'd be your wife, not mistress. I don't share well."

*If you were the man of my heart.* The words echoed inside Archer with a force that shouldn't have surprised him but did. He was discovering that he had rather deep feelings for this fierce, mysterious woman. Letting her walk out of his life wouldn't be easy when the time came, so it became his plan to delay that parting for as long as possible. "Well, if you won't tell me your name, what shall I call you?"

The jokester inside herself took over. "Zahra is a name I've always cottoned to."

"Zahra," he said, weighing the name on his tongue. "I like that too, but I will learn the truth, eventually."

"There will be no razors to help you this time."

"I'll find a way, don't worry."

That decided, the loving resumed.

The sun was just waking up when he drove her home. The pink sky and the clear morning breeze signaled a new day, and it was a new day for Zahra. Archer had unmasked Domino, and she and Juliana's third son were entering a new relationship; one linked by their concern for the race and their need to make love to each other until they couldn't move. Zahra had never had the attention of such a glorious man before, and she planned to enjoy it until it became time for her to vanish from his world and, ultimately, his life. The thought saddened her, but she set it aside. Sentiment could play no part in her plans.

At the house, Archer stopped the carriage and feasted his eyes on her. She looked tired—*and for good reason,* he thought with pleasure. Had he ever met a woman more determined, more beautiful? He couldn't say that he had. She was more than he was accustomed to handling, but therein lay the challenge. Most men would attempt to cage such a beautiful *papillon,* but he sensed that would not work with her. "I'm going to wire some friends I met during the war to help with the search for the Death Books. I know they'll want to help."

"That's fine. If we combine forces, it may hasten the process."

"And if we combine forces, I'll see more of you."

"As I recall, you've already seen *all* of me," she tossed back.

He laughed at that. "What a woman you are."

"Astounding, aren't I?"

He leaned over and kissed her sassy mouth until she saw stars. "You're all that and more. Now go inside before I see how astounding you really are."

They shared one more long kiss, then she got out. "See you this evening?" she asked.

"Yes, and no drawers allowed," he told her.

She was still standing there, stunned, when he let out a laugh and drove away.

That afternoon, Wilma brought over a set of petticoats she'd done for the twins, then she and Zahra sat in Zahra's office to talk and catch up. When Zahra confessed that Archer knew she'd been the Butterfly, Wilma was surprised. "How did he find out?"

"My daddy's razor."

"The one with the beautiful pearl handle? Are you still carrying that thing after all this time?"

"Yes. Apparently I used it to free him from General Crete's barn."

Wilma shook her head. "Guess the cat's out of the bag."

"I'm holding him to his word that he'll keep my secret."

"How can you be sure?"

"Because I am."

Then Wilma asked, "Any progress on the Death Books?"

"Not so far. My people are still trailing him. Le Veq has pledged to help with the search. I'm going to meet with him and some of his associates here tonight."

"You've taken him into your confidence quite a bit."

There was no mistaking her censuring tone. "Yes, Wilma, I have. This is such a serious matter I'd take help from Satan himself if it would help me get my hands on one of those books."

"Are you in love with him?"

"No."

"Are you lying to me or to yourself?"

Zahra met her old friend's blue eyes and said truthfully, "I have feelings for him, I can't deny that, but love? I don't know."

Wilma nodded at the logic and offered a smile. "Well, try and keep head and heart separate. There's much at stake."

"I will. Don't worry."

"Should I relay this news to Araminta?"

"Yes, and if she disagrees with my decision to add Archer to the game, she'll let me know in no uncertain terms, but she worked with his brother in the Sea Islands. I'm sure she'll see the advantage in including him."

"I hope you're right."

"And if I'm not, it's too late. As you said, the cat's out of the bag. We have no choice but to play the hand we've been given."

"Okay. I'm going back to the shop. I'll send the wire to Araminta this evening. I'd come to the meeting tonight, but I have a wedding party scheduled for a fitting at seven-thirty. I will probably be there for hours. Is there anything else you need assistance with?"

"Not at the moment. That's more than enough, don't you think?"

Wilma smiled. "More than enough. I'll see you soon."

"Thanks, Wilma."

"You just be careful."

"Yes, ma'am."

With a wave Wilma departed.

Alone now, the pensive Zahra sat at her desk and mused over Wilma's pointed question. Had Zahra fallen in love with Le Veq? The answer depended on which part of her did the answering. Her mind said emphatically no. Nothing good could come from loving a man like Archer Le Veq. As she'd mused before, were it not for her fancy clothes and her many secrets, he wouldn't have looked at her twice. The reality of that didn't sit well with her heart, because were it asked the question of whether she'd fallen in love with Le Veq, the answer would be yes. And therein lay her dilemma. How could she fill her heart with a man she planned on leaving at the first opportunity? Men of Archer's class preferred perfumed beauties who spent their days shopping and paying calls on women just like themselves. What could he possibly see in a swamp brat who lived in a house that was smaller than his bedroom and had tar paper in the windows instead of screens? No, if Archer knew the truth about the real Zahra Lafayette, he'd wish her luck and send her on her way. So, because the last thing she needed was to return to South Carolina with a broken heart, she vowed to keep her love for him to herself.

"She's who?" Raimond asked in an incredulous tone.

"The Butterfly," Archer repeated.

"Araminta's Butterfly?"

"One and the same."

"I'm impressed."

"So am I. She saved my life, remember?"

"Why's she here?"

Archer told Raimond the story, including the information about the Death Books. The news disturbed Raimond as much as it had Archer.

Raimond asked, "Does she know if there are any in New Orleans?"

"Not yet, but she's looking. I figured we could help."

"Most certainly."

Raimond studied his brother for a moment before saying, "So you were right about her not being a whore."

"Yes."

"I'm glad. I liked her."

"Thanks."

"But what's going to happen once she's done here? You're aware she's called the Butterfly because she never stays in one place."

"I plan to cross that bridge when it comes."

After Raimond left with a promise to be at Domino's house for the evening meeting, Archer thought about the woman he'd agreed to call Zahra. He had one more level of her identity to crack, and it would be the hardest by far. She'd be on her guard from now on and wouldn't surrender the truth easily. He knew enough about Mrs. Tubman to be certain that asking her for answers would be futile. She'd never reveal Zahra's secrets.

* * *

Domino's Gentleman's Club was closed Monday through Wednesday. The girls usually used the free days to sleep, shop, and make money on the side with private dates, sometimes at the man's home, but more often at one of the city's hotels. They all had dates tonight and were getting dressed. By eight that evening, everyone was gone except Matilda, who was waiting for Mitchell Isenbaum.

"I hope nothing's happened," Matilda said as she stood by the window. "He was going to take me to a little place he has up near Baton Rouge."

Zahra didn't comment. For all she knew, the man was out terrorizing freedmen. "How long are you planning to be gone?"

"He'll bring me back on Wednesday. I guess I'll just have to wait and see if he really shows up."

"Guess so. Oh, and you don't have to find out anything else about him for me."

"Are you sure?"

"Yes."

"You know, he'd be a nice man if he didn't have all that hate inside him."

Again, Zahra had no comment.

"I played with Colored kids the whole time growing up. My mama never saw a problem in it. Neither did my daddy. Mitchell and his family must have been raised different." She turned to look at Zahra. "That's too bad, because like I said, he could be a real nice man."

Miranda was still in the front parlor waiting when Archer arrived by the back door. He had his brothers with him.

"Archer, we'll have to do introductions later.

Matilda's in the parlor waiting for Isenbaum. If he arrives I don't want him to know you all are here."

Archer and his siblings headed up the back stairs just as Zahra heard Matilda shout, "Domino, Mitchell's carriage is here."

Zahra hastened out to the front parlor in time to see Matilda open the door so he could enter.

He greeted Matilda with a kiss on the cheek. Upon noticing Zahra, he nodded curtly, "Evening, Domino."

"Mr. Isenbaum. How are you?"

"Just fine. House is closed tonight, I see."

"As it is every Monday night."

"Then who belongs to all those carriages out back?"

Zahra didn't flinch. "A private gambling party."

"Didn't know you allowed that." He paused, his eyes narrowed in thought. "Anybody I know? I might want to sit in for a hand or two."

"It's private, Mr. Isenbaum."

"You didn't answer my question."

"I don't plan to."

"You're pretty uppity, girl. Been that way since you came to town. Lot of folks don't like uppity nigger whores."

"Mitchell!" Miranda gasped. "How dare you talk to her that way!"

He turned to her and drawled, "I'm not paying you to be my conscience, sugar, just to spread your legs."

Matilda said, "I may be a whore, but I have feelings, so pay somebody else. I'm not going with you." Picking up her carpetbag, Matilda hastily climbed the staircase and headed to her room.

Zahra surveyed him coolly from behind her black domino. "Consider yourself banned from the premises for as long as my name is on the sign, Mr. Isenbaum. Have a good evening."

Zahra knew Alfred was on the balcony behind her, so she called out as she walked away from Isenbaum, "Alfred, please escort the gentleman to his carriage, and if he ever shows up here again, toss him out."

"With pleasure."

Zahra climbed the stairs and did not look back.

# Chapter 10

**H**er anger must have shown on her face, because as she entered and removed her domino, Archer stood and asked with concern, "What's the matter?"

"Isenbaum. I had to have Alfred escort him out." She told them the story.

"Did he harm you?"

"No. I'm fine. He was just nasty." She then looked around the room at the men. They were all tall and handsome. "Thank you for coming, gentlemen. Alfred will be joining us shortly."

On the heels of her announcement, Alfred entered and closed the door behind him.

Archer made the introductions, and Zahra greeted each brother with a welcoming nod. She'd already been introduced to Raimond, but the others she'd never met before, except the youngest, Philippe. She recognized him right off because he

236

patronized the twins frequently. She'd had no idea Naomi's and Salome's favorite playmate was Archer's baby brother.

They all gathered around two of the room's small round tables. They began the meeting by drawing up a list of men who might be harboring the books. There were five in all, including Isenbaum. The others—Sam Banks, Hathaway Dawes, Wendell Thomas, and Zebediah Spain—were well-known supremacists according to the Le Veqs, and had high enough standing in the local White League and Democratic Party to merit being trusted with something as volatile as the Death Books.

In Zahra's opinion the Le Veqs proved their value there and then. It might have taken her weeks to ascertain who to target for this mission, but because Archer and his brothers were natives they knew the wheat from the chaff. Their knowledge had saved valuable time. She glanced Alfred's way. As if he'd read her mind, he nodded his approval as well.

According to the Le Veqs, some of the men on the list, like Dawes and Banks, owned businesses; Dawes ran a cigar shop and Banks owned an express company that delivered mail, packages, and parcels. Spain and Thomas were both firemen. "We'll need to search their homes, businesses, and offices," Zahra said. "Alfred and I had already planned to use the days of Carnival to do some looking around. We'd heard everyone in the area goes to the balls and other events in the evenings, so we thought it might be a perfect time."

"Excellent idea," Archer said. He then turned to Drake and asked, "Did you bring the map?"

"Sure did." Drake unrolled a canvas that depicted New Orleans and the countryside. He then pointed out the homes of Isenbaum, Banks, and Thomas, who didn't live inside the city.

Zahra noted, "Their homes aren't very far apart."

"No, they aren't," said Archer.

Alfred studied the map and said, "Ideally, we'd search them all the same night. If we do them separate nights, more chances they'll get wind of us."

Everyone agreed.

Raimond said, "What about the offices? Those will be harder to infiltrate."

Zahra shook her head. "Not really. Most businesses have cleaning people. We find out who they employ, we masquerade as one of their employees, and we go in."

Philippe asked, "And if there are no cleaning people?"

Zahra shrugged, "We try something else. There isn't a person in this city who doesn't come in contact with our people in one form or another on a daily basis. We're servants, barbers, laundresses. Yes, we have quite a bit of territory to search, but we'll find a way in."

Zahra saw Raimond Le Veq's grin and asked easily, "What's the matter?"

"Nothing. I'm simply impressed by you. Were I not already married, my brother and I would be dueling at dawn."

Archer drawled, "Then it's good that you are, *mon frère,* because we'd be burying you at noon."

The siblings laughed, and Zahra simply shook her head. She noted that the quip even made the usually taciturn Alfred smile.

Zahra took them back to the discussion. "I have two young women on my staff concentrating on Isenbaum servants right now. I'll have them begin investigating gaining entry to the other homes on our list, too."

"Sounds good," Beau said. "How many staff do you have presently?"

"Six, but we'll need more. Archer mentioned bringing in some others to assist us."

"I'll send wires in the morning. I wanted to wait and see how many additional folks we might need."

Drake said to Zahra, "Your six servants plus you and Alfred make eight. Throw in the five of us and you have thirteen. Shouldn't that be enough?"

Archer pointed out, "But our faces are so well known we couldn't infiltrate a Sunday school class."

"Good point."

So it was agreed that Archer would contact his friends in order to add more numbers to their forces.

By the time the meeting ended, everyone involved was confident their mission could be accomplished. If there were Death Books anywhere near New Orleans, they would be found.

Zahra escorted the brothers back downstairs. "Isenbaum was very interested in who those carriages belonged to, so let's hope he isn't skulking in the trees."

"Only if he wants trouble," Alfred noted.

"Well, just be on the alert when you leave."

The Le Veqs nodded, then all except Archer departed the same way they'd entered. Moments later, Alfred left to meet his cousin across town to enjoy their night off.

Once Zahra and Archer were alone, he pulled her into his arms and looked down into her unmasked face. "I'd love to spend the night, but I'm riding with the veterans tonight. So I believe I shall kidnap you in the morning."

"For what purpose?" she asked, as if she didn't already know.

"For the purpose of pleasure, of course, and for us to get to know each other better."

"Still fishing for clues, are you?"

He grinned. "Who, me? Of course not."

"Liar," she teased. Leaning up, she kissed him softly. "I must be back on Wednesday morning and no later."

"That's fine. I'll be here bright and early."

"I'll be ready."

Archer lifted her chin so he could memorize her features for his dreams tonight. "Now, the most important question of the night."

"Which is?"

"Are you or are you not wearing drawers?"

She burst into laughter. Zahra loved his wit and the passion that ran through it. "A lady never tells," she tossed back saucily.

"But she does show. Come on, raise the gown."

Zahra chuckled. "I will not. You are too audacious for your own good, arrogant Frenchman."

He leaned down to kiss her smiling mouth,

then murmured with sensual invitation, "I'll give you a reward. . . ." Still feasting on her lips, his finger began drawing languid circles around her breasts.

"Then maybe I should reconsider. . . ." She fed herself on his marvelous kisses until her eyes grew heavy and her body began to respond in kind. Stepping back, she held his hot eyes, then slowly drew the silk up her legs, showing off her shoes, black stockings, sassy black garters, and the fact that she had on no drawers.

Archer's manhood tightened instantaneously. Mesmerized, he walked forward and grazed a slow hand over the curls before sliding it in between. Her soft gasp rendered him even harder. In response to the age-old call, she rose sinuously, holding her gown aside, her eyes locked with his.

"To receive your reward, your legs need to be wider, *chérie* . . ."

In response to his hot voice, Zahra's eyes slid closed and her legs widened wantonly. He was touching, stroking, circling, and gently penetrating her with such possessive boldness that she thought her whole body might burst into flame.

Then he was on his knees, giving her her reward, and she was standing against the wall, coming, and twisting, and crying out his name.

"That ought to hold you until I see you in the morning," he whispered, standing upright now, his hand gently soothing the pulsating spot between her brown thighs. *"Non?"*

"Yes," she breathed, still reverberating. "A diet of this every day could kill a woman."

"You're welcome," he said with a pleased smile.

Once she finally found the ability to focus her eyes and rid her brain of its passion-induced haze, she let her skirts fall. She didn't want to move.

"I'll see myself out, *papillon*."

"Good, because I can't take a step."

He kissed her on the cheek. "*Bonne nuit, chérie.* Get some sleep, because tomorrow there'll be plenty more where that came from."

"I can't wait. Good night, Archer."

And he was gone.

After his departure, Zahra forced herself to climb the staircase. As she passed the statue of Adam and Eve, she smiled knowingly.

Before going to her room, Zahra stuck her head in Matilda's door and found the young woman seated on the bed. Her eyes were red and swollen. "What's wrong, Matilda?"

"I let Mitchell hurt my feelings is all."

"You shouldn't give a minute of thought to that bigoted bully."

"I just hate it when he talks to me that way."

"I wasn't pleased with the way he spoke to me either, so he's banned from the premises. You won't have to worry about him being mean to you anymore."

"Thanks, Domino. Whores do have feelings."

"I know, and that's why I told him never to come back."

Matilda met Zahra's eyes. "I heard you down there singing the orgasm aria, as Stella calls it."

Zahra was appalled. "You did?"

"Folks probably heard you in Baton Rouge," she

pointed out, smiling. "Your Mr. Le Veq seems real nice. I can't imagine him speaking to you the way Mitchell spoke to me."

"I can't either," Zahra said plainly.

"Well, he could make me sing anytime."

Zahra laughed softly. "I'm going to spend the day with him tomorrow, so I may be gone when you get up. Will you tell the girls for me? I should be back Wednesday morning."

"I'll tell them. Alfred know you're going?"

"No, but I'll let him know before I do."

"Me, I'm going to write my mama and then sleep."

"Pleasant dreams, Matilda."

"Thanks, Domino. You rest up your voice. I'm thinking you'll be doing lots of singing while you're away."

Grinning, Zahra said, "You're getting to be as bad as the twins. I'll see you on Wednesday." Zahra departed and closed Matilda's door softly.

As it turned out, the only person who raised their voice the next morning was Alfred.

"Fire!"

Zahra shot awake. His voice rang out a second time. She left her bed and smelled smoke for the first time. She struggled into a robe and grabbed a domino and her handbag just as Alfred burst into the room. Zahra's eyes widened at the sight of his battered face and swollen eyes. "You have to go off the verandah. Can't go out the front."

Taking his word for it, she hastened to the French doors and snatched them open. He was in the process of pulling the mattress off her bed when she turned back to look and froze at the wall of fire raging in the hallway.

"Out the way!" he shouted.

He pushed by her and tossed the mattress off the verandah and down to the ground. Zahra was already swinging her legs over the wrought-iron railing. He joined her. Flinging an arm around her waist, he pulled her to him and jumped.

Hours later, Zahra and her shivering girls stood before the smoldering remains of Madame Domino's Gentleman's Club. According to the firemen, the blaze had been deliberately set. Even now the air was thick with the smell of the kerosene the arsonist had used as an accelerant. The sky-high flames had put on quite a show and drawn a sizeable crowd of curious onlookers, but now the policemen, the firemen, and the crowd had all departed, leaving the women alone in the cool dawn air. Zahra knew that had she and the girls been something other than whores, the city's aid groups would have been dispatched with blankets and hot coffee to comfort them, but since they were prostitutes they had to fend for themselves. With that in mind, she'd sent Alfred to the Hotel Christophe to see if Archer had any empty rooms available, but so far, he had yet to return.

"Guess we're out of business," Zahra lamented.

"Looks that way," Adair said sadly.

"Too bad about our whore red coach," Stella added glumly. "Glad the horses got out though."

Matilda said, "One of the policemen asked me if you'd had trouble with any customers lately, so I told him about Mitchell."

"Thank you, Matilda."

Of course, Isenbaum had been the first person to come to Zahra's mind when she'd learned the fire had been deliberately set. She had no proof, of course, but in her gut she knew it had been him or someone connected to him and his cronies. With the need for shelter at the top of her list, Zahra knew that wondering how the loss of the house would affect her operation was something she'd have to explore later, but that didn't stop the question from weighing on her anyway.

The women were huddled near the smoldering ruins for warmth when Alfred drove up in a flat-bed wagon. Beside him sat Sophie, and they cheered his arrival. Zahra was even more delighted to see Archer, in his signature black barouche, pull up behind the wagon and get out.

Sophie said with concern, "I didn't know anything about the fire until Alfred came to get me. Are you all right?"

"We're cold but glad to be alive. It was arson."

Archer asked her, "Are you sure you're not hurt?"

His concerned manner softened her heart. "I am certain."

She took one of the blankets Sophie had brought and draped it over her shivering shoulders. "Do you have any rooms you can rent us?" Zahra asked the madame.

"Yes, and for as long as you need them."

Relieved, she saw that the girls were all wrapped up and being helped into the wagon by Alfred.

Sophie asked her, "Are you going with us?"

Zahra looked to Archer, who smiled. She replied, "No."

Sophie offered up her own smile, than said, "Make sure she gets a hot bath, Archer."

"Yes, ma'am."

After Sophie's departure, Archer pulled her into his arms. He was so grateful she hadn't been hurt. "Let's get back to the hotel and settle you in."

"I've heard you have a wonderful bed. Is it big enough for two?"

"Oh, yes."

As they drove away, a melancholy Zahra surveyed the charred remains. Being Madame Domino had been fun and she'd had a good time, but she looked upon tonight's incident as providential. Being Madame Domino would be a hindrance to finding the Death Books because she wouldn't be able to move around the city at night, a necessity in her line of work, but now due to the fire, Madam Domino would be leaving New Orleans on a train going west never to return, so Zahra could get on with the search.

When Zahra reached Archer's apartments, she immediately fell tiredly into one of the large upholstered chairs. Every inch of her body was exhausted. Still wrapped in the blanket she felt capable of falling asleep right then and there, even though the sun was coming up. "If anyone tries to wake me before noon, would you kill them for me?"

"Most certainly."

"I'm glad no one was injured."

"So am I." When Alfred pounded on the door to tell him her place was on fire, Archer's heart had jumped into his throat. Only when he'd been assured that she was alive and well had he begun to breathe again.

"I don't have any proof," she was saying, "but Isenbaum was involved, I can taste it. We need to find out where he went after he left the club this evening."

Archer watched her with a fond smile. Even though she'd survived a fire and looked asleep on her feet, she was still focused on her mission. "How about you sleep first, then we'll discuss what's to be done."

"Okay," she replied tiredly. Stumbling to her feet, she made her way over to him, kissed him soundly, then headed off to the bedroom.

Archer was weary too, but he didn't have the luxury of returning to bed. He had a hotel to run. The knowledge that while he was working Zahra would be upstairs asleep in his bed—and might also be in his rooms at the end of the day—gave him all the incentive he needed, though, so with that in mind, he washed up and changed his clothes.

In his office, thoughts of her filled his mind. The final veil over her identity still had to be lifted. Who was the Butterfly? Would he ever know? She'd made it clear that he'd get no help from her in his search, and she'd been true to her word. That he could have lost her in an arson fire before having the opportunity to know her as well as he wanted did not sit well.

André came in through the open office door and announced, "Aristide wants to know if Domino wants breakfast."

Archer was glad to see him. "Welcome back.

Tell him she made me pledge to kill anyone who attempts to waken her before the noon hour."

André laughed, "I'll relay the message. I heard about the fire. I'm glad she and her girls were able to escape."

"So are they. Police are pointing to an arsonist. I'll fill you in in a moment. Were you able to see Mrs. Dunn?" Archer had sent André with a letter, hoping she would receive him.

"Only long enough for her to send this reply."

He handed Archer a short, handwritten missive; when he read it, it made him sigh with resignation. "She wants to be left alone and would prefer that any further inquiries into Oscar's death be halted. Permanently."

Archer tossed the note onto his desk.

"Are you going to honor her request?"

"What choice do I have? If the family can't be convinced of the need for an autopsy . . ." He shrugged and sighed again. "We'll never know now, and that's a pity."

André nodded in silent agreement. "So, tell me about the meeting."

André had been a trusted family friend and an unofficially adopted sibling for most of his adult years. Rai's best friend, Galeno Vachon, had rescued the then youngster André from a brothel and taken him home and paid for him to be educated. After serving as Rai's aide in the contraband camps established during the fading years of the war, André had followed Rai to the Sea Islands and then back to New Orleans.

Archer told him of the plans they'd formulated the night before. "The fire's going to make us alter things, but I'm sure she already has it worked out. She's an amazing woman, Dré."

"I agree."

"Oh, did I tell you I found out who she is?"

"No!"

"She's the Butterfly."

André's mouth dropped. "Truly?"

Archer nodded. "I was shocked as well."

André was still speechless.

"So, that part of the mystery is solved."

"And do you know who the Butterfly is?"

"No," Archer groused.

André grinned. "She's not making this easy for you, is she?"

"Not at all, but I'll figure it out."

"Before or after the Second Coming? According to everything I've heard, her fame is well deserved."

"I agree, but I'm a pretty fair investigator in my own right."

"Is that why she had to rescue you from that barn?"

The teasing was good natured, but Archer shot him a look nonetheless. "You're as bad as my brothers."

André smiled. "If you don't need anything else from me, I'm going to my apartment and get some sleep. I rode all night to get back here."

"I've some wires to send, but I think I'll wait until I speak with Zahra before sending them."

"Who's Zahra?"

"Madame Domino. It's the name she's chosen to go by now."

The confused André shook his head. "Okay.

You can explain that to me after I've had some sleep."

Archer nodded. "Go home. We'll speak later."

When Zahra awakened, she was so disoriented that it took her a moment to figure out where she was. Then she remembered the fire. Lying there in Archer's big bed, she let the memories of the night roll across her mind until every detail was clear. She and the girls had been lucky. They could have easily been consumed, and because they were whores, few people, if any, would have mourned their passing. Zahra wondered how her staff had fared. They'd all been on assignment last night, so their lives had not been in danger. She trusted Alfred had informed them all, Wilma included. She thought about his battered face and wondered how it had come to be that way, but she knew she'd get the answer when she saw him. Because of the fire their plans for the Death Books would have to be altered somewhat, but she'd think about that later. Right now, she needed to wash, then search out food for her hungry stomach. Tossing back the coverlet, she got up.

Zahra was wearing a long paisley robe she'd taken from Archer's wardrobe when he arrived with her lunch on a tray. Alfred was with him; his face looked as bruised and beaten as it had last night. "What happened to your face? Were you hurt during the fire?"

He gave her a negative shake of his head. "Got into a fight."

"With whom?"

"The husband of a woman I've been seeing. Didn't know she was married."

Zahra didn't know he'd been seeing anyone. "Did he have to be hospitalized?" She could only imagine what the other man must look like.

"No. Not a scratch on him. I didn't defend myself, so he got in some pretty good licks."

"You didn't defend yourself?"

"She was his wife, so I had it coming. I'll be all right in a few days."

Speechless, Zahra stared at him, then over at Archer, who shrugged and said, "As a man, I understand it perfectly."

"You're a better man than I, Alfred."

He smiled through his swollen lip and said, "Got good news, though. Wilma will be by later with some clothes, and I found the strongbox from your office in the rubble. The heat fused the top so it can't be opened, but otherwise it looks okay. Mr. Le Veq is sure his brother can use welding tools on it."

Zahra sent up a silent cry of thanks. "Hallelujah! I can pay Wilma for more dresses, and maybe there will even be enough left over to give the girls money to help them start over somewhere else."

Alfred asked, "We're not going to reopen?"

Zahra shook her head. "No. We'd have to rebuild, or find another place that we'd have to furnish and do all the other things necessary to make it as fine as the old place, and we just don't have the time."

"What about the operation?"

"That won't change. I'm still committed to finding those books and getting them to the president." She also planned to continue in her role as the spider for Henry Adams and his volunteers. The times were too volatile for the web to cease disseminating its vital information.

While Zahra ate lunch and moaned with delight over the succulent quiche and catfish Aristide had prepared, they discussed how to alter the plan.

A few minutes into the discussion, a knock sounded on Archer's door. *"Entrez!"* he called out.

In walked the Le Veq siblings and a woman who resembled the portrait on Archer's wall.

A smiling but confused-looking Archer stood and greeted her with a kiss on her unlined cheek. "Afternoon, Mama. What brings you here?"

"I came to meet Zahra."

Zahra was surprised and even more so when Juliana announced, "Anyone who is not female will please leave the room."

There were a few guffaws, but the men complied.

Once their departure was complete, Zahra met the smiling black eyes of the Le Veq matriarch and wished she were wearing something besides Archer's robe.

Juliana took off her gloves and sat at the table across from Zahra in the seat vacated by Archer. "How are you, dear?"

"I'm well. Please pardon my attire. I lost everything in the fire but the nightgown on my back. So did my girls."

"So I've heard. And your plans?"

Zahra wondered where these questions were leading. "Why do you ask?"

"Because I'd like to help if I can."

"Why?"

"Because you saved my son's life, Zahra Lafayette, and I owe you the world."

Zahra was stunned. "How do you know my name?"

"Do not tell my sons, but they are not the only intelligence gatherers in the House of Le Veq." Juliana smiled.

"You are the Henry Adams spider, and I am one of the people who feed your web."

"And your sons don't know?"

"My dear Zahra, if you ever have children, keep your own counsel on some things. If you do, they can't interfere by attempting to save you from yourself."

Zahra smiled. So this was Juliana Le Veq. Her sons would undoubtedly throw fits if her secrets were revealed. "Are you ever going to tell them?"

She shrugged her elegantly gowned shoulders. "I've learned to never say never, but not in the foreseeable future, not if I have a choice."

Zahra shook her head in absolute amazement. "I applaud you."

"And I applaud you. I'm also honored to meet you. Had I known Madame Domino and the Butterfly were one and the same I wouldn't have been so upset with Archer about being seen with you."

"I understand appearances, ma'am, but I was still myself underneath."

Juliana paused. "Forgive an old woman for being of her times and class."

"I don't fault you. We agree that few mothers want their sons to be seen in public with a known whore, but aren't placees whores in their own ways?"

Juliana's face slipped into a rueful smile. "Tell that to our men. You are quite formidable."

"As are you. I believe we're going to get on just fine."

And they did get along fine for over an hour, discussing Zahra's future plans, the war, and the contributions made by female spies, both Black and White, to the Union cause—women like freed slaves Mary Touvestre and Mary Elizabeth Bower.

There was a knock on the door.

Juliana sang, "Come in."

Archer stuck his head in and asked, "Have you two forgotten that we're cooling our heels out here?"

"No, dear, but Zahra and I are getting along famously. That should put the sun back into your stormy face. You're behaving more and more like Raimond daily. I'd see someone about that were I you."

The defeated Archer hung his head.

That night, as Zahra lay in bed next to Archer, she yawned. "I'm still trying to catch up on my sleep."

He pulled her close and kissed the top of her head. "Then I'll let you sleep, but tomorrow I won't be so kind."

She smiled contentedly. "I like your mother."

"She seems to adore you. What were the two of you talking about so long this afternoon?"

"Oh, a little of this and a bit of that. Women things."

"I see," he said, though by his skeptical tone it was clear to Zahra that he did not.

"We didn't discuss you, if that has you worried," she replied.

"I'm not worried. I know what a good son I am."

Zahra chuckled and said sleepily, "Swelled-headed Frenchman."

He gave her a soft pinch on the butt.

She elbowed him in the ribs. "Be nice or I'll tell your mother."

"Okay," he chuckled. "Get some sleep, *chérie*."

She cuddled closer and whispered, "Night, Archer."

A few minutes later, they were both snoring.

The next morning, Zahra and the girls had breakfast in the hotel's staff dining room. Afterwards, Zahra started the process of saying goodbye. She'd informed them the night before that she wouldn't be reopening the house, and although the decision had saddened them, they were realists. Beau Le Veq had been able to open the fire-damaged strong box. Out of the money that remained, Zahra gave each of the women one hundred dollars to help them start over in a new place. When she finished, everyone, including Zahra, was in tears over the breakup of their unconventional family.

"You've been good to us, Domino," Chloe declared as she gave Zahra a fierce hug.

"And you all have been good to me," Zahra responded. And they had been. They'd also given her quite an education—especially Naomi and Salome. "Where are you headed, Chloe?"

"Chicago. No one knows me there. Maybe find a man who won't mind my age or that I'm from Virginia."

The girls had varying plans: Adair and Stella were off to New York to try their hand at being on stage. They thought they might find an audience there for their songs and recitations.

Matilda was going back home to Pennsylvania to take care of her sick mama. "Now that she's sick she doesn't much care about me being a whore anymore, long as I'm there to take care of her."

The tall, dark-skinned Lovey was headed for Canada. "My brother has a farm in a place called Amherstburgh. Think I'll go up for a visit and scare him to death. Then I don't know what I'll do. Maybe do like Chloe and find a man, start a family."

The twins, however, had definite plans. "We're getting married!" they said excitedly in unison.

Everyone stared.

Zahra was afraid to ask, "To whom?"

"A Mormon named Uriah Bennett. We met him one night at the house."

Zahra asked, "Which one of you is he marrying?"

"Both of us, Domino. Haven't you heard? Mormons can have more than one wife."

Zahra hadn't heard, and she shook her head.

Stella asked, "How old is he?"

"Sixty."

Adair drawled, "He'll be dead in a month."

The twins didn't think the quip was very funny, but the rest of the women howled until tears rolled down their cheeks.

# Chapter 11

The girls left on the next morning's train, and Zahra began preparations for her own temporary departure. She'd already decided that Madame Domino would have to disappear permanently, but she hadn't worked out the details of how it would be accomplished until she'd had an afternoon talk with Juliana. The plan they'd settled on was a simple one.

"Alfred is going to drive me to the train," Zahra explained to Archer that evening in his suite. "I'll take it to Baton Rouge, get off, transform myself into the country mouse daughter of your mother's old friend, and take the next train back to New Orleans. If all goes well, I'll be back on the three o'clock train tomorrow."

He shrugged. "Sounds simple. Then what?"

"Your mother, and you, probably, will meet me at the train here and take me to her home."

"You're going to be staying with Mother?"

Zahra laughed at the delight shining in his dark eyes. "Yes, I'm going to be her companion until your stepfather returns in April."

"Ah. Where will you sleep?"

"At your mother's."

"A pity."

She rolled her eyes. "You are insatiable."

"Yes, I am, and so are you." Then he paused. "Mama has a good-sized house, and there are many hidden places where you can spread your wings for me and we won't be disturbed."

"Archer, I will not be singing the orgasm aria in your mother's house."

He laughed, "The what?"

"Orgasm aria. The girls call it that." The recollection made her wonder about her girls and where they might be on their respective journeys. For the short time they were together, Lovey and the others were the sisters she'd never had. She missed them already but wished them Godspeed.

"Where are you, Zahra?" he asked softly.

Zahra met his concerned eyes. She wasn't accustomed to having someone so attuned to her. "Just thinking about the girls."

"Missing them?"

She nodded. "Probably will for a while."

He came over and took her in his arms, then kissed the top of her hair. "They're a good bunch. I'm sure they'll do fine."

"I know, but it doesn't stop me from missing them." Then she backed out of Archer's arms and wiped at the telling moisture in her eyes.

"Goodness, when did I become so sentimental? This is all your fault, Frenchman."

"Mine? Why?"

"Because you're the only one here."

He laughed and eased her back against his heart. "I sort of like the sentimental Butterfly. I also like the razor-carrying version, too."

She chuckled against his chest. "And the nude version? Where is she on the list?"

His face widened with mock surprise. "There's a nude version? Where? May I see her, please?"

Giggling like an adolescent, she said, "You are such a loon."

"Loons mate for life, did you know that?"

She paused and searched his eyes. "Really? Well, if I see a female loon, I'll send her your way."

He smacked her playfully on the behind. "Sassy woman."

She enjoyed their play but was immediately sobered by the knowledge that once the mission was over, there'd be no more of this.

"A doubloon for your thoughts."

She shook her head and placed it back on his chest. "It was nothing."

In the silence that followed, he asked softly, "You are coming back from Baton Rouge, aren't you?"

Zahra closed her eyes and unconsciously tightened her arms around him. "Yes, I'm coming back." But the time was coming when she wouldn't be. She didn't want to think about that now. "Do you still wish to see the nude version?"

She heard the low rumble of humor in his chest. He lifted her chin, and she swore she saw his heart in his eyes. "Thought you'd never ask."

Zahra raised herself on her toes so she could kiss him, and as it deepened, he swung her up into his strong arms and carried her to the bedroom.

The following morning, Archer watched her dress for her journey. The idea that she might not return was still in the back of his mind, but he pushed it aside. Knowing the threat the Death Books held, his worries were unfounded; she'd return, if only to find the books. Once that was accomplished the real battle would begin, but he set that aside for now, too.

"What are your plans for the day?" she asked, tying on the black domino that matched the black traveling costume she'd borrowed from Sable. Wilma had altered it to suit Zahra's needs.

"Help with preparations for a rally the Republican Party is having to denounce the violence."

"I thought you resigned your position with the party?"

"I did, but the hotel is hosting the speaker's luncheon."

"Ah." Her domino secured, she turned from the mirror and said, "Please be careful. Those thugs aren't above shooting into the crowd."

"I know. It's happening all over. I promise to be in one piece when you step off the train."

"I'm holding you to that."

"Question."

"Yes."

"You won't be masked when you return. How are you going to keep from being recognized by anyone who may know you as Butterfly?"

"I've been thinking about that, too. Being your mother's companion isn't as public a position as being Domino. I'm hoping to stay as much in the background as possible because that's the only option I have at this point. I must find those books. My personal safety is secondary."

Archer understood her dilemma, but he didn't agree with her last statement. Her personal safety was of the utmost importance to him. At least having her near Juliana meant that he and his brothers would be able to keep a close watch on her.

Since she appeared to be finished dressing, he asked, "Are you ready to go?"

"Yes."

He walked over and took her in his arms. He looked down at the face that had turned his life upside down. Never having known such strong emotion for a woman before, he lightly traced her mouth, then the eyes of her mask. "I'm going to miss Madame Domino."

"Then how about I save the domino I'm wearing? That way, you can see her whenever you like."

He smiled like a pleased male. "Good idea."

"I must go," she said softly. "I'll see you when I return." They shared a long, fervent kiss, then Zahra hurried away.

Archer went to the window and looked down on the street. He could see Alfred waiting beside the rented coach. When Zahra returned to the city under her country mouse persona to take the position as Juliana's companion, Alfred would be hired as Juliana's new driver and thus remain close to Zahra's side. The other members of her staff had been divided up between Archer's hotel, his mother's household staff, and Sable and Rai's orphanage. Their unfamiliar faces made them perfect for the positions; more importantly, the plans Zahra and Alfred had set into motion before the fire wouldn't be interrupted. Alfred's cousin Roland had found work at Sophie's place. His people were also spread across the city posing in various occupations until needed.

Archer turned his attention back to the busy street and saw her getting into the coach. Even though she'd only be gone overnight, he was pining for her already.

According to the plan, Zahra gave Alfred a big hug on the depot platform. She wanted everyone to see Madame Domino leaving town, even the biddies that had hissed at her when she was standing in line to buy her ticket from the agent. Her ticket designated Chicago as her final destination, so she worked that into her act too.

"If you're ever in Chicago, stop in and see me," she said to him as they broke the embrace.

Looking appropriately grim, Alfred shook his head. "I will. You take care of yourself, now."

"I will."

Alfred walked away, and Zahra waited for the train to arrive.

When it finally made its appearance belching smoke and embers from its stacks, Zahra got aboard and headed for the gambling car. No decent conductor was going to allow a masked whore to sit with the God-fearing passengers, so she'd have to settle for traveling with the godless ones.

The car was already filled with cigar smoke and the train hadn't even left the depot. The interior was no better or worse than ones she'd traveled in before, but at least it was clean. There were tables, chairs, and a bar with a bartender selling drinks. She had no idea how many people would eventually occupy the space, but as a woman traveling alone, she knew it best to be nice but to stay on her guard.

She took a seat at a table near a partially opened window and looked out. Passengers were still boarding. She saw tearful partings of men and women, and a woman clutching the hand of an adorable, chocolate-skinned little boy hurrying to get on. Her attention was then caught by the passengers entering the smoking car. There were Black and White men sporting fine, gentlemanly attire and laborers wearing faded work clothes and mud-stained brogans. There were even a few women, all looking to be soiled doves like herself. However, when Etienne Barber stepped inside, she cursed silently. Sensing her smooth little plan was about to become wrinkled, she met his eyes, and his immediately turned hostile. She hoped he had the sense to steer clear of her, because she would shoot him again. With that in mind, she slipped her hand into the pocket of her black skirt and waited.

She didn't have to wait long. To her displeasure he strutted over, stood right next to her chair, and in a voice loud enough for everyone to hear, said dismissively, "Well, if it isn't the whore."

Zahra could see that he'd caught everyone's attention. She assumed he was pleased by that, but she pointedly ignored him and turned her masked eyes towards the window.

He kept on, "Heard you and the rest of your whores were burned out. Couldn't have happened to a more deserving *bitch!*"

The force of Zahra's right cross connecting with his groin made him squeal like a fat piglet caught in a fence. He dropped to his knees. Holding his injured anatomy and keening in tremendous pain, he rolled on the floor of the car, gasping, bug-eyed and pale.

The rest of the passengers shook off their shock, then began to laugh. They had no idea what had precipitated the confrontation between the man and the whore in the black domino, but the whore had won this round, and for them it had been a good show. Short, but good; one they'd gleefully describe to their friends and family when they reached their destinations.

Zahra had no more trouble out of Barber; in fact, to the added amusement of the other travelers, he dragged himself to a table on the far side of the room and collapsed into a chair. She was content.

It was dark when the train pulled into Baton Rouge, and Zahra wondered how long it might take her to find a room for the night. She'd never been here before and knew nothing about the city. She and Juliana had failed to take that fact into account when they'd put the plan together, but she was confident she'd find somewhere to lay her head eventually. The train would resume its journey in the morning, but until then all of the passengers had to depart. Barber had recovered enough to shoot her simmering looks of contempt, but he didn't open his mouth or attempt to approach her. Holding her tapestry carpetbag and black cape, she stood and joined the rest of the passengers moving towards the exit. A few of the men stepped back politely to let Zahra depart ahead of them, and she gave them a smile of thanks.

When Zahra stepped out into the night air, she glanced back and saw Barber standing on the platform watching her, but she ignored him and joined the large group of women slipping off into the cover of the dark trees to take care of their needs. Zahra had other needs however. Distancing herself from the rest until she found a private spot she removed her cape and set it at her feet.

She quickly untied the domino, but held it with her teeth because she didn't want to lose it in the dark. Moving precisely, she undid the button on the waist band of her skirt, stepped out of the skirt, reversed it so that the blue inside was now the outside, stepped back into it and secured the waistband button. Bending, she opened the carpetbag, removed a blue, short-waisted jacket, took off her black jacket, and turned the bag inside out so that the paisley inside became the outside. She stuffed her black jacket and the domino inside. After shrugging into the blue jacket, she reversed her cape, making it now dun brown, and pulled up the hood.

Now she was ready. Making sure she exited the trees from a different spot than where she'd entered, she stepped back onto the dimly lit platform. Sure enough there stood Barber waiting near the trees where he'd seen Domino disappear. She smiled to herself and walked right by him.

The depot was badly lit, but there was just enough light for her to see the cabs with their lit driving lanterns lined up waiting for fares. Most of the drivers she approached wouldn't even look her way—the cabbies practiced segregation, she supposed—so stalking off, she saw two Black drivers and their poor-looking cabs waiting a distance away. She headed towards them, only to see one snapped up by a well-dressed man and woman.

She yelled at the cab that remained, waving and running towards it, hoping to catch his attention. It worked. Upon seeing her, he set his horse in her direction, and a grateful Zahra slowed to a walk. As she climbed in, and the old man pulled away from the depot, she saw a perturbed looking Barber standing on the platform, and she smiled to herself again.

The elderly cabbie introduced himself as Mr. Poole, and a short while later they reached the boardinghouse he'd recommended. She paid him, and he drove off into the darkness.

The owner of the boardinghouse, a tiny, brown-skinned woman with a bulldog face, showed Zahra the room. Zahra didn't care that the place was tiny; she simply wanted it to be clean. Pulling back the quilts and sheet on the small bed, she didn't see any bugs scurrying away, nor did she see anything moving around on the well-swept floor.

The landlady, who'd introduced herself earlier as Bitsy, asked, "This do for you?"

A satisfied Zahra nodded and paid her for one night's stay. "How do I get a cab to the train depot in the morning?" she asked Bitsy.

"I can send my grandson over to get Old Man Poole to come take you, or if you don't mind a wagon, my brother Tommy is going to the depot tomorrow to ship some livestock. You can catch a ride over with him."

"Who's more reliable?"

The bulldog face smiled. "Tommy. Old Man Poole don't get up 'til noon."

"Then Tommy has a passenger. I'll pay him, of course."

"That's fine. Anything else?"

"Not that I can think of."

"See you in the morning, then."

She closed the door, and Zahra released a sigh of relief. She'd made it.

The ride back was far less dramatic, thanks to Tommy and his livestock. The livestock turned

out to be pigs, and Zahra arrived at the Baton
Rouge station seated up front holding a small sow
and two piglets on her lap. She thanked Tommy,
paid him, and went to buy her ticket.

As Zahra made her way through the small depot, the passengers on the platform gave her
wide berth. At first Zahra attributed it to her attire, but when she reminded herself that Madame
Domino was no more and that she was presently
attired as primly as a deacon's daughter, she figured out what all the sour faces around her were
about. She smelled like pigs! Instead of being
alarmed, she found the situation amusing. It also
worked to her advantage. Her pungent clothing
and shiny, paint-free face gave credence to her
role as a country girl traveling to the big city of
New Orleans for the first time. Moreover, because none of the other passengers wished to
ride the ninety-mile journey anywhere near her,
Zahra had her row of seats, and the ones directly
in front and in back, all to herself. Smiling, she
looked out the window and settled in for the
ride.

The train arrived in New Orleans right on time
at a little past three in the afternoon. Remembering her role, she got off the train and peered
around, as if not knowing where to go or what
to do.

The White conductor who'd been kind to her
during the journey in spite of her smell stopped
and said, "Do you need some help, miss?"

Raising the pitch of her voice, as she'd been doing since stepping off the train in Baton Rouge

yesterday, she said, "I'm not sure. I'm supposed to be meeting a friend of my mama's, but I don't know what she looks like."

"What's her name?"

"Mrs. Le Veq Vincent."

He looked impressed. "They're a very prominent family. Come on with me, maybe she's waiting on the other end of the platform."

Carpetbag in hand, and wearing what had to be the ugliest pale blue jacket and skirt she'd ever had the misfortune of wearing, Zahra let the conductor lead the way. They didn't have to go far.

"I believe that is Mrs. Le Veq Vincent there. I've seen her on the train many times."

Zahra saw Juliana and Archer standing by the depot. Zahra fed her eyes on the tall, handsome Archer, then, remembering herself, asked the conductor, "You sure that's her?"

"Positive." He raised his hand to catch Juliana's attention; she was pretending not to know what Zahra looked like. The conductor escorted Zahra over and said to the Le Veqs, "Mrs. Vincent, this young woman said you were to meet her here at the platform?"

Juliana smiled. "Are you Zahra Crane?"

Zahra nodded. "Yes, ma'am."

Juliana hugged her and said, "Of course you are. Welcome to New Orleans. You look just like your mother, Hanna. This is my son, Archer." Then she drew away, and her nose wrinkled.

Archer asked, "What on earth is that smell?"

"Pigs," Zahra said brightly. "I had to ride to the

depot with my landlady's brother and his pigs. I had a cute little sow and her piglets on my lap the whole way."

The smiling conductor departed, and Zahra kept up a running conversation all the way to the buggy.

Archer was amazed at Zahra's transformation. Everything about her was different: her voice, mannerisms, the way she walked in that country ugly blue suit she was wearing. There was nothing about her that even suggested she'd been Madame Domino.

Once they were safely inside Archer's barouche, Zahra turned to them and asked in her signature black velvet voice, "So, what have I missed?"

He shook his head. She wasn't a butterfly; she was a chameleon.

The first thing Zahra was instructed to do upon entering Juliana's house was to bathe. Juliana waved her elegantly manicured hand in front of her nose to shoo away the stench and said, "Archer, show her up to Sable's room. I'll have Little Reba heat some water. Lord, Zahra, you smell."

Zahra smiled and stood there, matching grins with Archer, who said, "Mama's right, you know."

"Too smelly for a kiss?" she asked.

"Maybe."

Cocking her head, she put her hands on her hips.

He laughed. Coming closer, he eased her into the welcoming circle of his arms and kissed the top of her head. "I missed you, Madam Smelly."

"Missed you, too."

"Where'd you get that awful suit?"

"Wilma. It was the only traveling costume she had."

"I need to take you shopping and get you a proper wardrobe now that you're Mother's companion."

They pulled back and gazed at each other for a long moment, then he kissed her slowly and thoroughly. "Welcome back," he murmured.

Just as the kiss began to deepen, they heard "Ahem!"

Zahra jumped from embarrassment, and Archer gave his mother a pleading look, to which she responded by saying easily, "Take her up to the room and come right back so you can carry the water when it's ready. You all can *talk* after dinner this evening."

Pouting like a six-year-old, Archer took the silently chuckling Zahra by the hand and led her up the staircase.

The room was as beautiful as she'd expected. It was done in ivory and gold, of all colors, and in a way that was as subtle as it was elegant. "The colors make me feel right at home."

At first Archer was confused, and then he understood. "These were the same colors of the Club, aren't they? Never thought about that before. This started out as Rai's room, then Sable had it for awhile. Now, it's yours."

The layout, with the French doors and big canopy bed, reminded her of her room at Domino's, and once again she thought how difficult going back to her shack would be after being surrounded by all this luxury. She placed her carpetbag on the seat of the dressing table and took a seat beside it. "I'm tired," she said, yawning.

"How was the journey?"

"Uneventful except for Tommy's pigs and a human pig named Etienne Barber."

"Barber was on the train? Did he bother you?"

"Of course, but after I buried a fist in his piggies, he crawled away and left me alone."

Archer laughed. "Details, please!"

So she began at the beginning. By the time she got to the end of her tale, his laughter was echoing around the room. "Oh, I wish I had been there to see his face." Walking over, he gave her a quick kiss. "I'll go see about the water."

Smiling, she watched him leave.

Dinner that evening was a fun affair. All of the brats showed up, as did André Renaud, Raimond, Sable, and their children. Baby Desiré was an adorable five-year-old. Her big sisters, Blythe and Hazel, were poised young women, and the silent, eighteen-year-old man-child Cullen, with his watchful eyes, reminded Zahra of Alfred.

Zahra had seen Alfred earlier in the evening, and he'd welcomed her back with a rare smile and a hug. According to Juliana, he would officially be hired tomorrow as the household's new driver. He'd been invited to the dinner too, but he'd chosen to take his meal in the kitchen with Juliana's cook, Little Reba.

After dessert, Cullen drove his sisters home, and

the adults, including Juliana and Sable, settled in to discuss the plans surrounding the Death Books. It was decided that they would follow the advice Alfred had given at their last gathering and search the homes of Isenbaum, Banks, and Thomas on the same night if possible. They conceded there was no guarantee that all the homes would be empty at the same time.

Archer said, "But the Democrats are having their own ball this year. I think we can assume Isenbaum and his friends will be attending."

"Do you know the date?" Zahra asked.

"No, but I can find out tomorrow."

She then asked Alfred, "How are Caleb and Jesse doing with the shadowing?"

Because Jesse wasn't from New Orleans, all of Isenbaum's visitors were strangers to him, so he'd jotted down their physical descriptions and added a description of their vehicles. Archer and his brothers were able to put names to most of the descriptions because they fit men known to be either members of the local Democratic Party or city officials. The remaining descriptions were of persons unknown to any of the Le Veqs.

Alfred said, "This man Jesse refers to as barrel-chested and tall, and driving a beat-up buckboard, has been at the house every evening. According to the log, the man comes around at about the same time each time. Seven p.m." Alfred looked up, as if seeking an explanation, but no one had one because no one knew who the man might be.

Drake offered a solution. "How about I join

your man tomorrow night? Maybe I'll recognize him."

Zahra answered, "That's a good idea, Drake. Thank you." She then asked Alfred, "How are Suzette and Clare coming with the servants?"

"Nothing to report yet. I'm meeting them at the city market tomorrow."

Zahra nodded. All in all, it was a good start.

Beau Le Veq and André Renaud had slipped out of the meeting earlier. It was their night to join the patrols that had been formed to combat the nightly visitations of the White Leagues, but the normally gregarious Philippe hadn't said a word all evening.

His mother must have noticed. "Philippe, are you feeling poorly? You don't look well."

He shrugged listlessly.

Archer and Drake began chuckling.

Raimond asked, "What's so funny?"

Archer pointed at his baby brother, who in truth was taller than all of his siblings, and said, "Him. He's mourning."

Taking exception to the flippancy, Juliana said pointedly, "Archer, there's nothing humorous or amusing about someone's death."

Drake stepped up for his brother. "No one died, Mama. Phillie's mourning Naomi and Salome."

"Who?"

Zahra hid her laughter behind her hand. Philippe looked at once angry and bereft over having his business bandied about this way.

A confused Raimond asked, "Are they the twins from Madame Domino's?"

Archer said, "Yep."

Raimond leaned back and barked a loud laugh.

Philippe snapped, "It's not funny!"

Which of course made his brothers howl louder.

Even Juliana had trouble keeping her smile from showing.

Philippe turned to his laughing brothers and declared, "You three baboons can kiss my arse!" And he stormed out. Next came the sound of the front door slamming closed.

Sable asked, "So where did the twins go after the fire?"

"Utah. To marry a sixty-year-old Mormon named Uriah Bennett."

Juliana echoed, "Sixty?"

Zahra nodded. "Adair said the poor man will be dead in a month."

The room exploded in laughter. Even Alfred chuckled.

Shortly afterwards, Juliana yawned and told everyone good night. "Zahra, I will see you in the morning."

The others made their departures, and once they were all gone, Archer and Zahra were left alone sitting in front of the parlor fireplace, enjoying the flames, the crackling warmth, and the nearness of each other.

Zahra had her weary head resting on Archer's shoulder. "I could sleep for a week."

He kissed her forehead. "One last question, Madame Spy, and you can go to bed. Do you still want my friends to help us search?"

"If they can get here in the next few days."

"All right. I'll wire them first thing tomorrow."

She nodded, then said, "I would love to sit here with you all night, but I must go."

"Can I walk you to your room?"

She raised up and gave him a sleepy smile before shaking her head no.

He kissed her softly. "Why not?"

"Because as sleepy as I am, spending the night with you is still tempting, and I don't want us to end up in the woodshed with your mama in the morning. So you stay away from my bedroom door."

He chuckled softly, "Familiar with my maneuvers, are you?"

"Quite." She returned his kiss. "So good night, Frenchman."

"Good night, *chérie*."

They shared a few more kisses, then Zahra floated up the stairs and Archer left the house, closing his mama's door softly behind him.

When Zahra awakened the next morning, it was still dark. Feeling the chill in the air, she put on the night robe she'd been given yesterday by Juliana and walked across the cold floor over to the fireplace. She stuck the poker into the low-burning embers to see if she could wake them up, then added pieces of kindling. That did the trick, so she quickly crawled back into the bed and buried herself beneath the warm sheets and quilts.

The sleep had left her rested and refreshed. Were she at home, she wouldn't be lying here like a lady of leisure: She'd be up already, boiling water for the day's laundry and treating herself to grits and whatever else she could find to accompany it for breakfast. There'd be no beignets or café. Archer wouldn't be taking her shopping later either. Who had time for shopping when there was a pile of shirts to scrub? She gently rubbed the skin on her palms and fingers. The calluses and redness had finally disappeared, but she knew it wouldn't take long for the lye to return them to their normal state.

Zahra sighed. She knew she was going home when this affair ended; she was committed to that, but what should she do about Archer? Who would have imagined that she'd wind up in love with the *gens de coleur* she'd rescued from General Brandon Crete's barn? Certainly not she, yet here she lay, in his mama's house, madly in love with everything about him: his intelligence, his wit, his commitments to his family and to the future of the race. In her mind, there was not a finer man in the state of Louisiana, or anywhere else, for that matter. But she still planned on turning her back on whatever future they might have had together. Men like him did not marry swamp rats. The knowledge that Raimond had married Sable, a former slave, was a plus, but Sable appeared to have the grace and social niceties necessary to be the wife of a man as distinguished as Raimond Le Veq. Zahra wasn't certain about herself. Yes, she had set many a grand table while posing as a servant during the war; she knew which fork went where and where to place the dinner plates and such, but for instance, at last night's dinner, she'd had no idea what all the forks had been for! Dessert forks, salad forks. She'd wound up discreetly watching Sable. Whenever Sable had picked up a fork, so had Zahra. She'd done the same thing during her dinners with Archer. Yes, she was a spy and accustomed to masking shortcomings, but in this case she was also a fraud.

In her own defense, Zahra knew every which way to skin rabbits, how to build a snare, and she could scale and gut a fish in no time flat, but she didn't think that kind of knowledge was a necessity here in the House of Le Veq. She'd done well posing as the elegant and sophisticated Domino, but it had been a role. The real Zahra Lafayette didn't even wear corsets, for heaven's sake! And she preferred bare feet to shoes any day of the week.

Yet the thought of leaving Archer and never seeing him again left her morose. She supposed she should stop worrying over it, because no matter what her heart had to say, her mind was made up. Once this was done, she'd be going back to South Carolina to see her parents and getting on with the rest of her life.

Zahra had fun shopping with Archer and Juliana. They went to all the fashionable shops in the city, including Wilma's, where Archer introduced Zahra as his mother's new companion and secretary, Zahra Crane.

Juliana said, "We need to add some pieces to her wardrobe."

Wilma smiled. "It's nice to meet you, Miss Crane."

"Nice to meet you, too," the gregarious Zahra Crane replied.

"What will you be needing for her precisely, Mrs. Vincent?"

Archer answered for his mother. "Everything."

Zahra shook her head. "Just the necessities."

"Everything."

"No," she said firmly. "I'm sure clothes here cost a whole lot more than they do back home, and I don't want to be paying Mrs. Vincent back for the rest of my life."

Juliana said, "But Zahra, dear, the clothes are a gift."

Zahra Crane's face brightened. "Truly?"

Smiling, Juliana nodded. "Yes. So, Mrs. Gray, why don't you take her measurements, and Archer and I will look at your pattern books."

They spent an hour at Wilma's shop. Zahra thought Archer's talent for picking just the right style and color bordered on the magical. Whether he was eyeing capes, day gowns, or traveling costumes, she and Juliana wholeheartedly approved everything he selected.

When Wilma left them to add the selections to Archer's and Juliana's bills, Juliana said, "Do you see why I rarely go shopping without him, Zahra? Now, Raimond is a different matter. Don't ever shop with him. He'll want to put you in the ugliest colors and patterns imaginable. Ask his poor wife."

Archer added, "And he'll get angry because Sable doesn't wish to be mistaken for a circus clown."

Wilma returned with a receipt, which she handed to Juliana. "I will have Miss Crane's garments in a week's time even if I have to hire extra seamstresses."

"Thank you, Mrs. Gray," Juliana said.

"Miss Crane, again, it was nice meeting you."

Zahra smiled. "Same here. Good-bye."

After leaving Wilma's, they headed up the street towards the Hotel Christophe for lunch.

Archer said, "You two go on ahead. I need to send those wires off. I'll meet you at the hotel."

The women nodded, and he headed across the busy street to the telegraph office.

The sidewalks were crowded as they always were at midday, and Zahra and Juliana had to walk slowly in order to move in pace with all the people ahead of them. They didn't mind; they enjoyed each other's company, so they chatted along the way. The walk's two-way pedestrian traffic made for even more congestion, and sometimes folks going north bumped into folks going south. Zahra was accidentally bumped by a tall, older man in work clothes, who immediately reached out to grab her as she stumbled. "Sorry, miss. You okay?"

"Yes, I am. Thank you." And then, as she looked up into his weathered blue eyes, a cold dread coursed through her. She knew him. Immediately dropping her eyes lest he recognize her as well, she quickly made move to resume her journey, but he touched her arm to delay her departure.

"Do I know you?" he asked.

"I don't think so."

Without another word, Zahra moved off, and she and Juliana continued up the street.

Juliana said, "He must have mistaken you for someone else."

"No. He knew me." Zahra's heart was pounding. She really wanted to turn around to see if he was still standing in that spot watching her, but she knew better than to give herself away so easily.

Juliana must have picked up on Zahra's serious tone, because she asked with concern, "Who is he?"

"Confederate General Brandon Crete, the man who hung Archer in that barn."

Juliana appeared stunned.

"Don't look back, Juliana."

"Don't worry, dear. I won't."

"Are you certain it was Crete?" Archer asked gravely as they sat waiting for their orders to arrive.

"I don't forget faces, Archer. Especially not that one."

Juliana asked, "Maybe he won't be able to place you. And if he does, will it matter to him? He didn't appear to be a prosperous man. Maybe he's a simple resident now and is too busy rebuilding his life to worry much over a woman from his Rebel past."

"He *was* dressed like a common laborer."

"Then maybe Mama's right," Archer said. "But even if Crete does remember you eventually, he really lost nothing that night in the barn, except me. I never got the maps I was sent in after."

"But I did."

Archer stared. "What? You had them the entire time we were together?"

"Yes, and the North put them to good use during Sherman's campaign. The Rebs couldn't have been pleased knowing the Union army knew as much about the South's troop deployments and fortifications as the South did."

Archer was impressed by her admission. "So what do you want to do about him?"

She shrugged. "Not sure. Our people are already overtaxed. All we can really do, I suppose, is to keep an eye out for him. With any luck, we'll never see him again, but if he's up to trouble he undoubtedly knows you're here, too, Archer. You have ties to the Radicals—and it's no secret that you own this hotel."

"True, so let's alert our people to his presence in the city and play Wait and See."

The women nodded solemnly.

The dread stayed with Zahra for the rest of the day. She tried to set it aside, but the questions continued to occupy her mind. Was the middle-aged Brandon Crete just a common citizen now, or had he followed in the footsteps of former Confederate General Nathan Bedford Forrest, the man deemed responsible for the 1864 massacre of the Black Union soldiers at Fort Pillow, Tennessee, and the founder of the Kluxers? She wished she knew the answer.

That evening, as Zahra sat with Alfred in the parlor discussing what he'd learned from Suzette and Clare at the market earlier, Juliana entered the room. She was dressed for going out, but instead of the elegant and costly attire Zahra was accustomed to seeing her wear, she had on a simple brown gown and cloak.

Juliana pulled on a pair of dun brown gloves and said, "Alfred, I need to go out for awhile. Would you drive me?"

"Be honored." He left the room to ready the buggy.

Since Juliana hadn't mentioned anything to Zahra earlier about having an appointment this evening, Zahra was a bit confused.

Apparently, Juliana caught the look and explained, "Your General Crete worries me, so I'm going to talk to the keeper of the spiders. With your people concentrating on the books, you don't have the time to find out what we need to know about Crete, so I'll see if Henry Adams knows anything."

Zahra knew that whomever Archer married, the woman of his choice would be blessed with an incredible mother-in-law. The thought of Archer marrying some faceless woman in the future didn't sit well, so she ignored it. "When will you return?"

"Later tonight, more than likely. If any of my sons ask for my whereabouts, tell them I'm gone to see Aunt Vi."

"Who's she?"

"No idea, but she's who I go to visit whenever I set out to do something I know they wouldn't approve of."

Zahra laughed. "Juliana, when I grow up, I wish to be just like you."

"Why, thank you. By then you and Archer will have given me more *grandbébés* to spoil."

"Juliana," Zahra said warningly.

"What?" she asked innocently. "The two of you are so in love I fear the furniture will catch fire when you're together in the same room. Everyone notices."

Zahra hung an embarrassed head.

Juliana added, "I know there are many complications and wrinkles to smooth out before you can see your way clear, but love is a rare and beautiful thing, Zahra. Many women go to their grave never knowing what I had with my Francois—what Sable has with Raimond, and what you could have with Archer."

Zahra couldn't meet her eyes.

Juliana continued anyway, "And do you know why I find his feelings for you so fascinating?"

"Why?"

"Because Archer has never been in love. Never. He's never believed in it, never set any stock in it. Thought it nothing more than foolishness."

"But what about his mistresses?"

"He's had a string of them since he turned sixteen. None of them served any other purpose but to sleep with, buy for, and take to the Opera." She paused to add, "I'm not saying he didn't enjoy their company, but for you, my dear Butterfly, he would cut out his heart with a spoon and present it to you on a plate should you ask."

The force of that rattled Zahra in her chair.

"All of my sons are passionate, good men, and they deserve passionate, good women. You are both."

Juliana let the silence fall between them for a moment, then looked at Zahra kindly and said, "All I ask is that you give my words some thought."

Zahra nodded in reply.

Juliana smiled. "I must go. Alfred will have brought the coach around by now."

"Good luck," Zahra said genuinely.

"Thank you."

Juliana hurriedly made her departure, and Zahra was left alone to contemplate all she'd just heard. Did Archer really love her? She knew he had special feelings for her, but she'd attributed them to male lust and an appreciation for the fun they had together. She'd never considered it to be anything more, mainly for all of the reasons she'd mused on earlier this morning while lying in bed. Besides, Archer had never mentioned anything remotely tied to love, except his comments about loons mating for life. Then came the realization that even if he wanted to declare his feelings for her, why would he, in the face of her continued and oft-stated commitment to leaving when the task here was done? There wasn't a man or woman alive willing to subject their hearts to such certain pain, and Archer was surely no exception. *What a mess.*

There was no doubt in her mind that she was in love with Archer, though. But what might be set in motion if she were to let him know? She couldn't see him living in the swamps away from all the things he loved here, like his family, his hotel, and the vibrancy of his birthplace, but she couldn't see herself wearing corsets and shoes for the rest of her days either.

The dilemma was one that would have to be dealt with later, she told herself. Right now, she had to coordinate the search for the Death Books while staying in the shadows so she wouldn't be recognized by the Brandon Cretes of her life; love would have to wait.

But as is often the case, love had its own agenda. When she glanced up from the desk where she was working and saw him standing in the doorway, as if waiting for her to notice his presence, all she could see and want was him.

"Evening, *chérie*."

"Evening to you, too," she responded in soft welcome. "I thought you were working with the Republicans on their rally."

"We finished early, so I came to see you."

"I'm flattered."

Archer wanted to eat her up right there and then. She was wearing a plain white blouse and a dark skirt. He'd hardened from the moment she'd looked up and met his eyes, and nothing had changed. "Is the lovely Juliana here?"

"No, she went to visit Aunt Vi."

"Ah, the saintly Aunt Vi. Mother has been visiting her for as long as I can remember. The woman must be a century old by now."

Zahra hid her smile. "Little Reba left food in the kitchen. Are you hungry?"

He eyed her without shame. "I'm starving."

The pace of Zahra's heartbeat increased. "For food?"

"For you."

Her senses opened like petals in the sun. "Then lock that door."

Archer chuckled and did what he was told.

Now that they were secured in the small room Juliana had converted into an office for Zahra's use, Archer removed his coat and set it, with his hat and cane, on a nearby chair. Zahra was watching his every move.

"So, Miss Zahra Crane," he said, "have you ever made love to a man before?"

"No, Mr. Le Veq."

Archer's already attentive manhood stiffened like railroad steel in response to the velvety voice and the intensity in her dark eyes. "Never?"

"Never."

"Then we'll have to start from the beginning."

"Just tell me what to do."

"First, your drawers," he said softly. "Remove them, please."

Zahra slowly lifted her full skirt, undid the tapes, and worked the white undergarment down her legs and then off. The pulse between her thighs seemed to be synchronized with her pumping heartbeat.

"Very good. Now come here."

She crossed the room to him, and he kissed her with a soft heat that made her desire flower and bloom. Soon they were dual participants in an erotic, breathtaking coming together that wildly exceeded all other couplings of the past. And when they'd both experienced *la petite mort* for the final time, they lay against each other in the center of Juliana's imported Turkish rug and willed their breathing and heartbeats to slow. Zahra had never participated in such scandalous games in all her life, while Archer, the master of the bedroom games, realized he had finally found his equal.

Zahra said, "Your mother's going to come home eventually."

He slid his hand over a plump breast and replied, "I suppose we should get dressed."

Suddenly there was a sharp knock, followed by his mother calling, "Archer!"

His eyes widened, and he looked at Zahra and grinned. "Yes, Mama?" he called back.

"I'm going to assume you two are in there talking and not ruining the fabric on my sofa or rugs!"

Archer and Zahra looked down at the telltale signs they'd left on the rug. Zahra placed her hand over her mouth to keep her laughter from being heard on the other side of the door.

Then Juliana called, "Get dressed. I have something important I need to share with you two."

They heard her footsteps retreat. In the silence that followed, the naked lovers turned to each other, then laughed behind their hands until they cried.

Archer and Zahra joined Juliana in the parlor a short while later, and Zahra couldn't quite meet the mild censure in Juliana's dark eyes. Zahra was certain her own mother would be appalled knowing Zahra had repaid Mrs. Le Veq Vincent's kindness and hospitality with such scandalous behavior.

"You can stop looking so meek, Zahra. I know how tempting my sons are, I was married to their father, after all. We ruined more—".

"Mother!" Archer said, cutting her off. His eyes were wide.

Juliana said, "If you and your brothers wish to believe your births were by immaculate conception, that is your choice, but I know better."

He asked hastily, "What did you wish to discuss?"

Zahra tried to hide her smile and failed.

"Brandon Crete."

"And?"

"He is not a simple citizen. He's in the upper echelon of a new supremacist group calling themselves Sons of the White Star."

"How do you know this?" Archer asked.

"A friend."

He studied her. "Who?"

"Do you wish to hear this or not?"

"I do, but—"

"Then please stop interrupting."

He looked over at Zahra, but her attention remained focused on Juliana. He sighed and gestured for his mother to continue.

According to Juliana, Crete's group was small, but unlike other groups of its ilk, it was very selective about its membership. "They are based in Georgia but accept only the elite. Most of the members are former Reb officers, rich planters, and politicians from across the South."

Zahra found that interesting. "Any idea why he's here?"

"Unfortunately, no. He may be here recruiting. He may be here because there is a plot afoot."

Archer said, "So in other words, we're going to have to keep an eye on him as well?"

Zahra replied, "Might be a good idea."

"We have enough on our plate," Archer disagreed. "We can't investigate every supremacist in town—we have neither the time nor the resources."

"I know, Archer, but Crete's here for a reason."

He asked Zahra, "Did Alfred have an opportunity to talk to the women who have been trying to infiltrate the homes of Isenbaum and his friends?"

"Yes, he did, but so far, they've not found a way in. I wish we knew where Crete was staying."

"Zahra," he said warningly. "We're supposed to be concentrating on those books, remember?"

"I do, but if the two are related?"

"Then we'll find him out."

She knew he was right, of course, about spreading their forces too thin. Spying was in her blood, however, and she knew she wouldn't rest until the questions surrounding Brandon Crete and his reasons for being in New Orleans were resolved.

Juliana said, "Unless you two have any more questions, I'm off to bed. Zahra, you may want to seek your bed, too. It's late." She looked at her son. "And Archer, go home."

"Yes, Mama."

"Come, Zahra."

Zahra wiggled her fingers in farewell at Archer, and he winked and went to get his coat.

With the start of Mardi Gras only days away, incidents of violence and intimidation were increasing on the city's streets. The police had their hands full with roaming gangs of hoodlums harassing and intimidating Blacks young and old, rich and poor. Out in the countryside, White Radicals known to be working for change and equality were being subjected to nightly visitations by mounted masked terrorists blowing horns and carrying torches. Some Radicals had even been dragged from their homes and whipped like slaves. The Le Veq brothers and the bands of Black vets who were riding each night to meet the threats head-on saw only limited success, because their forces weren't large enough to patrol everywhere.

Thus the need for today's rally called by the Republicans to denounce the terror. Standing near the podium waiting for the next speaker to begin, Archer surveyed the crowd. He was pleased to see that hundreds of people had shown up; at more and more rallies across the South, participants were being shot at and, in some cases, killed by forces opposed to justice. People of all races and ages were in attendance today—even some of the Chinese now being employed on the docks had come, some with their families. There were signs and banners; church associations; Republican ward clubs; sisters from the Ursuline convent; and average citizens. All had come together this afternoon to say No More.

Archer found the speakers inspiring, and he wished Zahra were at his side, but she thought it best to stay in the shadows. He'd spent all morning discreetly looking into the faces of men he'd passed on the street, hoping to come across Brandon Crete, but so far his efforts hadn't borne fruit.

The rally lasted over an hour, and when it ended, the crowd began singing "Amazing Grace." As the voices rose to embrace the second verse, a succession of shots rang out, sending the screaming, terrified assemblage scrambling for cover. Then around the corner came a hundred or more masked riders, blowing horns and tin whistles and doing their best to run down any one who got in their path. Archer, who'd sought cover behind the elevated dais, began firing his pistol, as did other men nearby. Their combined shots and the answering fire of the supremacists, both in the crowd and on horseback, filled the street with a deadly hail. Suddenly soldiers on foot and on horseback joined the fray, and the masked riders wheeled their horses and fled. Their supporters did their best to delay the army's pursuit by blocking the way with commandeered vendor carts, backing wagons into the soldiers' paths and continuing to pepper the air with shot. As a result, the bulk of the riders got away, but Archer saw two angry-faced men being taken into custody by the police.

In the aftermath, Archer looked around to see if anyone nearby had been injured. A few feet away he saw a woman kneeling on the ground beside a small boy lying prone in the street. Hurrying over with a number of other people to see what kind of aid the child needed, they stopped when the woman brought the lifeless youngster to her chest and began to rock and wail. Filled with equal amounts of rage and despair, Archer watched as the authorities arrived to take charge. Then he turned and walked away, her cries of sorrow echoing in his head and heart.

Zahra's afternoon wasn't progressing much better. Seated at her desk, she was reading the reports sent to her by leaders and veterans groups across the South. None were uplifting; everything was violence, violence, violence, but some of the most disturbing news came out of South Carolina.

Her home state had made history after the war by electing the largest number of men of color to its legislature, passing color-blind laws and generally showing the nation what progress could be had if Blacks and Whites worked together. Now, however, the race was under brutal assault. In Piedmont County, five hundred masked men had rushed the local jail and lynched eight Black prisoners. In York County, where nearly every adult White male was a member of the Kluxers, eleven murders, along with hundreds of whippings, had been reported. To then read that thousands of her state's Black citizens were being forced to hide in the trees every night out of fear for their lives left her tight-lipped, grim, and worried sick about her parents.

When she glanced up, Archer was standing in the doorway. He looked terrible. "What's happened?"

"A child was shot and killed at the rally."

"Oh, no." She went to him and wrapped her arms around his waist, then let him pull her close.

He said quietly, "He appeared to be no older than Raimond's and Sable's Desiré. When will this end?"

Zahra didn't know, but she did know that she felt his pain as keenly as if it were her own. What if he had been killed, too? Could she have lived with herself knowing he'd died ignorant of her true identity? "My true name is Zahra Lafayette."

Archer pulled back and stared down. "What?"

"My true name is Zahra Lafayette."

He went still for a moment, then said, "Oh, really?"

"I'm a laundress in my real life, and if you laugh at that I will never speak to you again."

He had a soft smile on his face as he stroked her soft cheek. "Never is a long time, *chérie*."

She backed out of his arms. Having never revealed herself this way before, she needed some distance. "I'm from South Carolina."

"That I knew or at least thought I knew. The Gullah, remember?"

"Right." Zahra couldn't ever remember being this nervous. "I live in the swamps, Archer. I don't like corsets or shoes."

"Personally, I don't care for corsets either."

For a moment, the only sound in the room was the ticking of the wooden clock on the wall, then he asked, "Why are you telling me this now?"

"Because you've earned the right to know the truth. How would I have felt had you been killed too, never knowing who I truly am. Or what if I'm killed?"

"Don't say that."

"But it's true."

He crooked a finger and beckoned her back. She came willingly, and he folded her against his heart once more. "I'm honored," he said, and he was. For her to trust him with her secrets meant more than she could ever know. "So the Butterfly is a country girl."

"Born, bred, and raised, and I'm worried to death about my parents."

"Why?"

She told him about the reports she'd read.

"That's not good news." He pulled back to look down into her eyes. "Is that the reason you're so insistent on leaving me? Your parents?"

His question, so personal, made her heart flutter. "Yes, that and the fact that I don't fit into your world."

"You could have fooled me."

"Archer, I'm a swamp brat. I know how to spy, but I don't know all the little things women who are born into your class know."

"Such as? And I'm not trying to embarrass you, I'm just trying to understand."

"I don't know forks, or the dances, or how to arrange flowers. None of that."

"And you think that's important to me." It was a statement, not a question.

"I do."

"I see." He smiled. "And suppose I told you I don't care about any of the things you feel are shortcomings?"

She said softly, "Then I'd say good." What she didn't say was that she loved him. Even in light of Juliana's take on Archer's feelings, Zahra would not risk her heart by broaching the subject first.

Archer tightened his hold on her and let the pleasure of it fill his being. "So will you consider staying?"

Zahra looked up at him and said truthfully, "Only if you remember that considering and saying yes are not tied together."

His smile faded. "I appreciate your candor."

"I can't make promises I can't keep."

He traced her mouth with a fleeting touch, then pulled her back against his heart. After a long moment, he whispered, "Okay."

They stood that way for quite some time, but neither said another word.

# Chapter 13

The next day's meeting in Juliana's parlor brought together all of the players in Zahra's cast. As the meeting progressed and each group gave its report, good news followed good news. Roland and his group were now posing as night sweepers at the warehouse of the express company owned by White Leaguer Sam Banks, and Clare and Suzette had successfully infiltrated the households of two other Leaguers on the list—firemen Wendell Thomas and Zebediah Spain.

An impressed Archer asked the question on everyone's lips: "How did you accomplish it?"

Clare responded, "We worked separately. I concentrated on Hattie, who's the housekeeper for Thomas, and Suzette took Mary, Spain's laundress."

Clare explained that after casually striking up conversations with the women at the market,

299

they'd made a point to speak to the women each time they saw them thereafter. Over the course of the next few days, in talking about trivial matters such as where they'd each been born, relatives, and the like, Clare and Suzette had gathered all the information they'd needed.

Suzette took up the telling. "Hattie is from Birmingham, Alabama. Her mama lives there with a younger sister named Rose. I had Wilma send Hattie a false wire from Rose saying mama was ill. We did the same thing for Mary, only it was her grandmother in Tallahassee."

Zahra said, "Birmingham and Tallahassee, then they'll be away for quite some time."

"Yes, they will," Suzette said, "and more importantly, when we saw them at the market the day before their leaving, both were upset enough about the turn of events that they quickly agreed to give our names to their employers as replacements until their return."

Clare said, "Another thing in our favor. Neither Hattie nor Mary know each other well enough to have compared the similarities in timing or situations."

"Marvelous," Juliana said, smiling.

At first, Zahra felt bad about causing the women worry over their kin, especially considering all the concern she was carrying for her own. Knowing, however, that both Hattie and Mary would find their relatives in good health forestalled any guilt. "So, you're both in," Zahra said.

The women nodded, and Clare added, "Neither of the houses are very large, so searching them shouldn't take too long, we hope."

A satisfied-sounding Alfred said, "Then that crosses two houses off our original list."

A pleased Zahra looked to Archer and met his nod of satisfaction. She turned her attention to Caleb and Jesse, who reported that even with Drake's and Raimond's assistance, they hadn't been able to put a name to Isenbaum's daily evening visitor.

"I've no idea who he is," Raimond said. "He wears a beat-up planter's panama, so we can't tell his hair color or even if he has hair."

Archer asked, "How long did he stay the evening you all were there?"

"Three quarters of an hour?" Raimond looked to the others for verification, and they agreed; the man had stayed just short of an hour.

The thin, freckle-faced Caleb said, "Whenever the visit is over, Isenbaum always walks the man back to his wagon. They stand and speak for a few moments longer, then the man drives away."

Zahra said, "Describe him again."

Drake said, "When they said he was barrel-chested and big, that's him exactly. He looks like he swallowed a keg."

Zahra thought that could describe many men, then she remembered her encounter with Crete. He was a big man, but she'd been too busy looking into his eyes to say whether he was barrel-chested or not. Back in '63, the night she and Archer had met in the barn, Crete had been a large man, but his physique had been muscled. "I'm going to join you tomorrow, Caleb. I want to make sure he's not Crete—although I would love for the man to be him. That way all the fish could be on one plate instead of two or maybe three."

Everyone agreed.

Zahra then turned to Wilma. "Anything to add?"

"Only that Mr. Isenbaum visited my shop yesterday and castigated me for allowing Coloreds in my establishment."

"Oh, really?" Archer asked drolly.

"He said he and friends were encouraging White shop owners to draw the color line. Said he hoped I would follow along willingly and not have to be *convinced*."

"So he threatened you," Beau stated.

"Yes."

André said, "Arrangements can be made for a hired guard if you care for one."

She waved off the offer. "No. I'll be fine. The wife of one of the Union captains was in the shop at the time and heard Isenbaum. She said she'd definitely inform her husband."

"Good, the more folks watching Isenbaum the better," Zahra said. She continued to believe he'd torched Domino's place, but since there wasn't a thing she could do about it presently, she scanned the room. "Is there anything else?"

When no one spoke, she said, "Okay. We'll meet here again two evenings from now. Everyone be on your guard."

As she watched them spend a moment conferring with each other before departing, she was thankful that her chess pieces were finally making their opening moves.

Juliana left the house with Raimond. She and

Sable were traveling to Baton Rouge in the morning to seek sponsors for some of Sable's orphans and would be returning in a few days. As always, when Juliana traveled, Little Reba had the time off.

"So," Archer said as he and Zahra sat before the fire, "we have the entire house to ourselves for two whole days. What do you want to do?"

She grinned and placed her head on his shoulder. "I know what you want to do."

"As do you."

He was correct, of course, but she wanted to know more about him; more than how much he enjoyed her kisses. "What was it like growing up here?"

"Exciting. Fun. With so many brothers around, we always had someone to play with or plot mischief with. We four youngest spent many an evening lined up in the woodshed."

Zahra smiled. She could almost imagine Archer, Drake, Beau, and Philippe giving poor Juliana fits, but she was certain Mama Le Veq had had full control of the ship no matter what her sons may have believed. "Who was your first love?"

"Never had one."

She turned to stare. "What do you mean? The great Archer Le Veq never had a first love?"

"There were young ladies I was attracted to, but love? Never believed in it."

"I see."

"At least, not that can't-eat-can't-sleep-sonnet-writing love. No." He looked her way, and added, "Now, that doesn't mean there haven't been women in my life that I've cared for deeply. Present company included." He kissed her forehead.

He was so charming that Zahra smiled in spite of herself, but the backhanded compliment stung. Again she thought about Juliana's words. Maybe the mother did not know the son as well as she believed. *Well, at least I won't have to worry about you pining for me when we part*, she thought to herself.

Archer felt the subtle change in her and got the sense that he'd said something wrong. He wasn't sure what it might have been, so he moved the conversation on. "Did you have a first love?"

"I did," she said proudly. "I was twelve, and his name was Amiri. I thought the sun was in the sky because of him."

"What happened to him?"

"He and his family moved to Florida and I never saw him again. I was devastated. His name meant 'prince.'"

Archer rolled his eyes. "Does Zahra have a meaning?"

"Yes, 'flower.'"

"Not many people carry the old names any more."

"True. Now tell me about your name. Is *Archer* French?"

"No," he said, sounding amused. "According to family legend, I was conceived under the stars of Sagittarius. The symbol is the Archer."

"Really?"

"Yes. My father, Francois, was a seaman and spent his life following the stars. When is your birthday?"

"June first."

"Ah, Gemini. The twins. Since you are often two people, the sign fits you well."

His mentioning twins sparked a thought, so she asked, "Speaking of twins. How is Philippe faring? He wasn't at the meeting tonight."

"He sailed to Cuba the morning after storming out of here. Beau said maybe we shouldn't have laughed, but I agree with Raimond: that's what baby brothers are for. Besides, he falls in love three times a week. By the time he leaves the dock, he'll have given his heart away to someone new and Naomi and Salome will just be fond memories."

Zahra wondered how two brothers could view love so differently. Apparently Philippe fell in and out of love as easily as someone else put on his hat, while Archer placed no faith in the emotion at all. "So, since you don't believe in love, if you ever actually fell in love would you know it?"

He shrugged. "I've no idea." He then turned to her. "I can envision myself committing to be with a woman, but will it be because I love her?" He shrugged, then continued. "Raimond didn't believe in love either until Sable entered his life. Now he swears he can't live without her. I'm sure he believes that to be true, but my brother is the strongest man I know. I believe he'd survive if something tragic happened."

"But would he want to? That's the true measure of his feelings."

Archer went silent for a moment and thought about how devastated and inconsolable Raimond had been when Sable and the children had been kidnapped. Archer admitted, "No, he wouldn't."

"Then that's love. It's the kind of love my parents have. The kind of love I think your mother had with your father. The kind of love I'd choose to have."

"And I choose not to. I can't conceive of loving someone so much that if they died, I'd want to die as well. Mama was that way after Papa's death." He paused for a moment, as if thinking back, then said quietly, "I think if she hadn't had to care for my brothers and me she would have walked into the Mississippi to be with him. I was twelve and I'd never seen such pain. I swore then, I'd never love anybody that much."

The admission took him by surprise. He turned to Zahra. "I'd forgotten all about that until just now."

Zahra was silent, and she now understood. "Maybe a woman will come into your life who will show you that taking that risk is worth more than you could ever imagine."

"She'd have to be an amazing woman."

"I think so, too."

Archer thought she was pretty amazing. He eyed her thoughtfully for a long, silent moment. He felt different. He couldn't put it into words, and there was nothing he could put his finger on specifically, but something inside had changed. It was as if talking about Juliana's sorrow had opened up a closed place within him, and whatever had been imprisoned there had been freed. Deep in thought and not sure what any of this meant, he slowly lowered his head and touched his lips to hers. The kiss was sweet, tender, and then he slowly pulled away. In a voice as soft as the moment, he said to her, "I'm going back to the hotel for the night."

Zahra was surprised, but his pensive manner kept her silent. "All right."

"Will Alfred be here with you?"

"Yes, he went to take Reba home."

"I'll see you in the morning."

And then he was gone.

Zahra sat there for a few moments thinking about him, then got up and lowered the lamps.

Archer lay in bed, watching the moon through the window in front of him. The light was flooding the room, but that wasn't the reason he was finding it difficult to sleep. The conversation with Zahra was still resonating, and he'd come home alone so he could mull it over. He'd no idea why that particular set of memories had risen at that particular moment, but remembering the pain in his mother's eyes . . . there were no words to describe it, just as there had been none back then. The memories recalled the helplessness he'd experienced because no one, not even he, who'd loved her the most, had been able to put the light back in her eyes. She'd been strong through it all but she'd looked as if she'd died inside.

Was that why he eschewed the notion of love, at least when he was personally involved? Were all of his protestations about why he didn't believe in love just veneer over his fear of the pain and anguish he'd seen in the lovely Juliana's eyes? Archer had no way of knowing truly, but he was comfortable enough with himself to entertain the idea. This was all Zahra's doing. *It's the kind of love*

*I'd choose.* Archer knew that whatever this epiphany meant, it wasn't something that would be easily deciphered or dismissed, so he burrowed beneath the bedding and turned his head on the pillow. After vowing to revisit the subject over the next few days, he closed his eyes and slept.

The next evening, Zahra and Archer were hunkered down with Jesse in the thick brush near Mitchell Isenbaum's battered mansion, waiting for the mystery man to make his evening appearance. Spyglass at the ready, Zahra hoped she or Archer would be able to shed light on the man's identity—if the insects didn't eat her first. She slapped at the offending bugs and prayed the man would show soon. It had rained last night, and the mud and muck, combined with the bloodthirsty insects, made their hiding place a wretched one. She was dressed like a man, in overalls and brogans, which helped her move more comfortably and kept her feet dry, but she planned on soaking in a nice hot bath just as soon as she returned to Juliana's.

"Here comes a wagon," Archer said softly.

Jesse raised up a little and took a quick look down the road before dropping down again. "That's him."

The three of them waited silently as the sound of wagon wheels moved along the rutted, mud-filled road. Their hiding place was far enough away from the house so that they would not be seen. The sound of the wheels got louder as the wagon drew closer. Isenbaum's long drive connected to the main road, and the wagon turned onto it.

When Zahra deemed it safe, she carefully raised her head above the reeds and foliage. She could see the man's back atop the wagon. He had on the hat Raimond had described and a faded blue work shirt. Zahra raised the spyglass just in time to see the man step down from the wagon, and for a split second she got a clear look at his face. She smiled. It was Crete, all right. Her happiness not-withstanding, now came the crucial question: What were he and Isenbaum up to that made it necessary for them to meet every evening? "It's him."

"Good," Archer said, slapping at the beasties feeding on his neck. "Now we can get the hell out of this ditch."

Jesse and Zahra didn't protest in the least.

Back at Archer's apartment, Zahra didn't know which was finer—the feel of the nice warm bath-water or the feel of the man she was leaning back against in the nice warm bathwater. "A woman could learn to love this . . ."

"The water or me?"

"Since love is a concept you don't embrace, I suppose it would have to be the water."

"Touché."

"But you feel good, too, Mr. Frenchman."

He moved his hands over her budded nipples. "So do you."

While he played, Zahra did her best to come up with a plan that might decipher the questions surrounding Crete and Isenbaum. "Do you know an artist who could do a rendering of Crete for us?"

Archer was sliding wet hands over the caves, valleys, and peaks of her body with a maddening slowness that caused her hips to rise in response. "Brother Beau is a fairly decent artist. I'm sure he could. What do you have in mind?"

Because of the heat building inside from his caresses and fondling, she found it difficult to remember enough to answer him. Finally, she responded, "I want to show the likeness around town so we can determine where he's living and go from there."

"Good idea." But he had a better idea. With his touch, he silently coaxed her to part her legs a bit further for him so they could explore his better idea in depth. It didn't take long for them to delve further and even less time for Zahra to catch fire.

"We're supposed to be planning," she whispered.

"I am planning. I'm planning to make you kneel with your back to me just as soon as we do a little more evaluating. . . ."

She shuddered passionately in response to his heated promise and to the hands exploring her with erotic expertise.

Archer once again mused upon how beautifully uninhibited she was. It was every man's dream to find a woman whose intensity equaled his in the game of making love. Acher had found his. The sight of her naked and arching against him in the soft light cast by the dim lamp increased his desire a hundredfold. Her soft brown breasts filled his palms perfectly, and the unblemished skin was as seductive as the silk she'd favored as Domino. In reality she was three women: Madame Domino, the proper and prim Zahra Crane, and the fiercely independent Butterfly. Each persona was as delectable as the others, and the man who finally claimed her would reap the benefit of having such an incredible woman. As before, the idea of another man pleasuring her bothered him, but unlike before, it bothered him more than he wanted to admit.

"Kneel up, *papillon,* I want to fill you. . . ."

Zahra's eyes were lidded, and the fog of desire made it difficult for her to see, but she raised up onto her knees. He reached behind him and pulled a thick towel from the chair. Folding the towel, he placed it on the floor of the big tub for her to kneel upon. Once her knees were cushioned, he fit himself behind her and wrapped an arm around her waist. They melted into each other, kissing and caressing, then he turned her back and possessively arrowed his way into paradise.

The feel of her heated cove grasping him so sweetly took Archer's breath away. Savoring the sensations, he held for a moment, his hands on her hips, and never wanted to move; ever. She was too enticing, though; the skin of her back, smooth and damp, and the soft skin of her neck perfect to place kisses against. Soon his hands were moving over her and he was moving inside her; coaxing, inviting her to take up the rhythm of lovers.

Zahra needed no coaxing; she was already enthralled. His splendid length filled her with such glorious delight that she groaned and arched back to reward him with tender kisses. With him she could take her passion without shame. With him there were no boundaries or borders. Any man in her future would be measured against this skilled and seductive *gens de coleur*, and she instinctively knew they would be found wanting; no man would make love to her with as much fervor or adoration as Archer Le Veq.

And he proved it, beautifully, solidly, and wonderfully. An orgasm swept over her with such power that she knew she had died and gone to heaven. Her body splintered into a hundred glowing pieces, yet he didn't stop until he too was shaken apart and they went limp against the edge of the tub.

Later, in the bed, Archer held her close while she slept. He realized he never wanted to let her go. In his perfect world, she would be at his side every night, just like this until the end of time, but she wanted to leave. He knew she was worried about her parents and that her concerns for them came first, but then what? Would she come back to him or stay in the swamps where she was free to eschew corsets, shoes, and flower arranging? After all they'd been through together and all they'd shared, he couldn't imagine her not being in his life. He'd never felt this way about any of his former mistresses. When he'd grown tired of them or they of him, he'd simply moved on; no regrets, no guilt, no tears. But the razor-carrying woman sleeping beside him would not be so easily dismissed. Her keen mind, sense of humor, and the way she had of deflating his ego were unparalleled and therefore unique. Also unique was the fact that for the first time in his life, Archer wanted to keep a woman who didn't want to be kept.

At the next meeting, Beau took out paper and charcoal. With Zahra and Archer as his guides, he began drawing a likeness of Brandon Crete. It took them all a while to get the eyes right, the cut of his chin and the slope of his nose, but Beau eventually came up with a portrait everyone agreed was very close to the real thing. "I have a printer friend who can put this on a plate and make us some doubles. How many do you want?"

Zahra shrugged. "Fifteen, twenty? I don't want to circulate too many and chance Crete or his cronies seeing them and begin raising questions about their origin. What do you all think?"

Everyone agreed that erring on the side of caution would be the best approach.

Archer asked Beau, "How long do you think the printing might take?"

"Since he has to make the plate, I'd say no more than a few days. He has his own operation."

Raimond asked pointedly, "Is he discreet?"

"Yes."

Zahra was glad to hear that.

So it was decided that Beau would handle the tasks surrounding the portrait. He would get the duplicates back to Zahra as soon as he could.

Suzette and Clare were so far unsuccessful in their searches for the Death Books in the homes of Spain and Thomas. Suzette said, "I found his

Kluxers robe in a locked trunk in his cellar, but there was no book with them."

Clare added, "I've been cleaning the Thomas house top to bottom for the past two days, and so far, nothing. I've run out of places to look."

"Okay," Zahra said. "If you haven't found anything in two more days, pull out. That goes for you too, Suzette. There's no sense in beating a dead horse."

She turned to Archer. "Any word from the friends you wired?"

"Yes. None of the three can come for various reasons."

Zahra hid her disappointment.

André said, "Maybe we can get along without them."

Archer countered, "We're going to have to."

Zahra asked Wilma, "Has Isenbaum paid you any more visits?"

"No, but a soldier came by today and asked me about him. I guess the wife of the Union captain kept her word about speaking to her husband."

Zahra thought that good news. "What did he want to know?"

"What Isenbaum said to me. Did I know him socially, that sort of thing. He then said he would give the report to the captain, and should I have any more encounters with Isenbaum I was to let the army know."

Zahra thought that even better news. She then asked Alfred about his cousin Roland. He and his men were working at the express company warehouse owned by Sam Banks.

"So far, nothing. Banks has hired a gang boss who's paid to keep an eye on the fifteen sweepers who work at night, and his presence has been keeping Roland and the others from doing anything but sweeping. He's not sure if they're going to have an opportunity to look around or not."

That was not good news. "That leaves Isenbaum's home and the home and cigar shop of our last target, Hathaway Dawes, to still search," Zahra said.

Archer added, "Mardi Gras starts tomorrow. Probably be a perfect night to slip inside Dawes's shop and take a look around."

"André, Beau, Drake, and I are patrolling with the veterans tomorrow night," Raimond informed them.

Alfred spoke up, "And I'll be driving Mrs. Vincent to a ball. She and Miss Sable are due back on the morning train."

Zahra looked to Archer. "Guess that leaves you and me."

"Guess so."

"All right then. You all know what to do. We'll meet again in two nights' time. Wish Archer and me luck tomorrow evening."

With that, the meeting was adjourned.

The words *Mardi Gras* translate to "Fat Tuesday" in English. In New Orleans, Mardi Gras filled the city streets with floats, masked revelers, and the festive sounds of its signature hybrid music as the predominantly Catholic population embraced excess before having to put on the mantle of solemnity and reflection for Lent.

Masked and disguised as pirates, Zahra and Archer walked through the raucous crowds choking the streets. Holding hands so they'd not get separated in the sea, Zahra had to admit she'd never seen anything like it in her life. Everywhere she looked, people were drinking, laughing, and kicking up their heels. The buildings were decorated, and all the lights bathing the area made it seem like day instead of night. She skirted by people dressed in elaborate, expensive costumes and others wearing their everyday clothes and a simple domino covering their eyes. The air was filled with high-pitched laughter and shouts of glee. Off in the distance, the faint but strong beat of a drum echoed like the heartbeat of a city drunk on gaiety.

"It's up here," Archer called back to say. They turned off the street and down one far quieter and less lit. Zahra saw a masked Indian hurrying as if he was late for the throng and a few masked couples in formal wear slowly sauntering arm in arm, their eyes on each other. None of them paid the costumed Archer and Zahra any attention.

Zahra was glad of that, because she and Archer were on their way to search the cigar shop of Hathaway Dawes. Because the shop was not housed in a building on a main street, they were hoping their entrance would go unnoticed.

Archer had scouted the back of the place earlier in the day and had found it to have one small door secured with a standard padlock. Because Zahra had lost her lock picks in the fire, along with everything else she'd brought to New Orleans, they were relying on a set Archer had owned since the war.

They entered easily enough and quickly closed the door behind them. Due to the darkness of the interior it took a few moments for their eyes to adjust to their surroundings, but once they could see, they began slowly moving around. The sweet smell of tobacco permeated the place.

The shop was small and tidy. A wooden counter stood between the customers and the cigars, and that's where Zahra and Archer began.

Since it was impossible to do a thorough search in the dark, she fished out of her trousers pocket one of the stubby candles she'd brought along and some matches. She lit it and prayed the faint light wouldn't attract the attention of anyone who might be passing by.

After placing the candle on the floor to keep it from being seen on the street, they used its light to look through the many humidors stacked behind the counter. Nothing.

"Let's try his office," Archer said.

Zahra agreed. Picking up the candle, she quickly followed him into a tiny inner office. The desk was locked, but Archer and his picks conquered it quickly, and soon she was going through the papers in the desk and in the drawers. In the bottom drawer, Zahra reached her hand all the way into the back behind a stack of ledgers and felt a small tablet. From its position, it was hard to determine whether it had simply fallen behind the ledgers accidentally, or whether it had been put there deliberately. "I think I found something," she said quietly to her accomplice, who was concentrating on the contents of a small cupboard on the wall. She slid out the tablet, then sat on the floor to examine it.

He came over and hunkered down beside her. Both of them kept their ears open for trouble.

Zahra opened the first page. When she saw the words Deth List, her hands began to shake. The next page had a listing of names that began with Frederick Douglass and ended . . . there were so many names that it made her heart ache. "This is it."

"Then let's leave. We can study it later."

"Let's make sure we put everything back the way we found it. Maybe he won't notice it's missing for awhile."

As quietly and as quickly as they could, they tidied up the desk's interior and relocked it. Although they'd searched the place thoroughly, they were both trained not to leave notice of their presence behind; they replaced all the humidors in their original order and positioning. Giving the place one last sweep with their candle to make certain they hadn't forgotten anything, Zahra and Archer slipped out as easily as they'd slipped in. While she kept watch, he quickly replaced and locked the padlock. Then they walked back to the main street and let themselves be swallowed by the celebrating crowds.

Once they were safely back in Archer's suite, they sat and leafed through the pages. The names listed astounded them, not only because of how many there were but also because of whose there were. Frederick Douglass was at the top of the list, followed by others known for their outspoken commitment to justice for the race. Men such as James D. Lynch, a presiding elder of the Methodist Church and the secretary of state for the state of Mississippi; Henry M. Turner, who'd been born free in South Carolina and served as a member of Georgia's constitutional convention and the state's first Reconstruction legislature; Reverend Jonathan C. Gibbs, born in Philadelphia, educated at Dartmouth, who studied theology at Princeton and was Florida's secretary of state.

The next name on the list chilled her. "Your friend Dunn's name is here, and a line has been drawn through it."

Archer looked where she pointed and read Oscar's name. His jaw tightened. "Was the line drawn through his name because of his untimely death or because Dawes and the others played a part in it?"

Neither of them knew.

Zahra said gravely, "According to my source, these books are all over the South. Who knows how many men of the race are in the supremacists' sights?"

"Or how many plots are already underway."

It was a grim situation made even more grim by the knowledge that if there were plots afoot, there was no way to stop them even if she left for

Washington in the morning. An investigation into the matter would, without a doubt, take months to be officially commissioned, considering the volatile nature of the present political scene, and even though there were congressmen taking testimony related to the ongoing violence in many areas of the South, counting on the Congress to actually do something was another matter altogether.

Archer could see her thinking. "So what are you going to do?"

"Because we've found one of the books, I can now pull all of our people off the search and have them concentrate on Crete. If we don't turn up anything on him in the next seven days, then I go on to Washington." She met his eyes. "Does that sound reasonable?"

"It does." Although parts of him wondered if he'd ever see her again after she left New Orleans. With that in mind, he wanted to spend every waking and sleeping moment with her until her departure. The desire surprised him, because he'd never been obsessive with any other woman—but then he reminded himself that from the first time they'd met Zahra had never been just any woman. "Is there anything else we need to discuss?" he asked.

"Not that I can think of. Why?"

"Because I want to hold you."

The seriousness of his tone was reflected in his gaze. His mood drew Zahra to her feet, and she let herself be enfolded in his strong arms.

He whispered above her, "I'm hoping, if I hold onto you long enough, I'll awaken and find the Death Books nothing more than a bad dream."

She tightened her hold. "And if we do wake up and the Death Books are still what they are, it won't stop the race from going forward."

He kissed the top of her hair. "No, it won't."

# Chapter 14

❧

Drake's printer friend had the duplicates ready the following evening. At dawn the next day Zahra put the initial part of her plan for Crete into motion. With Juliana and Sable's help, Zahra transformed herself into an old woman with graying hair and a pronounced but dignified limp. The changes in her hair and face were brought about by the skillful application of a talcum-powdered wig and some theater paint Sable had left over from a skit put on by her orphans. The limp was achieved by cobbling another heel onto one of Zahra's brogans. With one shoe higher than the other, the effect was as real as she needed it to be. She'd also wound lengths of cotton batting she'd gotten from Wilma around her arms, legs, and thighs to give her body more girth.

Juliana looked at this newest persona and shook

her head at the amazing difference. "Are you still in there?"

Zahra's smile showed bright and clear through the new face.

Sable said, "You look like an old woman."

"Good. Now, let's hope everyone on the street thinks that as well."

Zahra had shared the contents of the Death Books with everyone last evening, and all had been as concerned and as stricken as Zahra and Archer. Juliana would be seeing Henry Adams this morning to bring him up to date.

Now, as Juliana handed Zahra an old handbag to go with her disguise, she asked, "You are going to be careful?"

"Of course. We've come too far for me not to be."

Sable would be accompanying Zahra. Because Sable was well known on the streets of New Orleans for her work with the area's orphans, she'd be able to give Zahra some legitimacy with the people Zahra planned to ask for help.

Juliana wished them both luck, then Sable and Zahra began their drive into town.

They found the early morning streets awash in litter from last night's Mardi Gras celebration but devoid of the revelers, who were now home sleeping off the aftereffects of too much celebrating. However, the vendors, cooks, laundresses, and other little people who didn't have that luxury were setting up their carts, opening their store-fronts, or heading into work.

Sable pulled back on the reins. "There's someone we can trust." After setting the brake, she got down from the wagon and hurried around to assist her elderly passenger.

Zahra climbed down as gingerly as a true old woman would, then walked over with Sable to a young woman setting up a cart that would display the pralines she'd have for sale.

Sable said brightly, "Morning, Delia."

"Mornin' Mrs. Le Veq. How are you? If you're looking for orphans I haven't seen any in the past few days."

"Thanks, if you do see any, you know where to contact me."

Delia nodded.

"Well, I'm here for something else this morning. This is Miss Minnie. Her granddaughter was taken from her a few days ago."

Delia said, "Sorry to hear that, ma'am. Did they take her and put her to work on one of the plantations?"

"I think so," Miss Minnie said in a wavering voice. "And I'm so worried I can't sleep."

Sable showed Delia the likeness of Crete. "This is the man we think may have taken her. Does he look familiar?"

Delia studied the face. "No, but do you want me to keep an eye out for him?"

"Would you please and let me know if you see him?"

"I will. Folks stealing our children like they were apples on trees. It has to stop."

Zahra reached into her handbag and took out a coin. She handed it to Delia and said, "For your trouble."

"Thanks."

With a wave of parting, Sable helped Zahra back onto the wagon seat, and they drove on.

The women spent the next hour talking to people Sable knew and leaving drawings of Crete behind. They spoke to draymen, sweepers, newsboys, shoeblacks, and barbers. Many expressed their sympathy for Minnie's plight and offered up stories of their own of youngsters they knew of who'd been kidnapped and made to sign work contracts that kept them indentured until they reached adulthood. All of Sable's contacts were advised to be discreet; if Crete learned he was being followed, he would move on. They heartily reassured both women that they would be.

By ten that morning, Zahra's leg was starting to ache from her uneven gait. "I think Minnie wants to go home and get out of these shoes. I'm also roasting inside this batting."

Sable smiled. "Whatever you wish."

"Thank you for your help. You seem to know everyone."

"It wasn't always that way, but my work with the orphans has made me quite a few friends on the streets, and I value them very much."

Zahra valued them as well. They all promised to leave Sable word at the convent or the orphanage should they see Crete or find out where he was staying. Now that Crete's face was on the drum, all Zahra could do was hope and pray that something on him turned up soon.

Sable looked Zahra's way and said, "Before we go back to Juliana's, how about we stop at the Christophe, get something to eat, and see how long it takes Archer to see through your disguise."

Zahra thought it an excellent idea. "I doubt he'll be fooled, but I'm in."

The restaurant was fairly empty because of the time of day. André greeted Sable warmly, then turned to her companion. "My name is André. Welcome to the Hotel Christophe, madam."

"Thank ya," Minnie said. "Name's Minnie Turpin. Miss Sable said you all have the best food in town here."

André smiled, "Miss Sable is correct. This way, please."

He led them across the restaurant to a table, and behind his back Zahra and Sable shared sparkling smiles. As they sat, Sable asked, "Is Archer here? I'd like for him to meet my friend."

"I'll get him. You all look over the menu. Your waiter will join you shortly."

After his departure, Zahra and Sable chuckled, then read their menus and waited for Archer.

When he appeared moments later, Zahra could only sigh at how handsome he was.

"Hello, lovely sister-in-law."

"Hello, Archer. I want you to meet a friend. Her name's Minnie Turpin and she's visiting New Orleans for a few days."

"Enchanté, Madam Turpin. I hope you are finding New Orleans to your liking."

"Very much so. All this walking's got my leg acting up, but I'll be fine." She then looked up into his dark eyes. "Miss Sable said you own this whole place."

"I do indeed." Then, as if noticing something amiss, he asked, "Have we met before?"

Minnie shook her head. "Nope. First time I ever been to New Orleans."

"You remind me of someone."

"You know more than one old woman with a bad leg?"

"Well, no, but—"

Sable said, "Archer, tell Aristide I'll have the catfish and the red beans and rice. Minnie, what would you like?"

Minnie ordered the same. Both women could see Archer still trying to figure out if or where he and Minnie had met previously.

He seemed to give up as he said, "I'll take your orders back to the kitchen." Turning his attention to Minnie, he bowed and said, "It was a pleasure meeting you, madam."

"Same here. Back home in South Carolina the men don't bow like that. Makes me feel real special like."

Archer smiled and nodded. "Enjoy your meals, ladies."

As he walked away, Sable and Zahra hid their laughter behind their hands. By the time he disappeared through the kitchen doors, both women had tears in their eyes.

After they finished their lunch, Zahra said to Sable, "I'm going to go up to his office for a moment. Will you wait?"

"Certainly. Juliana wanted me to stop in at the post office to see if she's received any mail. I'll do that while you see Archer and I'll meet you back here."

"Very good."

Sable paid the bill and departed. Zahra stood and waved over André Renaud.

"Yes, ma'am?"

"Is Mr. Le Veq still here?"

"Yes, he's in his office."

"You think he'd mind me disturbing him a moment so I can tell him how nice everything was?"

André gave her a smile. "I'm sure he'd be pleased to see you, just as long as you don't stay very long."

"Oh, no. I know he must be a real busy man. I'm going to pop my head in, say what I have to say, then come back and wait for Miss Sable to finish her errand at the post office."

"Good. Then come. I'll escort you upstairs."

André knocked on the closed office door. When Archer responded, he opened it and said, "Miss Turpin wanted to speak with you for just a moment."

Archer stood up from behind his desk, then gestured in the direction of one of the chairs. "Certainly. Miss Turpin, please have a seat."

André withdrew, leaving Archer and the old woman alone.

"What may I help you with?"

"You know, you're a fine-looking man, Mr. Le Veq."

"Um, thank you."

"You know an older woman knows a whole lot more than a young one."

Archer went still. "Was there something you wanted, Miss Turpin?"

Using her real voice, Zahra said, "I just wanted to say thank you for the lovely lunch."

His eyes wide, he choked out, "Zahra!"

"In the flesh. I'm glad I didn't set a wager when I told Sable you wouldn't be fooled. I would have lost."

He came around the desk and stared. "My God. Look at you."

"Not bad, eh?"

"Not at all," he echoed. "You look like an old woman."

"Thank you very much. It was what I was hoping for."

She then told him about the distribution of Crete's likeness. "Sable promises that all of her people will be discreet."

Archer approved of the plan, but he couldn't get over her transformation. "I have no idea how long it might have taken me to see past the disguise, if ever."

"The measure of a good disguise."

"How'd you make yourself plumper?"

"Cotton batting, and if I don't get back to your mother's soon, I'm going to wilt."

"When you told us last night that you were going to hand out the drawings, I was concerned that you might be seen by Crete. But if I couldn't recognize you, I know he wouldn't have been able to. That's a fantastic getup."

"Hope you didn't mind the joke at your expense."

"No, I'm too impressed to be offended." And he was—there wasn't an ounce of Zahra anywhere in the disguise. "I've never disguised myself. Maybe if I had I wouldn't have wound up hanging like a side of beef in Crete's barn."

"How were you found out?"

"I was playing the role of a Cuban planter touring the area looking to expand my holdings. In reality, though, I was looking for the maps."

Zahra knew that part.

"But when I walked up to Crete's door, one of the men with him was a man I thought to be working intelligence for the BMI, because I had seen him a few times on other missions. Apparently he was a counteragent for the Confederacy, because he gave me away as soon as Crete escorted me into the parlor."

Zahra shook her head. She'd heard tales that the first James Lafayette had encountered the same sort of situation; the man on the other side had just been pretending to spy for the British. "If you hadn't been found out, we might never have met."

"True." Still enjoying her surprising new persona, he asked, "So what are you doing for the rest of the day?"

"Sable's going to drop me by Wilma's so I can put Minnie Turpin to rest, and see if any reports come in that need to be passed on to Araminta. Wilma has already sent on the information about the Death Books. Araminta wired back her intentions to alert everyone who is listed."

"Good. They need to be made aware of the danger."

The book was now locked away in the wall safe in Archer's bedroom.

Zahra said, "I should get going. Sable will be back shortly, if she hasn't returned already. I will see you this evening?"

"Most definitely."

"Shall I wear this getup to bed for you?"

"No!"

His emphatic answer made her laugh. "Just thought I would ask."

He had amusement in his eyes.

Zahra said in Minnie's wavering voice, "Come, give Miss Minnie a kiss and you can get back to your work."

He walked to her, but when she turned up her lips, he planted the kiss on her cheek.

Zahra grinned. "Coward."

"Yes, ma'am. There's nothing arousing about you whatsoever. You look like I imagine mother's Aunt Vi would look."

Zahra's amusement increased. "Okay, but I expect a bit more enthusiasm tonight or you'll wake up to Minnie in the morning."

He laughed. "And you would do that, wouldn't you?"

"Without a bit of shame."

Archer studied her and again wondered how he was going to let her go. "I'll see you this evening and Minnie had better be asleep in another room."

"She will be." Waggling her fingers goodbye, Zahra left him and closed the door behind her.

Zahra waved good-bye to Sable then entered Wilma's shop. Her old friend greeted her, saying for the benefit of the other customers, "Hello, Mrs. Turpin, would you like to rest a bit in the back and have some refreshment? We can talk about hiring you after that."

"Sounds like a good idea. This leg of mine is paining me something fierce."

Wilma escorted Zahra to a small back room. "There's tea there. Rest a minute while I see to these customers then I'll come back and help you out of those clothes."

"Thanks."

Zahra took a few sips of the tea, then looked in her cup. The brew had a strange taste. She was about to bring the cup to her nose to smell the contents when a dizziness began creeping over her. She stood up intending to call for Wilma but she crumpled to the floor and everything went black.

When Zahra awakened her head was pounding and she had an awful taste in her mouth. Somewhere outside of the fog clouding her brain she heard Wilma say, "Drink this, lass."

Zahra pulled away. She wasn't sure why, but she didn't want anything to drink.

Wilma's voice grew firmer, "Drink Zahra, you'll feel better."

Her throat was so dry and felt so foreign she swallowed and tasted cool water on her lips, then she drifted back to sleep.

When she awakened again, she was more clear-headed and so opened her eyes. Startled to see that she was in a moving wagon, she stilled at the sight of her companions: Wilma, Brandon Crete, and the driver, Mitchell Isenbaum.

Wilma said, "It's good to have you back with us, lass."

Zahra could only stare.

"Aren't you going to say hello to my friends?"

Zahra didn't respond.

"And here I was just telling them all about your fine manners."

"Where are you taking me?" she asked angrily. Still dressed as Minnie Turpin she was hot and uncomfortable. She noted that both Isenbaum and Crete appeared to be very pleased with themselves but she ignored them for now.

"Where's the book?" Wilma asked Zahra.

"What book?"

They were traveling along a rutted country road Zahra was unfamiliar with.

"The Death Book."

"We never found it. It was all a ruse to see who would come out of the woodwork after it."

"You're lying."

Zahra remained cool. "Am I? I never showed it to you did I? I spoke of having found one, but you never saw it in my possession."

Wilma's eyes narrowed. "What about the wires you had me send to Tubman?"

"Did you send them?"

"Of course not."

Zahra hid her profound disappointment. "How long have you been working on the wrong side?"

Before the woman Zahra had always considered a friend could answer, Crete answered, "Long enough to be of great value to our cause."

Wilma inclined her head. "I'm honored to be able to serve."

Zahra seethed. Zahra had trusted her. Araminta had trusted her. Now it was quite apparent that she'd been in with the supremacists the entire time. Zahra could care less how Wilma's perfidy had impacted the information needed by the president, but the possible damage done to the spiders set up across the South by Henry Adams would impact lives. Had she passed on false information? Zahra had no way of knowing. She did know that Wilma hadn't passed along the warnings about the Death Books, thus leaving the men named ignorant of the danger. According to Araminta, back in the days of abolition, traitors such as Wilma had often been found floating face up in the rivers, lakes, and streams of places like Ohio, Michigan, and Pennsylvania after having been visited by agents of retribution. Zahra wished Wilma a similar fate.

Zahra wondered how long it might take Archer and the others to realize she was missing. She was certain once they did they'd mount a campaign to find and rescue her, but it was going to take all of Archer's deductive skills to do so. She looked for landmarks that might help her get home such as: the big bent Cypress they passed a few miles back, and a stand of magnolias that were just beginning to bloom. Granted she'd not be able to see any of that should she escape at night, but at that point Zahra was trying to file in her memory as much information as she could for future reference.

"Where are we going?"

Crete answered her by saying, "When Faye told us the Butterfly was in New Orleans all I could do was smile because I've been after you a long time.

When you stole those maps back in '63, some of the generals put a bounty on your head. Ten thousand dollars. That's a lot of money."

Isenbaum grinned. "Sure is, and I can't wait to get my share."

Zahra stilled. "So where are you taking me?"

"To collect the bounty and put you on trial."

"For what?"

"Crimes against the Confederacy. The war's not over for us."

The possibility of being made to pay for having been a agent of the government was something Zahra had feared since the end of the war, and now it had come to pass. If she were ever to see Archer and her parents again, she had to find a way to escape.

"Anything yet?" Archer asked Alfred anxiously.

Alfred shook his head. "It's as if she's vanished into thin air."

Archer didn't want to hear that, but it appeared to be true. No one had seen Zahra since Sable let her off at Wilma's this afternoon. She hadn't shown up at his mother's as promised and Archer and everyone else who cared about her had spent the afternoon combing the city for clues. The fact that the dress shop was closed and that Wilma seemed to have disappeared as well added more mystery to the riddle.

"Where could she be?" Archer asked.

"Do you think that mistress of yours could be involved?"

Archer shook his head. "No. Lynette and her

aunt left town right after Zahra scared them silly that afternoon."

"What about Etienne Barber."

Once again Archer shook his head. "Barber moved his operations to Biloxi a couple weeks back."

The Le Veq brothers entered Archer's office. "Anything?"

"No. Nothing," Raimond said. "Isenbaum's place is deserted and since we have no idea where Crete is living it's impossible to know if he's involved."

Alfred said, "I knew I should have gone with her and Miss Sable today, but she wouldn't let me."

Archer was certain that Alfred's anxiety matched his own.

"The fact that both she and Wilma have vanished points to them being together, wouldn't you think?" Drake asked.

Everyone nodded but they had no answers to the question as to where the women might be.

By evening they seemed no closer to finding Zahra than they'd been that afternoon and Archer knew the longer she stayed missing the higher were the chances that she'd become a victim of foul play. Not knowing where she was was wearing on him. He'd never been so fearful for someone he cared about. He and Alfred had spent the last few hours trying to locate some of Isenbaum's associates in an effort to track down the White Leaguer to see if he was involved, but it was as if all the rats had scurried into their holes and were nowhere to be found.

Archer's suite was the command center. He'd

just returned from another fruitless search when Raimond walked in. Archer could tell by his brother's solemn face that he had no news.

"How are you holding up?" Raimond asked.

"As well as can be expected, I suppose."

"Sable has all of her people on the lookout, too. Maybe we'll know more in the morning."

Archer hoped so. The knowledge that he might never see Zahra again was tearing him apart. "What does love mean to you, Rai?"

If Raimond was surprised by the query he didn't let on. Instead, he shrugged. "Waking up every day with Sable in my arms. Holding her close and thanking the heavens for blessing me with such joy. It's looking at a little girl who has her grandmere's face and her mama's eyes. It's all that, brother, and more."

"Then I suppose I'm in love. Except for the child part. Hopefully that will come later."

"I guessed as much."

"So what do I do now?"

"Find her and tell her how you feel."

"She's planning on leaving when this is over."

"Then find her and don't tell her, but at least admit to yourself how you feel."

The advice felt right to Archer and it offered him a modicum of peace. "When did you become so wise?"

"The moment I knew I couldn't live without her."

Archer nodded his understanding. He turned and looked into his brother's face. "Thanks, Rai."

"Anytime, mon frere."

Sable arrived moments later and her green eyes

were sparkling with excitement. She had a middle-aged man with her. "This is Mr. Mayfield and he saw the men who took Miss Turpin."

Hope filled Archer for the first time today. "When?"

"This afternoon," Sable said. "Tell them, Mr. Mayfield."

"I have a fruit stand and I sometimes dump the old crop behind the grocer next to the dress shop. I was back there today when I saw two men with Miss Turpin. She looked sick because the men had her between them and they were walking her to a wagon that was waiting there."

"How did you know it was her?" Archer asked.

"Met her this morning with Miss Sable. Miss Turpin was looking for her kidnapped grandchild."

"Did you recognize the men?"

"I did. One was that White Leaguer Mitchell Isenbaum."

"Are you sure it was him?" Raimond asked him.

"Real sure. I'm a Republican. Seen him on the corners and in the parks spouting his hate. Saw him at the rally where that little boy was killed. I know Isenbaum when I see him. That's why I hid myself behind the grocer's big packing crates when they brought Miss Turpin out."

He paused for a moment, then said earnestly, "I probably should have asked what they were up to, but I know those Leaguers don't like being questioned by us and I didn't want to wind up like that little boy."

Sable reassured him. "No one is faulting you, Mr. Mayfield. If you hadn't hid you might not be here now to tell us what you saw."

"My wife's right, Mr. Mayfield. Did you recognize the second man?"

"Yep, but only because it was the same face that's on the flyer Miss Sable and Miss Turpin gave me this morning."

And now Archer knew that Isenbaum and Crete had taken Zahra. "What about the lady who owns the dress shop, did you see her anywhere?"

Mayfield nodded. "Once the men laid Miss Turpin down in the wagon, the dress shop lady came out. She locked her door and got in with them. Then they drove away."

"Thank you, Mr. Mayfield," Archer said. On one level he was relieved by the story, but on another level he was even more afraid for Zahra because he knew what Crete and Isenbaum were capable of. Wilma's role would have to be discerned later.

Sable left to drive Mr. Mayfield home. She'd then return to Juliana's to await further word.

"Now what?" Raimond asked Archer.

"We need to find out where they might have taken her. We know they're not at Isenbaum's. If we can flush out some of his friends we might learn something useful."

"You found the Death Books at Dawes' cigar shop. Let's start with him."

"Good idea. He wasn't home earlier. Maybe he's returned."

\* \* \*

Zahra and her captors traveled until it became so dark the lanterns on each side of the buggy had to be lit in order to see their way clear. From the confidence Isenbaum showed as he drove, Zahra believed he knew where he was going. From her days as Domino she remembered Matilda referencing Isenbaum's cabin in Baton Rouge. Was that where they were taking her?

Cigar shop owner Hathaway Dawes awakened to a nightmare. A dozen men wearing black hoods were circled around his bed. And in the dark they looked like demons from hell. "Where is she?" one of them barked.

He was confused but wide awake. "Who?"

"The woman Crete kidnapped. The woman known as the Butterfly."

"I don't—"

The man who'd spoken reached down and roughly dragged Dawes' five foot three frame so close Dawes swore he could feel the heat blazing from the demon's eyes. The man voiced coldly, "I am going to kill someone tonight. Shall I begin with you?"

Dawes let out a squeak of fear.

"I'm going to ask you one more time—"

"Baton Rouge," he cried. "Mitchell has a cabin there. That's where the trial's going to be."

Archer stilled. "Trial? What trial!"

Dawes was shaking violently. "She's going to be tried for crimes against the Confederacy. Please don't kill me!"

Archer made him give them directions to the

cabin then threw him loose and stepped back. "Were I you, Dawes, I'd leave New Orleans. If she is harmed, I'll be back to send you to hell."

Dawes squeaked again and the man departed.

Outside, Archer and the others mounted their horses and rode towards the road. Archer was about out of his mind. According to Mayfield's story Zahra had been taken around two in the afternoon and now it was nine hours later. Archer knew how resourceful Zahra was and that under most circumstances she was more than capable of taking care of herself, but this was not a normal occurrence. Crete represented hate. He and his followers stood for the basest of human values and they had Zahra. His Zahra. If they harmed her he would hunt them down like the rabid cowards they were.

When Zahra awakened, it was morning. The sun was shining, the birds were chirping and Crete was driving. She was surprised she'd been able to sleep but she didn't feel rested or renewed. Although stops had been made to accommodate her physical needs, no food had been provided so far. She was hungry. The last time she'd eaten had been at the Christophe with Sable. She knew she had to set her hunger aside, though. What she was facing would be far more deleterious to her health than hunger, by far. *Tried for crimes against the Confederacy*, Crete had said. Were he and the others hunting down all the Black dispatches who'd spied for the Union or just her? Was there a death book of sorts listing their names, too?

The sun was directly overhead when the wagon left the main road and took a rutted track that led through the trees. An hour later, they stopped before a small cabin set out in the middle of nowhere. There were no other houses nearby for as far as the eye could see. She had no idea where she was, but she knew she was a long way from New Orleans and Archer. She pushed him out of her mind again. Thinking about him and what he and the others must be going through only made her despondent. She needed to remain clearheaded and alert if she was going to survive this, and the Good Lord willing, she would.

# Chapter 15

Zahra had been locked inside a small room since their arrival at the cabin a few hours ago. They had at least allowed her to remove the wig, cotton batting, and the uneven brogans, but at the moment her comfort was the least of her problems. She had to get out. Staying here and being put on trial was not anything she wanted to participate in, but the room had only a six-inch cut in the wall serving as a window and the door was locked. Besides, so far there'd been no opportunities to escape.

Suddenly, she heard a key scratching at the lock, and moments later the door was opened. It was Wilma, and behind her stood an armed man whose face was hidden beneath a dirty white pillow slip with cutout openings for his eyes. Hanging across Wilma's arm was what appeared to be a garment made of fine white satin.

She walked into the room. "This is for you, lass." She offered Zahra the garment, but Zahra didn't take it.

"What is it?"

"A simple robe. It's what you are to wear for your trial. I made it myself."

"And if I refuse?"

"Then you'll be presented as naked as a niggress on the slave block. The panel of judges would enjoy that, no doubt."

Zahra hated the triumph shining in Wilma's eyes, but she took the robe.

"You always were smart. Now get dressed and someone will come for you soon."

The man behind Wilma placed a small bucket of water on the floor just inside the door.

Wilma explained, "So you can wash off that paint. The judges want to see the face of the woman who helped defeat the South."

That said, she and the man withdrew. Zahra heard the lock click, and she was alone again.

Zahra washed her face with the rag and the small sliver of soap that had been in the bucket, then she removed the clothing she'd worn as Minnie. She took a moment to run the rag over herself in an attempt to rid her skin of sweat and grime, then she held up the robe. It was long and designed to be put on over her head. In the center, a large white star had been appliquéd to the fabric, and the rays beaming off the star were blood red. Grim, she shook her head and put the thing on. It was long sleeved, voluminous enough for her to move in comfortably, and flowed to her feet. Dressed now, she waited.

* * *

Archer and his contingent were on their bellies, hiding in the rushes about one hundred yards from Isenbaum's cabin. They could see by the light being cast from fires burning in two large pits on the side of the place. People were preparing for some kind of outdoor activity. Two men appeared out of the darkness, carrying a long trestle table. They set it a ways back from the fire, then returned carrying stools—five in all, by Archer's count as he looked through the spyglass. He was glad for the fires, because without them the glasses would be useless.

Beside him, Raimond, another glass to his eye, asked, "How are you, brother?"

"I'll be better once we have her back."

All he wanted was to hold Zahra in his arms again and never let her go. The ride here had been an anguishing one. He'd had to let his anger rule, otherwise despair would have taken over. The thoughts of never seeing her again, never hearing her laugh, never having the chance to tell her that he loved her as much as his life had ridden with him the entire way. And he did love her, he just wished the fates hadn't dealt him such a dangerous hand to make him realize it.

Archer continued to watch the scene playing out before them, hoping for a glimpse of Zahra. Until they saw her, they couldn't be certain she was here. Instead, a line of five people dressed in white hooded robes came out of the darkness. The firelight shimmered eerily off their satin costumes. After the five took seats on the stools behind the trestle table, another group filed in, carrying lit torches. Archer counted twenty-five. There were eleven in his group.

"About two apiece," a pleased-sounding Raimond whispered.

Archer liked the odds, too. Now if he could just see Zahra.

By the time Zahra was finally escorted from the room by two costumed men carrying burning torches, she was almost relieved. Almost. During the war, she'd had to extricate herself from some dangerous situations, but none as dangerous as this.

They led her outside into the cool night air. She saw the fires and the white-robed individuals gathered around them. All were turned and looking her way. She knew her captors were hoping the scene would frighten her, and it did, but being frightened and surrendering were two different things.

The wind picked up slightly, blowing embers into the air, and Zahra was grateful for the breeze. It felt good after being cooped up all day. Zahra stood silently before the robed judges. Her training kept her eyes focused on the one man, now rising from his seat. Outwardly, she looked calm. Inside, she was more afraid than she'd ever been in her life, but she held her head high.

As the man began to speak, Zahra recognized the voice as Crete's. "Sons and Daughters of the White Star," he called out commandingly against the night. "I present to you the woman known as Butterfly."

Horns blew and whistles trilled in response.

The Sons and Daughters were having such a good time celebrating her capture that when the riders came charging into the camp with guns firing, it took them a moment to comprehend what was happening. Then they began to run, screaming, yelling, tripping on their snow-white robes as they fled the riders and their big mounts. Zahra took the opportunity to push over the table, then she ran for her life. She heard Crete scream, "Get her! Get her!"

Zahra turned back to see if they were gaining on her and was stunned when she saw Wilma fire a pistol at Crete, then fire again. Crete staggered back, then sagged against the table before sliding from view. It all happened so fast, and she was taken by such surprise, she didn't realize she was standing still until she heard Wilma scream, "Run lass! Run!"

Zahra forced herself into motion and ran towards the tree line.

The Sons and Daughters had by now regrouped and were returning firing. But the riders having the advantage of surprise, speed and height were a more formidable and efficient force.

In the chaos of bullets and mayhem, the mounted Archer set his sights on Zahra. He could see her running fast. A man in a robe was right behind her. Spurring his horse on, he shouted her name. She looked up and ran towards him. He fired his pistol, the man dropped. Zahra held up her arms and let herself be scooped up and placed down hard on the saddle in front of him. "It's about time!" she said happily.

"Hang on!" Archer yelled, and then they were

galloping towards the trees. His mounted companions were right on his heels.

On the slow ride back, Zahra cuddled against Archer and savored the feel of being near him, Standing before Crete's judges, she'd doubted ever being able to do this again, but Archer and his companions had ridden to her rescue like the Black cavalry that toppled Richmond during the war. "Thanks for the rescue."

"You're welcome."

"You brought your own army I see." His brothers were with him, as were Alfred, and his cousin Roland, and some of the Black veterans from the night patrols.

"Had to."

She was grateful for the rescue. Being with him filled her heart. "How'd you know where to find me?"

Archer told her the story of Mr. Mayfield, and then about the bedtime visit they paid on Hathaway Dawes.

She asked him, "Did you see Wilma shoot Crete back there?"

Archer was surprised by that. "No. When?"

"During the melee. Shot him at least twice." Then Zahra related Wilma's role in her capture. "She had Crete convinced she was on their side."

"Was she?"

"Seeing her shoot him makes me say no, but I'm not sure of anything about her anymore."

"Whatever side she's on, I'll never forgive her for putting you in their clutches. Did she escape?"

"I don't know that either." Zahra had quite a few questions for Wilma, but she didn't know if she'd ever see the Irishwoman again.

Archer asked, "So, is there a reward for your rescue."

Zahra smiled up and purred, "Oh, yes, and as soon as we get back to New Orleans, I'm going to give you such a boon you won't be able to walk."

He chuckled. "Then let's get you home. He looked down into her face and his voice took on a more serious tone. "I'm glad you're safe, Zahra."

Reaching up, she cupped his unshaven cheek. "So am I."

Back in New Orleans, Zahra was greeted with hugs and joyful tears from Juliana and Sable. The next day, Juliana threw a small party to celebrate Zahra's successful return that was attended by the Le Veqs and the men and women of Zahra's staff.

Afterwards, Archer and Zahra returned to his suite and fell tiredly onto the sofa. "Can I sleep for the next two weeks?" Zahr asked wearily.

"Only if I can join you."

Zahra's rides to Baton Rouge and back to New Orleans had taken a physical toll compounded by her lack of food and sleep. She'd recovered a bit in the two days since her return but she was still very tired. When Archer leaned down and kissed her however, she was infused with a rush of sweet energy so familiar she leaned up to receive more. She'd missed his kisses almost as much as she'd missed him and she wanted to show him how much. Soon hands were undoing buttons, and tongues were mating and as always, Zahra wound up wearing no drawers beneath her beautiful plum-colored gown.

Archer carried her towards his room, lingering in the darkness on the way to taste her kiss swollen lips, then placed her gently on the bed. Just like the first night he'd made love to her there, the moonlight streamed through the large windows. Archer removed the rest of his clothes and fed his eyes on her partially nude form. Her breasts were bared and the gown was rucked up on her thighs. She was a vision of erotic loveliness he couldn't wait to pleasure.

And pleasure her he did, from the passion hardened nipples of her breasts to the damp hidden treasure between her thighs, Archer lavished her, aroused her. She climaxed the first time in response to his fingers and lips, then came again while positioned lustily atop him. He turned her over, and it didn't take long for him to yell his own release.

They spent the rest of the night in a sensual, uninhibited world all their own, and when they were both too sated to do more, they clung to each other and slept.

Zahra awakened first the following morning and smiled over at the sight of him asleep. His light snores gently broke the silence. Last night's lovemaking had been the stuff of dreams. She had never felt so cherished, so wanton. It was the kind of loving that could bind two people for life she sensed, which was why leaving him in the next few days was so imperative. He was the type of man who could make a woman turn her back on everything else just to see his smile, and Zahra's ties to her family precluded that. He also didn't love her, another serious issue for her because she loved him like she loved breathing. Filled with uncharacteristic regret, she gave him a bittersweet smile, then snuggled back under the blankets for more sleep.

The next day, Zahra received a letter from Wilma.

*Dear Zahra,*

*I am on my way back to Boston but I couldn't leave without explaining. I am aware you think I betrayed you, but my actions were for reasons you may or may not find sound. Grant and his people have been looking for Crete for some time, but our agents couldn't find him. I was sent down ostensibly to help you, but in reality my mission was to get a line on Crete and to eliminate him if I could.*

Very surprised by what that meant, Zahra read on.

*I knew when I arrived in New Orleans that he was rumored to be there. I'd hoped to learn where he was living to no avail. When your people verified that Isenbaum was in cahoots with Crete, my only choice was to convince Isenbaum that I was a supporter. To do so, I gave him your coded name to pass along to Crete, hoping he would take the bait and want to know more about you. He did. Crete came to my shop the very next day. I could*

*have eliminated him then, but the president
wanted to know who else Crete had recruited and
how many others were involved with his organization. My sincerest apologies for making you a
pawn and for participating in your capture, but I
had my orders. My apologies to Miss Tubman,
also. I did send her the wire about the Death
Books, Zahra. Too important not to.*

*Sincerely,*
*Wilma*

Archer sensed Zahra was withdrawing from
him. There'd been nothing specific really but she'd
seemed preoccupied and distracted for the past
few days. A week had passed since her rescue
and return to his life, but he wasn't sure how long
she planned to remain, and he cared for her too
much to broach the subject without cause. At dinner in his apartments that evening, she said, "I've
sent all of my people back to their homes."

"Even Alfred?"

"No, he's going to stay around for a few more
days before heading off."

"I'll miss having your giant around."

"As will I."

He studied her. She'd gone silent and was looking off in the distance in a way that made him
think her thoughts were far away. "Zahra," he
said softly.

She met his eyes.

"If you're leaving, I need to know." Archer
hadn't wanted to press the matter but knew the
time had come.

Zahra had hoped to not have this conversation but knew that had been unrealistic. She'd never been one to not meet a situation head on, but she'd never been in love before. Her feelings for him were making her walk in unfamiliar territory. "I am going, Archer."

The declaration twisted both their hearts.

"I'm going first to Washington and then home to South Carolina."

"And then?"

"I don't know."

"I need you in my life, Zahra."

The pain made Zahra look away. She needed him as well, but she couldn't be his mistress and watch him marry someone else. She also had to go home. Crete and his people had planned to try her, find her guilty and end her life. While locked up in that room awaiting her fate, wanting to see her parents just one more time had been as important to her as seeing Archer again. As it stood now, James and Marie Lafayette didn't know whether their only child was dead or alive, and with all the turmoil going on in South Carolina, she wasn't sure if they were still living either. She could take the easy way out and send a letter, but in her heart, she knew she needed to go and see for herself. "I have to see my parents, Archer."

"I know, but will you return to New Orleans?"

"I can't say." They were the hardest words she'd ever had to utter. Another consideration had to do with Araminta, Henry Adams and his spiders. What if her services as a dispatch were needed again. Upon her return here to New Orleans, she'd had the opportunity to talk with

Juliana and had been assured that the network would remain in place so that the information the race needed would continue to flow. Yes, Archer had been an agent and he knew its inherent dangers, but how might he handle the woman in his life having to disappear for long periods of time to do lord knew what.

Archer slid his disappointment at her answer beneath his love for her. He wanted to ask her how or when she might make the decision to come back to him, but he knew badgering her would only lead to bad feelings neither of them wanted. So after dinner, he made love to her slowly, torridly, and as completely as he could because he sensed it might be their last time.

Filled with a singular sadness, Zahra slipped from the bed and silently gathered her clothing. With movements that echoed the quietness in the room, she dressed and prepared to disappear from his life. Leaving this way was better, she'd decided. Were he awake and aware of what she was about, he'd be doing his best to make her change her mind and she would undoubtedly acquiesce for a time, but he would still be a man who didn't believe in love, and she would remain a woman who did.

Dressed now, she stood by the bed and watched him sleep. The urge to touch his cheek was strong, but she forced herself to remain still. She was certain that some women would declare her foolish for opting to turn her back on the comfortable life his wealth could provide, not to mention his talents in bed, but if she stayed she'd be his mistress and Zahra had no desire to be a Lynette. The

Lynettes of the world were easily replaced by others of their kind. What if one day he did discover love—with someone else. Her heart would break even more than now. She viewed him tenderly. If she never found another man to replace Archer in her heart and mind, she would still have her memories.

Giving him one last look, she slipped from the room and softly closed the door.

Archer waited until he was certain she was gone before tossing aside the covers. Picking up a robe, he hastened to his study where the windows looked down on the back of the hotel and gently pulled back the drapes. Illuminated by the light from the street lamps he saw Alfred waiting on the seat of a small coach. A few minutes later she appeared below, her form all but hidden beneath a hooded cloak, and his heart twisted with pain. Seemingly sensing his presence, she looked up at the window and her eyes met his. She slowly pulled back the hood as if wanting him to see her face one last time, and that too added to his pain. There seemed to be a sadness about her that matched his own and it took all he had not to throw open the windows and beg her to stay, but he respected her enough to respect her decision, so he simply nodded farewell, letting the gesture say all he could not, and she nodded solemnly in reply. Their gazes held for a few moments more, then she disappeared inside the coach and Alfred drove away.

On the train ride to Washington, Zahra thought about Archer day and night. What was he doing? How was he faring. How soon would he find someone else? She shied away from that one, but all of her questions and more mingled with the memories of their time together. She'd begun missing him as soon as she left his bedroom, and it would probably take a lifetime to stop doing so.

For the next few weeks, Archer moved through life as if a voodoo spell had rendered him a zombie. He ran the hotel with his usual efficiency, but it seemed as if all the color had been stripped from his world, leaving everything varying shades of gray. He missed Zahra so much, his heart ached like an open wound.

The night she left, he began consoling himself with cognac. By the end of the month, he'd stopped shaving or going to work thus making André responsible for the day-to-day management of the Christophe. Archer was such a mess that Juliana sent Raimond and the Brats over to intervene. She knew Archer was the most sensitive of her sons and that Zahra's leaving had hit him hard, but she was worried he'd never get over it unless someone made him hold up a mirror to himself and force him to take a good long look.

A drunken Archer was seated on his sofa in the dark when Raimond and his brothers filed in. "What do you want?" he groused in a slurred, sullen voice.

A lamp was lit and as if in answer to his question, he watched Drake and Beau go over to the armoire holding his liquor and begin taking down the bottles. They placed the bottles in a carpetbag.

"What the hell are you doing!" He got up and wobbled for a moment before gaining the momentum he needed to cross the room. "Put those back."

Raimond drawled, "They will when you come to your senses."

"Got to hell, Raimond. Nobody likes you anyway."

Philippe came out of the back carrying Archer's dirty bed linen. "I'll take these to the laundress."

Raimond nodded.

Archer stared around in drunken confusion. "Who invited you here? Everybody out!"

Next he knew, the stern-faced André appeared seemingly out of nowhere. Behind him looked to be a line of people holding buckets, but Archer was so inebriated he wasn't sure what he was seeing.

"Water's ready, Rai," André announced.

Raimond turned his attention to his brother. "We have plenty of hot water here. Do you want to take a bath and start resembling a person again, or do I have to give it to you?"

"The only thing you can give me, Raimond His Majesty Le Veq is the sight of you leaving me the hell alone. Now like I said, everybody out before I put you out."

An amused Drake said, "Did he just say he was going to put us out?"

Beau replied, "I believe he did."

Raimond said, "Archer, every minute I'm here fooling with you is time away from Sable and my children, so don't test me."

"Kiss it, Rai."

"Get him!" Raimond snapped.

Because the odds were five to one and the one was too drunk to be much of a challenge, the cursing and twisting Archer was summarily carried into his bathing room. He was stripped of his dirty smelly clothing and dumped into the tub where six buckets of ice cold water were poured without mercy over his head. His howls of rage were ignored.

Two days later, Raimond returned to find Archer packing his bags.

"Going somewhere?"

"Yes." Archer was still angry at his brothers for their visit even though he understood why they'd been sent to do what they'd done. He was also grateful. Because of them he was his self again, well almost. "I'm going to find Zahra."

A grin split Raimond's dark face. "Good for you, brother."

"Whether you think it's good or not, I have to see her and let her know how I feel."

"I knew you'd figure out what to do."

"If she turns me away, so be it, but this has to be resolved one way or another, so we can both get on with life."

Archer then looked to his brother and said solemnly," Thanks Rai. Without you I'd be still on the sofa drowning my sorrow in cognac."

"Thank Juliana. She was the one most worried."

"Will you let her know I'm gone?"

"You're not going to see her before you leave?"

"No. My train leaves within the hour."

Raimond assessed his brother and, upon seeing

the determination in his face, said, "I will. Do you need a ride to the station."

"Yes."

"Then I'll take you."

When Archer stepped off the train in Columbia, South Carolina, it was raining, hard, but he didn't mind. He was there and that much closer to finding Zahra. He hailed a cab, was driven to a local boardinghouse that catered to folks of color and got a room. Because the house had no other boarders upon his arrival, Archer sat down in the dining room to enjoy a simple meal of collards and pork. The landlady, a gregarious woman named Miss Opal, joined him at the table after he finished. "What's a fine bred man like you doing in Calhoun County?"

Archer smiled, "Who said I was fine bred?" He was dressed as a common laborer in order not to draw untoward attention. Supremacists often targeted well-dressed travelers of color.

"Table manners will a give a person away every time."

He chuckled. "Very astute, Miss Opal."

"You here visiting kin."

He saw no reason to lie. "No, ma'am. I'm looking for a woman."

"Is she from here or did you just stop here for the night so you can travel on in the morning."

"She's from here. Her name's Zahra Lafayette. Do you know her? Or someone who does?"

Miss Opal studied him with her creek green eyes. "Maybe. Why're you looking for her?"

"Going to ask her to marry me."

Surprise flooded Miss Opal's face. "Truly?"

"Sure as my name is Le Veq."

"Marriage, huh?"

Archer nodded.

"We'll go in the morning."

The grin on Archer's face matched hers.

"This is as far as I can take you, Mr. Archer."

The time was just past dawn. The small track of road they'd been following for the last two hours had petered out into nothing and he was seated on the wagon looking at the dense forest ahead.

Miss Opal said, "Trees too thick for the wagon from here on, so you'll have to walk."

Archer wasn't pleased by the knowledge, but he'd not come this far to turn back now, so he grabbed his travel bag and got down from the wagon. "Thank you, Miss Opal."

"You're welcome, son. You got a long walk ahead of you, so I wish you luck. Remember what I said. Those Lafayettes been in this swamp for generations, they have all kinds of tricks and traps to keep their place hidden. A city man like you needs to be careful."

"I will, and thanks again."

"You're welcome."

She turned her wagon around and headed back. Archer watched her go then headed into the trees.

Miss Opal had drawn him a crude map. Armed with that, Archer was fairly confident of his ability to be able to find the place she called Sanctuary, but he hadn't taken into account the heat that began rising the moment the sun came up or the vast undeveloped expanse of Zahra's home.

After a few hours of falling into bogs, fighting off bloodthirsty insects large as his hands and sweating in his too warm clothing, he was pretty certain he was lost. He never saw the twin oaks Miss Opal described as the gateway to Sanctuary, nor had he found the small creek she suggested he follow. It occurred to Archer that maybe this hadn't been such a sound plan after all. He was surrounded on each side by heavy vegetation and the soft filtered light inherent in a place like this, but he had no idea which way to go. Above his head the towering trees offered no help nor did the ever present insects. Smacking one feeding on his neck, Archer began walking again.

Another two hours passed and still no sign of anything resembling a community. He was hungry, tired and mad at himself for not having planned this better. He blamed it all on love. He obviously hadn't been thinking straight to attempt this but he had to find Zahra. Had to. He took a seat on a mossy green fallen log and pulled the two sandwiches Miss Opal had given him this morning out of his pack. He'd lost his prized pocket watch earlier in a fall down a slippery ravine so he had no mechanical way of determining the time. The sun which had been playing peek a boo with the clouds most of day appeared to be on the wane so he estimated the time to be long past noon. He ate the sandwiches, washed them down with the water in his canteen and set out again.

The world was alive with the sounds of bird calls and the incessant buzzing of insects. He saw a few deer, rabbits and heard something growling off in the distance that sounded for all the world like a big cat. He had his pistol in his pack but hoped he wouldn't have to use it.

Miss Opal had warned him to stay alert for the traps set by Zahra's people but he'd been walking for so long and was so tired he didn't see the noose of the ground snare until it was too late. The thick vine immediately tightened fast around his ankle and he cried out with alarm as he was yanked up into the air and left dangling upside down amongst the trees. Breathing hard from shock and surprise he fought to calm himself so he could think. The ground looked to be a good fifteen feet down, and even if mangaged to cut himself free he'd probably break several bones when he fell back to earth and he wanted to avoid that. The blood was rushing to his head, he was angry, wet and in desperate need of assistance.

Assistance arrived a short while later in the form of a tall Black man with bushy gray hair. He was carrying a walking stick and a rifle. "Well hello there!" the man called up. "Looks like you're in quite a pickle there, son."

"Can you get me down?" Archer was so dizzy from hanging upside down he was on the verge of blacking out.

"Have to ask you questions first about who you are and what you're doing here."

"Whatever you want. Just find a way to get me down!"

"Name?"

"Le Veq. Archer. I'm from Louisiana."

"Well, Mr. Le Veq Archer, why are you sneaking around here?"

Biting back his anger, Archer gritted out, "I'm not sneaking. I lost my way. I'm looking for someone."

"Who?"

"A woman I want to marry. Zahra Lafayette."

"Oh really?"

"Sir! Can we please have this interrogation on terra firma?"

"Answer me this first. Why would a swamp girl want to marry a fancy pants like you?"

Archer knew that if he got out of this he was going to strangle the man with his bare hands for his lack of sympathy for Archer's upside down plight. "Because I love her! And I'm hoping she loves me!"

Then he heard a voice that was as familiar as his own heartbeat. "You love me?" And to his anger and yes, extreme delight, Zahra Lafayette stepped out of the trees. Even as his heart swelled at the sight of her he swore, "Dammit, woman. Cut me down!"

Zahra and her father James had been out hunting and she'd been trailing him by a few yards. She'd heard him talking up ahead but had no idea he was talking with Archer until she stepped out of the bush. Knowing the man she loved more than anything else in the world was here filled her heart with joy. He certainly looked comical hanging up there twisting gently though, and she didn't have to see his face to know that he was also furious. But her surprise at finding him here paled in comparison to what she'd just heard him say.

He barked, "Zahra, if you don't cut me down, I'm going to make you wear corsets and shoes every day for the rest of our married life!"

She chuckled, then said to her father. "Let's get him down, Papa."

James looked down into his daughter's happy eyes and asked, "You sure?"

"Positive."

Once they lowered him to the ground, Archer was too dizzy to do anything more than lie there. When she came to kneel at his side, he took in the simple patched dress she was wearing and the beauty of her face and he felt his world right again. He smiled and asked. "Will you marry me?"

Zahra looked down at him in his dirty clothes, the profusion of raised insect bites on his golden face and replied, "Yes, Archer. I will marry you."

Relieved and satisfied, Archer gave in and blacked out.

# **Epilogue**

**Z**ahra and Archer were married a month
later at Saint Louis Cathedral. Her parents
were in attendance as were dispatches from
across the nation. That night as Archer carried
her over the threshold of his suite above the
Christophe, he asked, "So, what ever happened
in Washington? Did you give the Death Book to
the president?"

Zahra was the happiest woman in the world
and kissed him to show him how much before
replying, "No. He was in Boston, and I wasn't
leaving the book with his secretary and maybe
have it disappear, so I gave the man my written
report and left. Araminta has the book now."

He set her down on the sofa, kissed her soundly
then sat beside her. "She'll know what to do with
it."

"Yes she will."

Archer was slowly undoing her gown and placing sweet heat-filled kisses on her mouth, throat and the tops of her breasts.

"Who will you be in bed tonight, ma chérie—Domino, Zahra Crane, Zahra Lafayette?"

Feeling arousal taking hold in response to his expert kisses and caresses, Zahra purred, "I think I'll be Zahra Le Veq, the virgin bride."

Archer chuckled and bit the lobe of her ear gently. "Virgin?" he asked with amused interest and delight.

"Yes, which means you'll have to show me what to do."

"I believe I can handle that task."

"Are you sure?"

He slid the top of her gown down and brushed a kiss over her soft skin. "Most definitely."

"I love you, Archer," she breathed as his mouth pleasured her.

"I love you, too, Zahra."

And, later in the bedroom, he proved it until she screamed.

# Author's Note

Archer Le Veq was first introduced in my fifth novel, *Through the Storm*, published in 1998 by Avon Books. That story revolved around Sable Fontaine and Raimond Le Veq, but Archer and the Brats made such an impression that fans have been demanding a sequel ever since. I've been waiting for Archer and Zahra, too, so I hope you had as much fun reading about them as I had bringing their story to life.

To my surprise, the institution with the most complete information on Black Dispatches, male and female, turned out to be this nation's Central Intelligence Agency! An article by P.K. Rose titled *The Civil War: Black American Contributions to Union Intelligence* can be found at: *www.odci.gov/cia/publications/dispatches.dispatch.html*.

It's filled with fascinating little known facts of

the race's contribution to the war, and I'm pleased to have my tax dollars contributing to the preservation of such an important aspect of American History.

Dorothy Sterling, in her book *The Trouble They Seen: The Story of Reconstruction in the Words of African Americans*, published by Da Capo Press, describes Henry Adams as a "one-man investigating committee." Those of you who have read my first novel, *Night Song*, know that he played a significant role in the Great Exodus of 1879, and that my fictional town in which *Night Song* takes place is named for him. However, I'd no idea he was so politically active before the Exodus, nor was I aware of the covert activities he and his volunteers conducted during the dark days of Redemption until I read Ms. Sterling's book. Adams mentions his investigators in testimony before a committee of the United States Senate. (For further information please see: Senate report 693, 46th Congress, 2nd Session and/or Sterling's book.)

The Death Books Zahra and her forces were hunting were real, and they are referenced in Adams' Congressional testimony, as well. In my humble opinion, a full historical treatment of Henry Adams and his contributions to the race is long overdue, so all of you true historians out there, the ball's in your court.

The name and accomplishments of Oscar J. Dunn have faded so much over time, he has all but disappeared from the history books. The controversy surrounding his untimely death remains unresolved. No one knows why his family refused the autopsy, or why considering the numbers of other Republicans who claimed to have had the same symptoms, Dunn was the only one to die. The only article I could find on the circumstances of his death was published by the journal *Phylon*, and written by Marcus B. Christian.

Reconstruction is one of the most compelling eras of American history but trying to include all of the facts and stories is impossible, so please consult my partial list of sources below for more information.

Blassingame, John W. *Black New Orleans: 1860–1880*. University of Chicago Press, Ltd., London, 1976.

Foner, Eric. *Reconstruction: America's Unfinished Revolution. 1863–1877.* Harper and Row, New York, 1988.

Gehman, Margaret. *Free People of Color of New Orleans*. Margaret Media, New Orleans, 1994.

Quarles, Benjamin. *The Negro in the American Revolution*. University of North Carolina Press, 1961. (See this book for information on the original James Lafayette.)

Writing this book became very personal for me. While I was working on it Hurricane Katrina entered our lives. My heart goes out to the Americans impacted, especially those in New Orleans.

For all those who sent cards and wishes to me after the publication of *Something Like Love*, please know that I am alive and doing well. Thank you for the outpouring of love, concern, and support.

Stay Blessed,
B